Critical Acclaim for Nina Bawden

'Miss Bawden has a sensitive appreciation for the inner world of an adolescent as well as for the gritty complexities of the middle-class suburban scene. To both of these realms she brings a Dickensian relish for the joys and disasters of family life' — *New York Times*

'Nina Bawden is a past mistress at conveying the raw, unformed impressions of a child's mind. She is also a delicate, thoughtful writer, quite without sentimentality' — *Books and Bookmen*

'Nina Bawden's readers should be numbered like the sands of the sea' — *Guardian*

'Throughout her long writing career, Nina Bawden has depicted with ruthless precision the dysfunctional family lives of the English middle classes . . . She is a disquieting moralist with the gift of making the potentially disturbing scenes wildly funny' — *Sunday Times*

'Among the most perceptive and accomplished novelists writing today' — *P. D. James*

NINA BAWDEN

Nina Bawden was born in London in 1925 and evacuated to South Wales during the war. She was educated at Ilford County High School for Girls and at Somerville College, Oxford.

Her first novel, *Who Calls the Tune*, appeared in 1953. Since then she has published nineteen other adult novels including: *Tortoise by Candlelight* (1963), *A Woman of My Age* (1967), *The Birds on the Trees* (1970), *Walking Naked* (1981), all of which are also published by Virago; *Afternoon of a Good Woman*, winner of the Yorkshire Post Novel of the Year Award for 1976 and *Circles of Deceit*, which was shortlisted for the Booker Prize in 1988 and has recently been filmed by the BBC. Her most recent novel is *Family Money* (1991).

Nina Bawden is also an acclaimed author of sixteen children's books. Many of these have been televised or filmed; all have been widely translated. Amongst them are: *Carrie's War* (1973); *The Peppermint Pig*, the recipient of the 1975 Guardian Award for Children's Fiction; *The Finding* (1985), *Keeping Henry* (1988), *The Outside Child* (1989) and *Humbug* (1992).

For ten years Nina Bawden served as a magistrate, both in her local court and in the Crown Court. She also sat on the councils of various literary bodies, including the Royal Society of Literature — of which she is a Fellow — PEN, the Society of Authors, and the A.L.C.S., and is the President of the Society of Women Writers and Journalists. In addition she has lectured at conferences and universities, on Arts Council tours and in schools.

Nina Bawden has been married twice and has one son, one daughter and two stepdaughters. She lives in London and in Greece.

VIRAGO
MODERN
CLASSIC

NUMBER
333

Nina Bawden

A LITTLE LOVE,
A LITTLE LEARNING

Published by VIRAGO PRESS Limited 1990
20–23 Mandela Street, Camden Town, London NW1 0HQ

Reprinted 1990, 1992

First published in Great Britain by Longmans Green & Co. Ltd 1965
Copyright © Nina Bawden 1965

A CIP catalogue record for this book is available from the British Library

Printed in Finland by Werner Söderström Oy

for Austen

*'Innocency hath its present answer,
wisdom requires time'*

Sir Henry Yelverton

Chapter One

The year Aunt Hat came to us, my main ambition – apart from rescuing someone from drowning or winning the Victoria Cross – was to go down to Jock's Icecream Parlour in the main street of Monks Ford and eat as many Knickerbocker Glories as I could pay for. Ellen, our mother, said this was a pretty limited ambition for a girl of twelve and that I ought to have learned by now that icecreams made me sick. Boyd said that was why I wanted them: it was a clear example of a man's reach needing to exceed his grasp, what else is heaven for? Ellen said that if I got on with my school work and didn't waste so much time, I would have better things to think about. Boyd said wasting time was the best occupation he knew, for someone my age.

Ellen said he spoiled me. Our mother was always worried that Boyd was spoiling us and that his easy ways were distracting us from the main purpose of our lives, which was to work hard at school and pass our exams well. Joanna said that worrying was a symptom of middle age.

Joanna was almost eighteen and worried herself, about getting old. She had a theory that twenty was the beginning of the dull, dangerous age in life. Young people under twenty were all right, and old people over sixty. In between, if they weren't careful, they became faceless and boring, empty envelopes filled with worries and unpaid bills. She didn't blame them, she just knew it was the common fate and intended to avoid it herself. It wouldn't be easy, she said: Boyd was the only person she knew who had grown old without losing his sense of proportion.

Boyd was our stepfather. His name was Archibald Arthur Boyd and we called him by his surname because when he and Ellen married, Joanna who was eleven then, and shy, had called him Mr Boyd. We – Ellen, Joanna, Poll and I – were the only family he had ever had. His grandparents were dead when his parents married, his mother died when he was born and his father had been killed in the First War, when Boyd was six years old. He had been brought up by his mother's uncle, an ex-Army Colonel who had retired to Monks Ford. Once, when we asked Boyd what his uncle was like, he said, 'He was the sort of man who would bury nails in his front lawn to teach the errand boy not to ride his bicycle across it.'

The old man died in 1939. Boyd joined the army as a doctor and served in the Far East until he was invalided out towards the end of the war. He took a temporary job as house surgeon in a London hospital while he studied for a specialist exam in gynaecology and met my mother in an Outpatient's Clinic with Poll, five months old and suffering from colic. She used to scream with pain every time after her bottle. Boyd told Ellen to stop leaving her in the council nursery and stay at home with her for a while. Ellen thanked him for his good advice, but said it was impracticable. She worked, teaching in a Junior School, because she had to.

We were living then, as we had done for a year, in a flat off the Mile End Road. The walls were stained like a map; lying in bed, we could see the whole of the Americas on the opposite wall. The windows had panes missing that were filled with corrugated paper, there was no bathroom and we shared a lavatory with an old man on the ground floor who suffered from stomach trouble: the whole house was filled with his smell which was sour, like cooking cabbage. The street, with its bombed, half-derelict houses, was a desert that filled Ellen with despair.

'The end of civilization used to be just a phrase I read in the newspapers,' she said once when we were walking Poll

8

– pram-pushing was the only thing that soothed her – through a labyrinth of ugly streets and ugly houses to the only green space for miles, a graveyard at the back of a bombed church. Sometimes, on fine Saturdays, we took sandwiches there and ate them sitting on the fallen tombstones. The grass was rank but green, and there was a smell of earth.

To some extent, we shared our mother's misery. We had been country children and found London a terrifying waste. We went to a school where the other pupils, though they were no worse dressed than we were, sneered at our la-di-da airs: we said 'Please, Miss Piggot' instead of 'I say, Miss', and carried clean handkerchiefs every day. Being small, I was treated with a certain rough kindness, slum children are not cruel to babies, but Joanna had suffered. Apart from the handkerchiefs, she had braces on her teeth: fancy bridgework at that date, betrayed your bourgeois origin. There was one fat girl with a runny nose who fell upon her every morning as she entered the playground and pummelled her until the bell went. Though Joanna fought back, she got the worst of it. She was always in trouble, with her teacher for coming into class dirty-faced, and with Ellen for coming home with torn clothes. For pride's sake we never told the truth, but bought needles and thread with our pocket money and stopped at a bomb site on the way home to cobble up the worst of the damage before Ellen saw it. The bomb site was overgrown with willow herb. Joanna told me, years later, that she could never see a crop of that pink weed, waving in the breeze on a railway embankment, without a suffocating tightness in her chest. Joanna was not brave, on the farm where we had lived she had always refused to go into the field with the bull in it, but that year she was forced to be. One morning she picked up a broken milk bottle from the gutter, spat on the ground for courage, and went for her tormentor. After that her life was not easy, but it was better.

Boyd married our mother within a month of meeting her at the Clinic, and took us all to live with him at Monks Ford. When we asked Ellen about it, she said that he married her to cure Poll of her stomach pains. We found this answer perfectly reasonable: it seemed to us that any man would be glad to re-organize his life for Poll.

Although he rescued us from circumstances which had been, for a whole year, somewhat disagreeable, our stepfather got no gratitude from us. Nor, I imagine, did he expect it. He was a sensible man. We liked him because he made no demands. Ellen was always complaining about our behaviour – she had unnecessarily high standards – but he never did. Indeed, I never heard him complain about anything except the war wound in his leg, sometimes when the weather was cold.

It was cold the beginning of that year, a long, sharp cold. We ran home from school in the afternoon with the hairs freezing in our nostrils. Our shoes squeaked on the blue, hard snow.

Joanna and I had to fetch Poll from her school on our way home. Her class was late out and Poll last of all. She was a bustling but disorganized child whose hat was never on the peg where she knew she had put it. When she finally appeared she was red with the effort of collecting her possessions and disposing them about her person; her coat was buttoned askew, her open satchel stuffed with the books she took to school as an insurance against boredom during lessons; she clutched her khaki painting smock, her rubber shoes, and George, her bear. I re-buttoned her coat and Joanna knelt on the snow to tie her shoe laces while Poll talked full tilt in her curious, husky voice that cracked sometimes, like an adolescent boy's.

'I got a gold star today but Gilly got two. It's not fair but Miss Carter says I'll get one tomorrow if I try to write nicely but I can't because my poor hands get so tired. Miss Carter says we've got to be specially good this year because it's a special year, the Queen's going to be crowned in Westminster Abbey and they're going to roast a whole cow on the floody field down by the Water Works and we're all going to get a bit.'

'Not a cow, an ox,' Joanna said.

'Miss Carter says an ox is a sort of cow.' Joanna grinned and Poll said passionately, 'Oh, you can laugh if you like, but Miss Carter knows more than you do, she's a teacher.' Her eyes, which were a fierce, deep blue, blazed at us. 'She says this is a very important year, one we'll remember all our lives, so there.'

'I expect that's right, if she says so,' Joanna said soothingly, getting up and dusting the chipped snow from her skirt. She glanced across the playground. 'We'd better hurry.'

I saw why. Miss Carter herself had emerged from the door marked 'Infants' and was making a bee-line for us. She was a very tall, very thin woman, with a tortured face; high forehead and beaky nose, white and shiny like bone, and a big, grimacing mouth that sprayed spit as she talked. She was Poll's teacher and our neighbour. She was also in love with our stepfather and a great trouble to us.

It was too late to run: she was upon us. We composed our faces into blank, pleasant smiles.

'What nice girls to fetch your little sister!' She spat effusively. 'I'm sorry if you had to wait, but we were having such an interesting lesson, weren't we, Poll, that we couldn't bear to stop?'

Resigned to her company, her ghastly, ingratiating brightness, we left the playground. Joanna said, 'Poll says you were telling them about the coronation.'

'Yes, dear. I was explaining that they were going to be the New Elizabethans and telling them about this year's Project. We are going to put up big sheets of paper all round the Assembly Hall and write down on them the great things that are still to be done. All the advances we hope to make, in medicine, housing, education. . . . I want them to look forward. I believe this year will see the beginning of a great upsurge of energy, as there was in the time of the first Elizabeth. New poets, new discoveries. . . . I want to rouse them up, to make them see they can be doctors, teachers, explorers, that there are mountains to be climbed, great areas of the world to be civilized, diseases to be conquered . . .'

'Aren't they a bit young to be told they've got to climb Everest or discover a cure for cancer?'

Miss Carter laughed, as if Joanna had said something clever instead of something rude, and lifted her wild, sad face to the sky. We were walking along the side of the park; the wind swept across the snow-buried football pitch and made her eyes water. The light from the street lamp was reflected in the tears on her cheek and glinted on her prominent white teeth.

'Of course we won't mention cancer, dear, or anything dreadful like that. My idea was to tell them about the children in *Africa* who don't have enough to eat and who have diseases like river-blindness and leprosy. Ah – the misery that still lurks in the dark places of the world!'

She gave an inappropriate, loud laugh, and glanced sideways at us. 'I expect your poor Papa is very busy just now, so many poor people must be ill, in this dreadful weather.'

I looked at Joanna, who fixed her gaze on the ground. We had known she would mention Boyd sooner or later. There had been other ladies in love with him – he was a sympathetic doctor – and we knew the symptoms of the malady. Miss Carter was still in the early stage of trying to edge her way into our regard in order to bring the conversation round to him. She had not yet begun to pester Ellen, calling at the front door on the pretence of having mistaken the hour of the surgery and lingering, with lamentations about missed buses and cries of false regret, until asked in to wait. The ladies who did this were middle-aged; they had a record of minor illnesses but what chiefly ailed them, Ellen said, was that their children were grown and their husbands no longer noticed them. Ellen always asked them in though she knew it would mean weeks of misery ahead, offerings of home-made jam, cakes, not brought as neighbourly gifts, but as an entrance fee. Often, these ladies sat in the kitchen and cried, while Ellen poured tea. Our mother was a sharp, easily irritated person, and social occasions bored her, but with Boyd's hangers-on she was gentle, even going so far as to shield them by pretending they had really come to see *her*,

12

or by finding some hidden talent in them and displaying it before us like a talisman to dispel our scorn. 'Really, she's very gifted, she plays the piano beautifully,' or, 'She does the most marvellous embroidery.'

We dreaded the time when Ellen would begin to unearth Miss Carter's special abilities; it tired her so, and when she was tired she was hard on us. And we could see that Miss Carter was likely to be more of a nuisance than any of the others had been. Once winter was over, all she would have to do would be to linger in her garden, on fine weekends, and pop up behind the privet hedge. Her infatuation, therefore, must be nipped in the bud before summer began, and Joanna and I had already settled on a plan to achieve this. It was a good plan, but we could not put it into action while Poll was with us, so I merely answered her, politely, that Boyd was no busier than usual, for January.

Joanna said, 'Of course there's 'flu about. But not many night calls, not many confinements. We don't get a rash of babies till April. Nine months from the August holidays.'

Miss Carter said that she didn't think Joanna ought to talk that way, in front of her little sister.

I said, 'Why not? Childbirth's a natural function. Boyd says children are old enough to know things as soon as they want to know.'

'Why do you call your father Boyd? That's rather unusual, Kate, isn't it?' Miss Carter said.

'Because he isn't our father.'

Joanna glared at me. This was something she hated to get about. I thought it stupid of her. I was proud we had a step-father, it marked us off from other people.

Miss Carter said she hadn't realized, we looked so much like him.

'We look like our mother,' Joanna said.

Both Boyd and Ellen were light-haired and brown-eyed, as we were. Only Poll was different from the rest of our family; her hair was so dark that it was almost black, and her eyes were a rich, pure blue. I saw Miss Carter look down at her and knew she was guessing who Poll must be like. Embarrassed, I began to skip ahead, dragging Poll with me.

'Don't *pull* me, I want to walk with Miss Carter.' Poll freed her hand and ran back, smiling up at her teacher in a sycophantic way.

I felt stupid because I had run on ahead, so I ran faster, pretending to be absorbed in jumping the cracked paving stones. I was too old to behave like that, so perhaps it was reasonable that Miss Carter, when they caught me up at the traffic lights, should speak to me as if I were a child, Poll's age.

'A little bird tells me you're having a visitor today,' she said, coyly rolling her large, pale eyes.

Joanna said, bitter because she had had to apologize for me, '*I* told Miss Carter Aunt Hat was coming, that's why you're in such a hurry to get home.'

'She's not really our Auntie,' Poll said. 'She's an old sick friend. She's been in hospital having her insides out.'

Miss Carter looked startled. We were passing Boots'. 'Look, Poll, I began, but there was nothing to draw her attention to except a display of hot-water bottles in the main window.

'Her womb,' Poll said. 'Ladies have to have that done sometimes when they get old. I know what it's called but I disremember the name.'

'Shut *up*, Poll, I muttered.

Boyd had explained the functions of the body to us and also, when suitable occasions arose, what could go wrong with it. He always used exact, medical terms. His theory, and our mother's, was that this would teach us not to be afraid of disease, but, like many educational theories, there were disadvantages in practice. People were rarely shocked when we paraded our learning – that would have been gratifying; they were more often merely uneasily amused, and I hated to be laughed at.

But Miss Carter seemed neither amused nor put out. She only murmured, 'Oh, the poor thing!'

'We've got to keep quiet and not bother her too much,'

Poll told her, as the lights changed and we crossed the main road.

Passing Woolworth's, Joanna's eyes met mine. We both had the same fear, that Poll would go on and spill out the rest of Aunt Hat's story, or a garbled version of it, anyway, which was all she could have overheard by chance – a blow by blow account of Aunt Hat's hysterectomy might have been thought suitable for Poll's ears, but the true reason for her visit was not. And, certainly we did not want Miss Carter to know it. Joanna thought it shameful, but I had a different reason. I was not too young to know that nothing pleases people like a good disaster, especially if it is still fresh and smelling of blood, so to speak: I did not like Miss Carter well enough to want to give her that pleasure. Besides, I had been warned not to tell. . . .

Luckily the coffee-roasting machine was working in Cullen's window and Poll forgot Aunt Hat to look at it. Joanna and I were glad to stop too. Joanna could see Will Saxon inside the shop, buying his mother's groceries, and knew that if she waited until he came out, she could affect surprise at seeing him and linger, talking, until we went on ahead and they could walk home together. I was prepared to indulge her, and Poll, because I still enjoyed watching the coffee machine too, though I was too old to admit to it. The rattle of Cullen's roaster, and the smell of coffee, remains one of the good memories of my childhood.

There are plenty of others. Monks Ford is twenty-five miles from London. There was once an abbey there, on the River Lance, and a prosperous community based upon it and upon an earthenware industry. Like the abbey, it no longer exists, but when we lived there some of the pots were still displayed in the town museum, a dim, close-smelling room above the Council Offices, along with several cases of stuffed birds and a collection of Zulu weapons dating from the Boer War that had been presented by General Claud Archer Fantom who had also given the town the stone drinking trough, inscribed with his name, that stood beside the Market

Cross. The trough was no longer filled with water, only sweet papers and icecream cartons and empty cigarette packets. The Mental Hospital, the Fire station, the Junior School and the Grammar, had all been built in the years 1901–1906, during General Fantom's reign as Chairman of the local Council. That was the time, too, that the old houses in the main street had been pulled down and the ugly, flat, yellow ones built. The pots in the Museum and the Market Cross remained the only signs that Monks Ford had a past before General Fantom's heyday – it was said that he would have pulled down the Market Cross if the Antiquarian Society had not been active in organizing local resistance.

There was no industry except a timber mill down at the lock, where the Lance flowed into the Thames, and, behind the station, a dental factory which had a window where sets of false teeth were displayed on small plinths, like archaeological specimens. All the same, the town was growing, new housing estates spreading slowly across the surrounding fields like a skin disease. Most of the men and working girls commuted: factory hands to Slough, professional middle-class and typists to London.

Monks Ford was 'dead', most people said. We could never understand why. There were seven public houses, three churches – Anglican, Roman and Methodist – two cinemas, a golf course, a tennis club, a Dramatic Society. What more did they want? Brothels? Casinos? Whatever the dissatisfactions of our elders, it seemed to us that Monks Ford was a satisfactory place and superior, not only to the Mile End Road, but also to the country where we had lived before. There was so much more to look at. Boots, Sainsbury's, Woolworth's, Jock's Icecream Parlour – the shops in the main street were Aladdin's caves; winter afternoons, before curtains were drawn, the houses in the residential roads were theatrical shows, put on for our benefit. If we wanted trees and grass there was the park which was better than a country field: there were no cow pats in it. (Cow pats had no virtue, unlike horse dung which was a lucky thing to step into.) We could even, if we wished, gather blackberries – slightly dusty

16

and shrivelled, but tasting as good to us as the bilberries we had picked in Shropshire – from the high hedges in the lane that led from General Fantom's house, now lived in by his son and daughter, to the lock. Unsurprisingly, the Fantom's house was called Lock View: it looked directly down the lane to the river, over a stretch of what was almost country. There were country smells there, may and dead nettle instead of laurel and privet, and there were no buildings except the Water Works, a great, high, solemn building, aloof as a cathedral, standing alone in the flat field; Poll's floody field, where, this summer, they would roast the ox.

Watching the coffee machine, Poll forgot about Aunt Hat and remembered the ox. Turning to Miss Carter, she said, 'Will we have to take what bit we're given? What if we don't like fat?'

I expected this question to floor Miss Carter and watched her face for that look of stupidly superior, amused puzzlement with which adults conceal their lack of mental agility, but she said that though we should have to take Pot Luck, perhaps there would be separate portions set out for people who liked lean, and people who liked fat. She spoke sensibly, as if she had given the matter some thought, and I was disappointed: I hated to concede her any good qualities.

Will came out of Cullen's, blushing at the sight of Joanna. He had thick, sandy hair that fell straight from one point on his crown, like a wig. I thought he was undistinguished because of his blushes and the bi-focals he wore, and wished Joanna could have picked on someone better-looking to love. I had decided that her trouble was that she rated herself too low because she was miserable about her figure: she was only a little plump, but when she looked in the glass she saw, not a pretty girl, but a grotesque distortion, a comic postcard horror. She went without vests in winter and, however hot the summer day, always wore her school blazer over her frocks, to conceal her silhouette. Now, as Will approached her, scarlet between his freckles and nonchalantly swinging his shopping bag, she glanced furtively in the shop window and assumed a curious, unnatural posture, sucking in her stomach and hunching her shoulders forward to conceal her bosom.

Miss Carter spoke brightly to me. 'We'd better hurry on, hadn't we, Kate? We'll freeze if we stand here much longer.' She gave me a small, meaning smile, which I ignored. Although Poll protested that she was not cold, but boiling to *death*, she allowed Miss Carter to lead her away.

I lagged behind, anxious to avoid the moment when we would reach our respective gates and Miss Carter would say, archly, wistfully, 'I wonder if Anyone could find room for just one teeny,weeny piece of cake?' Or sweets, or icecream, or cinnamon toast. Joanna and I were always embarrassed when she coaxed us like that. She was exposing herself to our pity, and it made us ashamed for her.

All we could do was to keep out of her way as I was doing now, more determinedly than usual – when we turned into our road, I dodged into the Saxon's driveway – because I had an additional reason for not being trapped today. I had wasted enough time, waiting for Poll, watching the coffee grinder; suddenly I could not bear to waste another minute. I had to get home to see Aunt Hat.

My motive was not affection. Aunt Hat was a dim figure from our Shropshire days, pre-Mile End Road, pre-Boyd, when she had been evacuated from London with her stepson, Dick, and rented the cottage next to ours. As far as I could remember, we had only seen her once since, but she and Ellen must have remained close, or she would not have turned to our mother in trouble, nor would Ellen have reacted with such distress when she received her letter. She had said, 'Oh, no, Oh *no*,' repeating the words with stunned disbelief, and there were tears in her eyes as she handed the letter to Boyd, across the breakfast table.

He read it and said, 'She'd better come to us, as soon as she's well enough.'

'*Can* she? We haven't really room.' Ellen reddened slightly: she was often forced, with Boyd, into putting the ungenerous side of an argument. Boyd was generous to a

18

fault, as they say, the fault in his case being that his generosity was so natural, his goodness so easy-seeming, that he could make more practical people seem mean and carping. But in this case Ellen's objection was not merely practical. Once we had left the table and she thought we were out of earshot, I heard her say, 'It's a dreadful thing for the children to have to hear about. What can we tell them? It's no good expecting Hattie to keep quiet.'

'Tell them the truth, they won't be able to do enough for her,' Boyd said.

We did not find the truth so dreadful. Parents are forgetful – or, perhaps, ignorant is a better word: they prefer to forget what their own memories could tell them, which is that children are not so easily harmed. Unless it takes place in their immediate vicinity, they are not shocked by violence; it only whets their appetite for life which is, they suspect, rather different from what they have been told.

Aunt Hat's third husband, Jack, was an infrequently employed docker whom Aunt Hat supported by charring and taking in lodgers at her house in the East End of London. Among them, when he was home on leave, was Dick, the son of her second husband who had been killed at Dunkirk. One night, when Aunt Hat was just out of hospital, Jack had come home in a sour mood; he had attacked Dick, and, when Aunt Hat tried to intervene, knocked her senseless. A neighbour had called the police and Aunt Hat was in hospital again, suffering, not so much from her injuries as from shock and weakness. The husband had been remanded in custody.

'I hope he gets a good, long stretch,' Ellen said savagely. 'Oh – it makes my blood boil! When I think what she's taken from Jack all these years!'

'Has he always knocked her about? Why didn't she leave him, then?' we asked practically.

Ellen shrugged. 'She's the sort to put up with things. There are a lot of women like that, they put up with things, often because there's nothing else they can do. That's one of the reasons why it's important that girls should be properly educated and trained. . . .'

Here followed the familiar lecture on how necessary it was that we should not fritter our time away, but work hard at school and get into good universities so we should always have 'something to fall back on.' We often felt, though I think this was not Ellen's conscious intention, that we were only being educated so that later on we could run away from our husbands if we wanted to.

Since we knew what Ellen was going to say, there was no point in listening. I watched the fire that was giving out little puffs of green smoke and brooded on Aunt Hat and her fascinating situation, only returning to my own when Ellen said, 'If I were you, I shouldn't say anything about this at school.'

'Why ever not? It's the sort of thing everyone would be interested to hear about.'

'You mean it's the sort of thing you'd enjoy telling,' Ellen said, rather more tartly, and Joanna chimed in: it wasn't exactly the sort of thing we wanted to get about Monks Ford, was it?

'For Aunt Hat's sake,' Ellen said quickly. 'Use your imagination, Kate. How do you think she'd feel, if she thought everyone round here knew all about what had happened? And a bit extra, I expect, if you have a hand in it.'

Though I was hurt by the implication, I saw this was reasonable. But I knew I would find silence hard to bear. I had a taste for a good story which was not often satisfied in Monks Ford. In the time we had lived there things *had* happened, of course: there had been a robbery in the Post Office, some boys had got into the timber mill and started a fire which blazed gloriously all one summer night, and, three years ago, Mr Saxon, Will's father, had run off with the pretty girl in the chemist's shop but had got no further than the big roundabout, five miles beyond the town, when his car was hit by a gravel lorry. Though the girl was unhurt – and, in fact, returned to the chemist's the following week – Mr Saxon was doomed to carry round for the rest of his life the visible consequences of his one misdemeanour: his spine had been injured and his neck enclosed in a pink, plastic collar which rose up round his chin and gave him a jointed appearance, like a ventriloquist's doll.

But that was all. You could count the good, meaty scandals on the fingers of one hand, and none of them had been *personal*, in the sense that we had inside knowledge to give us stature. I remember that we did what we could with the fact that the Saxons lived next door but one and that Will stayed with us for a week at that time, but Will, just fifteen then, had volunteered no information and Boyd – this was one time he was stern with us – threatened Joanna and me with hell and high water if we asked him so much as one single question, so we really knew nothing beyond the plain facts, and everyone who was neither an infant nor senile knew those. . . .

'Promise me, Kate,' Ellen said.

'All right,' I agreed reluctantly. I thought a minute. 'Why should he go for Dick in the first place?' I asked, but Ellen went suddenly deaf, looked at the clock and said she hadn't realized how late it was, we would have to run if we were to be at school on time. She followed us into the hall and said, 'Now remember, Kate,' before kissing me suddenly on the cheek, surprising me: she didn't kiss us very often.

I had kept my promise for more than a week now, though once or twice I had been sorely tempted. It would have helped if I could have discussed it with Joanna, but she wouldn't talk. At first I thought she was being prissy, then I began to wonder if she knew something I didn't. Had I been given an edited version? Thinking along these lines, I came up with Ellen's refusal to answer my question about the stepson: perhaps there was a relationship between Dick and Aunt Hat that Ellen thought unsuitable for me to hear of. Though I knew such things took place in literature, I did not really believe they could happen in life, but the idea served to lift Aunt Hat into the realm of tragedy and invest her, in my mind, with glory. A woman who had been through such an experience could not be ordinary. How would she speak, behave? Not like other people. I imagined her, walking the

21

house at night, groaning and wringing her hands like Lady Macbeth.

By the day of her arrival I was bursting, not only with excitement, but with dedicated resolve: I would be so good to Aunt Hat. When she was uttering great Shakespearian cries she might not mind an audience, but there would be other times when she would just want to sit and cry quietly by herself. I would be good to her then, and make her tea, and keep Poll out of the way. If she wanted it, I would sit by her chair as she mourned and let silence form a tender bond between us. I would be her companion, her comforter. . . .

I longed to begin. Peering from behind the Saxon's gate post, it seemed an age before Poll and Miss Carter disappeared through her gate. Immediately, I dodged out of my hiding place, raced the few yards to our house, through *our* gate, up the path. . . . The front door was always left on the latch. I catapulted across the hall and into the living room.

Aunt Hat was sitting by the fire, alone. She said, 'What's the matter duckie-doo? Got a train to catch?'

Chapter Two

She sat with her skirts lifted to the flames and looking quite ordinary. I felt a slight disappointment – only slight, because Lady Macbeth would really have been rather difficult to live up to – and then shyness. She was a complete stranger to me.

She said, 'I don't suppose you remember your funny old Aunt Hat, do you? Well, here she is, turned up like the proverbial bad penny.'

For a moment I had the queer feeling that there was someone else in the room. It was a feeling that was distantly familiar, a faint echo in my mind. Then I remembered slices of fresh bread, buttered, and stuck with brightly coloured hundreds and thousands. I could almost taste the grittiness of the sweets on my tongue: it went with grazed knees, consolation, and a strange habit of talking about oneself in the third person.

'Now, which of the kiddies are you? No – don't tell Aunt Hat. You must be Kate. Fancy! How the years roll by!'

She was rosy and plump with soft, cow-brown eyes that had a tender, liquid look. Her hair, a rich copper colour which looked false, but was not, had been arranged in little curls on her forehead in a way that made her appear like a slightly aged, Botticelli angel. She was dressed in the fashion of a few years before, known as the New Look: a full, tight-waisted skirt and girlish, frilled blouse, fastened at the neck by a brooch of painted shells. The curls and clothes gave her a romantic air. Her talcum powder smelt like icing sugar and, indeed, she reminded me of a frosted cake, soft and meltingly sweet, as I came shyly into her arms and she kissed me.

'So you've met Kate,' Ellen said, coming in with the tea trolley and kicking the door shut with her foot.

Aunt Hat held me at arm's length and looked raptly into my face. Her gaze was so ardent and searching that I imagined she must have gipsy gifts and was about to tell my fortune. But all she said was, 'She's like you, Ellen, she's got your nose,' a remark that she followed with a deep, satisfied sigh as if great intellectual effort had enabled her to make a major pronouncement. 'Your colouring too, bless her little cotton socks,' she went on, and pinched my cheek. I didn't mind, because I could see she meant to be nice, and it was pleasant to be told I looked like Ellen. I thought my mother beautiful.

Ellen said, 'Joanna, too,' and hesitated before she added, 'Not Poll, though.'

There was a warning note in her voice which I recognized as the one she used to me when she was afraid I might say something tactless or unkind.

Aunt Hat said quickly, 'Oh, I wouldn't speak out of turn, dear,' dropping her use of the third person as we were to discover she often did, when upset, and colouring a little. I felt an immediate affection for her: I could see that like myself she was used to criticism that assumed she was going to do things she had no intention of doing.

Ellen apologized, as she never did to me. 'Sorry, Hattie. No offence meant.'

Aunt Hat said, 'None taken, dear, I'm sure,' and they both smiled as if at some private joke between them.

Ellen asked where Poll was and I said next door. Ellen said we really mustn't bother Miss Carter and I was going to point out that it was more a matter of Miss Carter bothering us, but Aunt Hat diverted me. She put a napkin on my lap and a plate and, to my astonishment, began to coax me to eat. 'Have one of these dear little scones, my duck. Look, they're lovely and fresh. Shall Aunt Hat jam it for you?' she asked strangely, as I glanced at Ellen to see how she was taking this behaviour: she objected to children being treated like babies.

But she only smiled as Aunt Hat spread my scone with jam and watched lovingly as I ate it as if I were doing something clever. Then she dropped two lumps of sugar into her tea, sighed happily and said, well this was nice, wasn't it, the cup that cheers. Though the trolley, with scones and chocolate cake on it, had been placed in front of her, she took nothing to eat. When Ellen offered her cake, she said, 'Oh, no dear, Mr Avoirdupois, you know.'

Ellen said, 'Go on, Hattie, just a small bit of cake won't hurt you,' which surprised me as she usually accepted one's refusal as final on these occasions, and actually cut a piece of cake for Aunt Hat and put it on a plate and brought it over to her.

Aunt Hat shook her head in mock disapproval, said, 'Oh, you temptress!' and proceeded to cut the cake in tiny squares and eat them, her little finger elegantly crooked. When she caught me looking at her, she winked. 'Sweets to the sweet,' she said.

Later, we were to become accustomed to her gentle, irrelevant archness, but it was strange at first. This time, I worried how to respond to her – I smiled, but felt I should say something jolly as well – but only for a minute because, as she turned towards me, the light from the table lamp beside her shone full on her face and I saw, marring the rosiness of her skin, the remains of a dark, disfiguring bruise.

I felt myself go red to the roots of my hair. Fear that she would notice my colour and understand the cause of it, made matters worse: my cheeks burned shiny and hot like chilblains when you come out of the cold. I contemplated dropping my tea cup, or spilling the sugar bowl on the carpet to create a diversion, but Joanna and Poll came in then, and did it for me.

Aunt Hat's delight at their arrival could not have been greater if they had been her own long lost children, torn from her by some terrible circumstance and miraculously returned, after a lapse of years. In the space of the first few minutes, she called Poll her duckie-doo, her angel-pie, and in an odd American accent, her honey-chile. These endearments temporarily disorientated Joanna who stood stock still in the middle of the room, awkwardly fingering her Prefect's badge and looking as if she did not know where to put herself, but they pleased Poll who could take any amount of fuss without shame. She didn't hesitate when Aunt Hat said, 'Hasn't someone got a little kiss for her funny old Auntie,' but went straight to be hugged and kissed and then sat, very composedly, on Aunt Hat's lap while she held out her free hand to Joanna, who moved forward and took it, her fingers stiff with reluctance. Aunt Hat said, 'Goodness, how the years roll by' – her version of the more usual, 'Haven't you grown?' and then, 'Well, well, and how's Joanna?'

'*Dead*. Working my fingers to the bone,' Joanna said in the drawling, nasal voice she assumed when shy. She withdrew her hand gently, plumped heavily down on the sofa and blew out her lips. 'Actually, I'm working for my A levels. Latin and Greek. It's a fearful sweat,' she said.

Aunt Hat widened her pretty eyes. 'Fancy! What a clever young person. Beauty *and* brains, I see.' The fringe of copper curls danced as she shook her head gaily. 'Let's hope it's not all work and no play. *That* makes Jill a dull girl, doesn't it? But I expect you have lots of fun, too, lots of parties and boy friends, don't you? Ah – don't look shy. Aunt Hat remembers what it's like to be seventeen!'

Joanna stared at her blankly for a moment and then, suddenly, smiled. I saw she had decided to like Aunt Hat and was glad, because she easily might not have done. There was an awful, self-conscious coyness about Aunt Hat's way of speaking which almost concealed her innocent intention to give pleasure.

Ellen said, 'She'll have plenty of time for that sort of thing later on. Just now she's got enough on her plate, working for her university entrance. So don't put ideas into her head, Hattie. Please!'

I was astonished by the fierce abruptness of her tone – as if poor Aunt Hat had been tempting Joanna into an orgy of meaningless frivolity. That was not only unfair, it was also silly, I thought indignantly, and then, looking at Ellen, saw that she was really upset: her eyes had grown huge and dark in her thin face and she was sitting tensely on the edge of her chair. I decided that she was disturbed, as grown-ups often were, not by something that had actually been said, but by something else altogether. I was afraid Aunt Hat might not understand this and would simply feel she had been snubbed, but she only said, mildly, that she hoped Joanna wouldn't pay any attention to her, she was a great tease, and proceeded to pour Poll a glass of milk and spread jam on a scone for her as she had done for me.

Later, when we were doing our homework upstairs after supper, Joanna said that the trouble with Ellen was that she worried too much about our future. 'She's scared stiff that if we start thinking life ought to be just fun, we'll get slack and not bother and it'll make things hard for us later on. Though how Plautus is going to make it so bloody easy, *I* don't know. Dirty old man.'

I said, quoting Ellen, that classics were a good training for

26

the mind and that once she was through university, she would be able to get a good job, teaching or in the civil service.

Joanna looked gloomy. She wasn't sure she wanted to go to a university, she said, and added quickly, because this was a near-heresy in our family, 'It's just that sometimes I get bored with thinking years ahead and never being able to relax and have a nice time.'

'But we do have a nice time,' I protested. I knew Ellen had sterner ideas about our upbringing than most mothers, but they had not incommoded me so far. 'We have birthday parties and go to the pictures.'

'Saturdays,' Joanna said. '*Saturdays*.' She got up from her chair and began to pace up and down the room, swinging her arms and breathing deeply. There was not much room to pace as Aunt Hat was to sleep in my room and my desk had been brought into Joanna's and a safari bed set up against the wall. 'Oh,' she cried in a wild, demented voice, 'Sometimes I feel like . . . like a young horse, tethered.'

'You look more like a caged elephant to me,' I said, not meaning to be disagreeable, but because her cramped, swaying movements had reminded me of just that: a sad, grey beast seen at the Zoo, lurching rhythmically backwards and forwards in a cruelly small space. I was not altogether sorry I had said it, though. I did not object to Joanna striking theatrical attitudes, but she was so bad at acting that it embarrassed me. Poll was a natural actress, had been since birth, and I had a good sense of timing and a feeling for the right phrase, but Joanna always overstated everything; she made large, irrelevant gestures where a shrug or a lifted eyebrow would have served the purpose better, and falsified her emotions by the use of loud, extravagant words. She was cleverer than Poll or I would ever be, but she did not know a good performance from a bad one.

Even when Joanna was acting properly, on the school stage, she ruined her parts by dramatic vulgarities, forcing her voice to soar too high or sink too low, and drawing in her breath with a terrible hiss when a simple pause would have been more effective. She had been Portia last year, chosen, I suppose because she was statuesque and striking and could be trusted to learn her part conscientiously. Afterwards she asked me if she had been good and, because she had been praised enough and it was bad for her, I said it would have been all right if the Merchant of Venice had been grand opera. She burst into tears and Ellen was angry with me. She said it was petty to be jealous, but Boyd took me aside later on and told me that he did not think I was jealous, only stupid. He said it was silly to be too critical of an amateur performance and, for an amateur, Joanna had done very nicely; it was not her fault if she had not inherited our father's talent for the theatre as Poll and I had done. I asked him, then, if our father had been a good actor and he said he had never seen him, but he believed he had been very good indeed. He hesitated a minute and then added that he thought Joanna was anxious to act, when she could, because she wanted to be like him.

It seemed a silly reason for wanting to do something you were bad at, but I knew people often made themselves unhappy for silly reasons and now, looking at Joanna, I was sorry I had called her an elephant. She was crouching in front of the gas fire with her back to me and her shoulders miserably hunched. As I did not care to apologize, it seemed best to ignore her dejection and the cause of it, and return to what we had been discussing before.

'I don't see why Ellen has to jump on Aunt Hat, though, she only tries to be nice.'

'Oh, it doesn't matter, they understand each other,' Joanna muttered. She straightened her back a little and held out her cramped hands to the fire which was an old second-hand one, all pops and hisses. It gave out so little heat when the gas pressure was low as it always was in cold weather, that you could barely thaw out your frozen fingers in front of it. Joanna's were white to the knuckle bone; she had bad circulation which wasn't helped by the temperature of her room – this evening, away from the popping fire, our breath puffed out like smoke. She began shaking her hands from

28

the wrists to get the blood back, and, turning from the fire, looked at me thoughtfully.

'Don't you really see? Aunt Hat bothers Ellen because she's such a different sort of person. Ellen's a worrier and Aunt Hat's the easy sort. She's a talker and Ellen's quiet, and she's sentimental and Ellen isn't.'

I knew sentimentality was bad. It was the way one should never recite poetry, as Joanna sometimes did, in a false, shuddery voice. I said, indignantly, that I didn't think Aunt Hat was sentimental at all.

Joanna sat on the floor and ran her fingers through her slippery blonde hair. 'Oh, but she *is!* Look how she talked at supper, about her husband!'

While we ate supper, Aunt Hat had chattered on about the price of fish, the scarcity of coal, a film she had seen with Gary Cooper and how we girls had grown since she had known us in the country. What little dears we had been! Did Ellen think I was taller now than Joanna had been at my age? Though Ellen said she could not remember, this did not deter Aunt Hat from speculation; she was sure, she said, Joanna had only come up to her shoulder last time they had met and I was taller than that, wasn't I? She herself, of course, was such a little dot! Knee-high to a grasshopper! But then, at *that* time, Joanna had only been ten and now I was two years older, so it was difficult for her to make a comparison, wasn't it? She would have thought it impossible, Ellen said, not sharply but gently, the way she was gentle with Poll, and Aunt Hat sighed and said, well it didn't really matter, we were both going to be right old bean-poles, she could see that.

Then she fell silent. I became very conscious of the tick of the clock on the mantelpiece as I ate my pudding. Aunt Hat only toyed with hers; after a little, Ellen glanced questioningly at Boyd who asked her if she was tired. Would she like to go to bed and have a glass of warm milk brought up to her? Aunt Hat said no, she wouldn't hear of it, the last thing she wanted was to make trouble. She gave one of her long, tremulous sighs and said, 'I didn't mean to be a wet-blanket, but it just came over me about Jack.' She put down her pudding spoon and her soft eyes misted. 'Poor Jack, poor Jack. I wonder what he's feeling now. It must be terrible for him, shut up in that place, a man of his nature. He was always one for great long walks and open air, he would never stick at an inside job, ever, that's why he left the factory, you know, though he was getting good wages and overtime. But he couldn't abide being closed in, he couldn't bear to see anyone shut up, not even a bird or a dog in a kennel. . . . Oh, that'll be the worst thing for him, worse than the dry bread and the hard words. . . .'

I was startled by this, because the dramatic reason for her visit to us had receded from my mind under the impact of her gentle, garrulous presence. Though I went on, stolidly eating my pudding, I peered at her through my lashes in wonder. The pretty colour had not gone from her cheeks, but she looked tired and somehow shabby, like an old doll. One tear slid shinily from her eye. She said, 'Oh dear, I'm so sorry, such an old silly.'

Ellen said, 'For God's sake, Hattie.' But she got up and went round the table to put her arm round Aunt Hat's shoulders. Though as a gesture this was clumsy and un-finished – she did not know what to do next but just stood awkwardly, her face on fire – I was impressed that she had made it. Ellen was unpractised in showing affection. We took her love on trust: a good-night peck or an occasional nervous pat on the cheek were all the demonstrations of it she could manage. She must care for Aunt Hat very much, I thought, and this surprised me because I was at the age when it is hard to believe anyone can be really fond of a person outside their own family, but I knew Ellen would not have gone to her like that, even though she loved her, and was sorry she was unhappy, if she had thought Aunt Hat was being sentimental. And, indeed, it seemed to me that Aunt Hat had been simply speaking of what she thought and felt, and that had nothing to do with sighing over poetry or silly postcards of kittens with bows round their necks.

I said this, or something near to it, but Joanna answered

scornfully, 'Don't be stupid, Kate. I mean, could any person in their right mind be really sorry for someone who'd knocked her unconscious and nearly killed her stepson?'

I observed, righteously, that I thought one was supposed to turn the other cheek, and then the rest of what she had said clicked into place. '*What* did he do to Dick?'

Joanna looked at me and then looked away. She said slowly, 'He knocked him down and Dick hit his head on the brass fender. He cracked his skull. They were afraid, for a bit, he might die.'

The room was still. Then I stammered, 'But if he had, it'ud be murder. I mean if he killed Dick, he'd have been *hanged*.'

I was awed by the thought of the glory that would have attached to us in this event. A murderer's wife in the house! Then I realized that the chance to contemplate this glory had been deliberately denied me.

'Why didn't you tell me?' I raged.

'Ellen told me not to. Oh – don't go black in the face. She was right. You know what you are.'

I longed to launch myself at her to wipe the smug look from her face, but the desire to hear more was stronger. Controlling myself, I said, 'What'll happen to him, then? Will they just let him *off*?'

'Ellen says he'll get nine months at least. I expect we'll have Aunt Hat here for ages and ages.'

'Don't you like Aunt Hat?'

'Oh, I *like* her. You couldn't not.' She paused and added in a surprised voice, 'But I can't *think* how she and Ellen ever became friends. *Really!*'

'Why, she was living next door to us in the country.' I said, but Joanna shook her head impatiently; she didn't mean that.

It struck me she had a guilty air. 'D'you mean because Aunt Hat is common?'

Joanna blushed. 'No, of course not. It's just they're such an unlikely pair. I mean, Ellen reads the *New Statesman* and worries about the world. Aunt Hat'll drive her mad, talking and talking about nothing.' But she avoided my eye and I knew Aunt Hat's common-ness was, in fact, in her mind. Joanna was peculiarly sensitive about people's accents and the kind of words they used. (We mustn't say 'toilet', we must say 'lavatory', she had argued one day, as passionately as if something of importance was at stake. 'Toilet' was common. I did not much care what we called it, but I had appealed to Boyd; he said it was a matter of fair indifference to him too, but, just for the record, both were middle-class euphemisms.)

Joanna said faintly, 'It's all very well, but someone in this house has to take account of what people think. What will the patients say if Aunt Hat answered the telephone and calls them dearie and duckie-doo?'

I answered, coldly, that I imagined they would be pleased to be addressed so affectionately. I thought Joanna's attitude disgusting. I turned to my homework and pointedly ignored her. Since she minded what I thought, too, she attempted to ingratiate herself by offering me half a Crunchie Bar, but I resisted temptation and applied myself to a problem about A, who could run faster than B, but slower than C. Just to open a mathematics textbook gave me the sensation of creeping slowly through a thick, yellow fog, but I stuck at it heroically until bed time.

Once in bed, I was sorry I had been so determined to punish Joanna for snobbery, because she went to sleep at once and left me awake and lonely. The safari bed was tolerably comfortable but the room was unfamiliar and far too light: my room, now Aunt Hat's, looked on to our garden and the Fantom's garden that backed on to it, but Joanna's faced the road and the headlamps of passing cars made cobwebby patterns on the ceiling.

I could hear them talking downstairs and, through the wall, the droning sound Poll made in her sleep, when she was not grinding her teeth. Our house was one of six new houses that had been built just after the war on part of the big garden that belonged to General Fantom's house; the walls and floors were thin and, because the wood they had used was unseasoned, the doors either sagged or bulged.

Boyd was waiting for a licence to build a surgery against the garage; meantime, he shared one with his partner in the town, and saw private patients in the dining-room. His uncle's house, on the main street of Monks Ford, would have been better placed for a doctor, but Boyd had sold it for offices because, he said, it was unsuitable for a family. Ellen said he had been so unhappy in that house that he did not want us to grow up there, but this seemed strange to me: I could not imagine that Boyd, or any grown-up, could be really unhappy.

The front door bell rang and I heard Boyd's step, and his voice, and then the car revving in the garage as he went out on a call. I watched the headlights move dreamily across the ceiling and lay, sleepily awake, listening to Aunt Hat murmuring downstairs and Ellen's voice, occasionally and briefly answering. It was a pleasant, comforting sound, in no way strange, and that puzzled me until I thought: Of course, when we lived in the country, Aunt Hat used to come in, some evenings, to sit with Ellen. Once I had remembered that, other things came crowding in; some I remembered, and some Joanna had told me when we talked about that time.

Aunt Hat's cottage was warmer than our's and full of cooking smells. She taught Joanna to make crinoline ladies: cakes, turned out of pudding basins, decorated with icing-sugar skirts and topped with waist-length, china models of Victorian ladies with piled hair and blouses. Aunt Hat made beautiful cakes and was generous with them in spite of rationing; she fed them, not only to us, but also to the Italian prisoners who lived on the farm and often called on her, when their day's work was over. Ellen never went in to Aunt Hat when the Italians were there and forbade us to go. Joanna thought this short-sighted of her, since, if she had been friendly with them, like Aunt Hat, they would have chopped her firewood too.

Joanna found Ellen's attitude especially peculiar because we were allowed to talk to the prisoners when they were in the fields or the yard. One, who was small and monkeyish and sad, was always displaying pictures of his wife and children in Naples. He left to go back to the camp when his family were killed by a British bomb: he had turned sulky, the farmer's wife said, and idled at his work. The other Italian, Giovanni, was much younger, dark and handsome with beautiful, white teeth. He was Aunt Hat's favourite; summer evenings, when the windows were open, we heard them laughing in the cottage next door.

He came to visit Aunt Hat the time Ellen left us with her. It was the first time she had left us, ever, but I don't remember that we missed her, perhaps because living with Aunt Hat was like a holiday: we stayed up late and ate at unusual times. Giovanni brought a pheasant one night and we were up long past our bedtime while Aunt Hat cooked it and roasted little rounds of bread in the fat and joked with Giovanni in the kitchen. She shut the door into the living room, to keep out the cooking smells she said, and we could hear them laughing through the closed door. Later on, we went to bed gorged with pheasant, and I fell asleep at once. Some time after, I woke up with a stomach ache and heard Ellen's voice downstairs. We hadn't been told she was coming back and I was half out of bed with excitement, my pain forgotten, when I realized she was angry. She was shouting. Her voice grated. Aunt Hat was crying. I froze on the edge of the bed until I became aware that Joanna was lying awake beside me. I stretched out my arm to take her hand, and we lay side by side, listening. The cottage had one living room and a tiny hall, containing the narrow stair. Ellen must have come into the hall because suddenly we heard her more clearly. All I know is that her tone made my stomach feel like a lump of lead but Joanna remembered her words and told me, years later, 'You say you meant well, but you couldn't have done worse if you'd wanted to ruin me, could you?' The front door slammed. Aunt Hat was still crying when we went to sleep.

It was very soon after that – Joanna says only a week – that we left the country and went to live in the Mile End

Road. We only saw Aunt Hat once again. She came to see us in the flat and brought a golliwog for me and a chicken for Ellen. I remember the occasion perfectly. It must have been about eight months after their quarrel, because I was five years and four months when we left our cottage, and she came on my sixth birthday, which was a week after Poll was born.

Lying awake in the safari bed, which seemed less comfortable than it had been earlier, I wondered why they had quarrelled. I had the feeling that I had known more at the time than I could remember now. Now, the whole of that time was as vague in my mind as the war itself which had passed over my head like a dull, adult conversation.

'Joanna,' I said into the darkness, 'Joanna.' I stopped. Joanna never remembered anything, she was too old. Even if she did, she wouldn't talk about it, she would say she had too much on her mind to want to poke into other people's business.

I sighed and wriggled and the struts of the bed creaked. I told myself it was silly to stay awake, worrying over something that was over and done and that, anyway, could not have been very important or Ellen and Aunt Hat would not have stayed friends in spite of it. But it was no good. I stayed awake, listening to the voices downstairs and straining to hear what they said, until I heard the car drive in, Boyd's step in the hall and his voice. It stopped me heaving and tossing at once, partly, I suppose, because in my half-awake, nightmarish state, I was afraid Ellen and Aunt Hat would start quarrelling again if he were not there to stop them. But it was chiefly that it was always a comfort to know he was safe home, and would be there in the morning.

Chapter Three

'I shan't be home tea-time,' Poll said. 'I'm going to tea with my lover.'

I caught Boyd's eye and smiled discreetly to show I knew this word had a different connotation from the one Poll placed upon it.

Ellen said, 'It's the first I've heard. Are you sure?'

Poll nodded. 'His mother said, Walt told me yesterday. I'm glad he's asked me to tea.' She crunched up her last piece of breakfast toast and gulped milk to turn it pleasantly soggy in her mouth. It was something I still did when I thought I could get away with it. She sloshed the mixture round her mouth. 'I thought he'd gone off me the other day.'

Joanna glared disapproval of Poll's manners, which she thought were too indulgently overlooked. 'Was that why your borrowed that shilling? You said you wanted to buy Walter something.'

'He was playing with Gilly all the time because she brings sweets to school. *Her* mother doesn't think they spoil your teeth. So I bought him an ice lolly. But he still wouldn't play with me. So I punched him in the chest and he was nice then. He told me a new song, about knickers and kippers.' She giggled insanely. 'Like to hear it?'

'No thank you, Poll,' Joanna said.

Poll shrugged her shoulders, folded her napkin and got down from the table. When she had left the room, Boyd said, 'Poll belongs to the knock-down, drag-out school,' and laughed, not so much at his own joke, as with love for Poll. He loved Poll more than anyone. It wasn't that he made a difference between us, but you could tell from the way his eyes followed her.

'Is Walter the warty one?' Ellen asked.

'Yes. All over his hands. It's disgusting. His name's Walter Tanner,' Joanna said, 'and he lives down on the caravan site. It's horrible, nothing but mud.'

'I've not noticed Poll minding mud.'

Joanna fiddled with her coffee spoon. 'I do wish you'd send Poll to a private school, Mother.' She only called Ellen 'Mother' when she was on the war path about something.

'She'll learn more at the Primary. Kate was happy there.'

Joanna turned her mouth down. '*She* didn't naturally gravitate to the lowest elements the way Poll does. A boy like Walter could be a terrible influence. He is already. Look how she was eating this morning, like a pig! We were never allowed to . . .' She looked at Ellen, then at Boyd. 'Don't you want Poll to grow up ladylike?' she asked in a tragic voice.

I started to laugh but Boyd froze me with his eye.

'I shouldn't worry, Joanna. Swearing and rude rhymes and eating like a pig are phases people go through. And I don't think Walter will influence Poll.' He chuckled. 'You might as well try to influence the wind.'

Joanna didn't answer for a minute. Her face was shadowed with worry. Finally, she said, 'They're so *rough*, Walter and his lot . . .'

I said, 'It's not Walter that's rough, it's Poll. You should just see her and her gang in the playground. She looks like a rogue elephant in a herd of cows.'

'You've got elephants on your mind, haven't you?' Joanna said venomously, and I was startled because it was at least ten days ago, the night Aunt Hat had arrived, that I had called her an elephant. I decided against pointing out that she certainly had a memory like one and awarded myself an extra spoonful of sugar in my coffee, for virtuous restraint.

Joanna gave a little, pointed sigh, intended to convey that it was a hopeless situation about which she had done her best. She followed the sigh with a too-sweet smile to show our parents that she forgave them for their irresponsibility, and stretched out her hand to the toast rack.

Ellen's tone suggested that she had been as irritated by the sigh and the smile as I was. 'Joanna, don't you think you've eaten enough?'

Joanna's hand whipped back from the toast rack as if it had burned her and her straight hair swung like curved wings on either side of her cheeks as she hung her head.

'I'm sorry,' Ellen said, more gently, 'but if you really want to lose weight . . .'

Joanna muttered, 'I've got mock A-levels today. Greek. You burn up a lot of energy in exams.'

Boyd said he thought, on the whole, that she'd absorbed enough calories this morning to write Gibbon's *Decline and Fall*.

Joanna groaned loudly, got up and flounced from the room. She slammed the door, opened it, and closed it again with elaborate, insolent gentleness.

Boyd said, 'If those extra pounds are ruining her life we've got to help her lose them.'

'Oh, I know.' Ellen pushed her plate aside, stuck her elbows on the table and looked dejected. 'And I know she feels it her duty to be critical of Poll's upbringing. But I wish she wouldn't feel it her duty at breakfast. Not just at the moment, anyway.'

Boyd said, 'Shall I take Hat to the hospital today?' I can get Philips to take my surgery.'

Ellen shook her head. 'No – I don't mind, really. But I do wish she wouldn't always tell the nurses that I'm her friend who's married to a doctor. I know it's petty, but it embarrasses me.' Suddenly, misery raked lines across her pale face and made her look much older. She said passionately, 'And I hate to sit with her, at that young man's bedside, and hear her telling him she's sure poor Jack didn't really mean to hurt him, it's just that he's a bit hasty sometimes. Oh – how can *anyone* deceive themselves like that?'

'Perhaps she couldn't bear it otherwise,' Boyd said.

'But it's so weak and silly.' Her lips curled. 'Oh, she's not a fool, why does she behave like one? And it's so *wrong* – what does she want that boy to do, commit perjury?'

Boyd said, 'Kate, take another cup of coffee up to Aunt Hat, will you?'

I was glad to go. It disturbed me to hear Ellen speak of Aunt Hat like that. I could not understand why she did, when I knew she loved her – her love was evident in a hundred little things she did for her, like putting hot-water bottles in her bed, 'sugaring' her tea and pressing her to eat cake. And yet she had spoken of Aunt Hat as if she despised her. This puzzled me: I had always assumed that if you loved, you must be partisan.

Even when I knew better, I still could not understand her despair over Aunt Hat's behaviour. There are some gulfs that are too wide. I was born too late to appreciate my mother's feminist sense of outrage that any woman should have to endure what Aunt Hat had endured, from any man. Though Joanna and I were shocked and sorry that Aunt Hat had a cruel husband, we assumed she could have left him had she wanted to. But to Ellen, Jack was an archetypal tyrant, an archetypal brute, a scourge of woman. Intellectually, Ellen was liberal and gentle, she abhorred the idea of retributive punishment, but faced with someone like Jack her blood boiled: prison was the place for him.

She was incapable, therefore, of understanding Aunt Hat's dilemma which seemed to me pitifully simple: she loved 'poor Jack' and she loved her stepson. The thought that he would testify against her husband was terrible to her.

'If only I can get Dickie to see things my way,' she said suddenly, when I had given her the coffee and lifted the breakfast tray off her knees. 'I've been thinking about it all night. He's young, dear, and young people can be hard.' She looked at me earnestly, sitting up against the pillows in a pink bedjacket, her forehead fringed with small, steel curlers. 'Though to be fair to Dickie, he's not bitter against Jack for himself. He thinks I've had a bad time. That's what I can't get him to understand. Oh – I'm not saying Jack's been easy, he's had a hard time in his life, all kicks and no ha'pence. He had a rotten drunk for a father, he took off his belt soon as look at him, and then he was wounded in the war and couldn't lift properly after. He ought to have had a disability pension, by rights.'

'That's no reason why he should knock you about,' I said, slipping over to the door and closing it.

Aunt Hat watched me doubtfully. 'I shouldn't really be talking to you like this. . . .'

Though we had had this out before, I reassured her for form's sake. 'It's all right. I'm old for my age.'

She sighed comfortably. 'Yes, you're a sensible kiddie.' She sipped her coffee and we smiled at each other.

She said, 'You mustn't run away with the idea I think it's right, what Jack did. My Dad used to say no decent man would lift his hand against a woman, but my Dad was a countryman – I can remember him at eighty up a ladder picking apples and straight as a man half his age – he'd not known a day's sickness and there'd been nothing hard in his life but the weather. He'd not understand Jack and what it's like to live in a dirty slum with every man's hand against you and no hope of justice this side the grave. But you're a clever kiddie, you can understand it. It's not natural for men to take things as they come, they have to kick against the pricks, fight back, it's their nature. Of course, Jack shouldn't have taken it out on me, but there was nothing personal in it.'

Apart from his drunken father and being wounded in the war, I was not sure why Jack's life had been so hard, but I took her word for it. I felt, though, that Aunt Hat did not altogether stick to the point. I said, 'It was Dick he wanted to take it out on, wasn't it?'

'Well, yes, but Dickie riled him, you see. Not by anything he did, Dickie's a quiet one, it was more my fault, really. I made more of Dick than I should, his Dad being killed in the war and him having no one but me. It got under Jack's skin. I used to think it would be better when Dick was grown but it wasn't. It was all right when he was at sea, out of sight, out of mind, but when he came home on leave, things were worse than ever. It would have been better if he'd been a girl, really,' she said in a thoughtful, considering voice, as if

40

Dick's sex had, at some point, been a matter over which she had exercised choice. Then she gave a small sigh and the curlers on her forehead tinkled against each other as she went on, 'Jack had been off work a lot – there was a bit of bad luck but a lot more of jealousy and spite on other people's part – and seeing Dick, a young man in a steady job and earning good money was like a living insult. Dickie did well, you see, he's well thought of by the Company and when he came home this last time, he'd just had a raise. He was pleased as Punch. He came right in and told us and said, 'Mum' – he always called me that – "Mum, I can give you a bit more now and you won't need to go out so much!" Well, Kate, I couldn't help being pleased, could I?' She looked at me anxiously, as if she really wanted my opinion. 'I didn't want to take his money, but it was a bad time you know, things were tight with Jack not working and me just out of hospital, I'd had this little operation.

'A hysterectomy's a major operation, not a minor one,' I said, showing off and prepared for chapter and verse, but she eyed me delicately and said it wasn't really the sort of thing she could discuss with someone my age.

'Anyway,' she went on hastily, 'I only mentioned it to explain I wasn't feeling quite myself. So I said, without thinking, that I was glad, I could really do with resting up for a bit. I could have bitten my tongue off, soon as I'd said it, but it wouldn't have helped, the words were out and the damage done. Jack got up – he was sitting in the corner. He didn't say anything, he just got up, gave me a look and went out. . . .'

Her eyes returned to my face. 'Oh, I should have had more sense, Kate. The times I've choked back words for the sake of peace! I should have known.'

Earlier, her manner and voice had been those of someone engaged in the cosy re-telling of an old story and I had listened as if it had been only that, fitting what she was telling me now into what she had told me on other occasions, with a pleasure which was rather like that of completing a highly coloured jigsaw puzzle. (Quite early on it had been established that I was a 'sensible kiddie' – and she did not mean by this that I would not repeat her confidences to Ellen, but that I would come to no harm from them. Nor had I. Indeed, I found it comforting to learn that someone could go through such dreadful experiences and emerge as apparently unscathed as Aunt Hat: only the fading bruise below her eye bore witness to what she had suffered, she herself did not. The more she talked to me, the less real the tale she unfolded became, perhaps in her own eyes as well: she had begun to see herself as a character in a fable, a play, rather than as the main protagonist in a real disaster.)

Now, suddenly, it was different. She repeated, 'Oh, Kate, I should have known,' and she spoke simply and, somehow, terribly, as if she had seen her fault and knew, for the first time, that it was past rectifying. Her face had lost its animation, her eyes stared: she had what I thought of as her shabby doll look.

I said, stumblingly, 'But you couldn't have known he'd go to the pub and get drunk and come home and ... I mean you couldn't *know*.'

'I didn't say I knew, I said I should have known,' she said, quite sharply. She set her empty coffee cup down on the table beside the bed and leaned back against the pillows, pleating the sheets between her fingers. When she had come to us, her hands had been very grimed and rough; now they were whiter, I could see how prettily shaped they were. She said, nervously pleating, 'I knew *him*, you see. Jack always took offence so easily. And any man would have felt the hurt – an unskilled boy offering his wife the bit of comfort he ought to give her himself. You mustn't think my poor Jack didn't *feel* his failings. ...'

'Even if he was hurt, he ought to have been pleased, Dick had offered. If he was a *nice* man. ...'

She shook her head, sighing. 'Oh, Kate, you don't know. Some men have too much feeling in them, they can't help themselves, even when they know something's wrong, a kind of devil drives them to it. One thing about Jack, he always regretted things after. I know he regretted *this* ... he was crying when the police took him away, my neighbour said . . .' She stopped and added after a minute, 'That's Jack all over. I'm sure as soon as he'd done it he'd have given his right hand . . . it was only an accident, after all, he didn't mean real harm, not in his heart. But I can't get Dickie to see that, he won't listen. Oh . . . his mind's so hard against Jack.'

I remembered what Ellen had said at the breakfast table and conceived it my duty to set Aunt Hat right. I said sternly, 'You mustn't persuade Dick to commit perjury, though. That would be dreadfully wrong.'

'Wrong?' She looked at me in astonishment. 'Oh, I don't see that, dear. As I see it, the police want to put Jack in prison and they want Dick to help them. So it's only fair to Jack I should put the other side.'

I opened my mouth to speak but the door opened and Joanna came in. 'Gabbing again?' she said amiably. 'Oh, you two . . .' She looked at me. 'I thought you were fetching Aunt Hat's tray. Ellen's fussing. She says you're to fetch Poll for school, she's gone across to the Fantom's.' She smiled at Aunt Hat. 'Ellen says if you want a bath, the water's hot.'

She took the tray and went out, closing the door with her foot. Ellen's trick. I stood at the end of Aunt Hat's bed. She said in a worried voice, 'Don't run away with the idea I want Dick to tell *lies*, dear. I only want him to see it was an accident.'

I could see it would take more time than I had at my disposal to thrash that one out. 'I've got to go . . .'

'Come and give Aunt Hat a kiss, then.'

She smelt warmly of bed and sweet talcum. As I bent over her, she whispered, 'All I want is for Dick to understand things look different once they're out and public from what they do in private.'

'Yes?' I said, coldly inflecting my voice as Ellen sometimes did, to express disapproval.

But Aunt Hat embraced me tenderly and said I would understand what she meant later on, when I was older.

43

Chapter Four

The little trees in our garden, apple and peach and pear, bristled with frost. The lawn was grey and flat, the diamond-shaped beds, graveyards of young roses. When General Fantom's son, Claud Connolly Fantom, had sold off some of his land for building, the contractors had moved bulldozers in and laid what had once been a fine, Edwardian garden, flat as an asphalt yard. They had left nothing except the spreading cedar at the back of Miss Carter's house and they would not have left that, Boyd said bitterly, if it had not been too costly to remove. Apart from the cedar, therefore, everything that grew in our garden and in the gardens of the six other houses in the development, was new and young; each garden had its herbaceous border, its rose beds, its staked fruit trees and its oblong lawns that fathers mowed at weekends. There were no trees to climb, there was no place to hide; if you sat on the lawn and spoke above a whisper, each word was clearly audible through the privet hedging and whatever you did, unless you confined your activities to the square yard between the coal bunker and the kitchen door, you were visible from a dozen windows. Joanna did not seem to mind this lack of privacy, indeed, last summer she had clearly enjoyed it – to my disgust, she had taken to changing her dress and brushing her hair before going to sit on the lawn in a deck chair – but Poll and I found it inhibiting: we spent very little time in our garden.

The Fantom's was quite different. Our feet had worn a track across the lawn to the hole in the wooden fence: once through you were in another world. The shrubbery that pressed up to the fence was wild and old: laurels and rhododendrons planted sixty years ago and untended since. To the

44

right of the hole was a clump of rhododendrons where, summer after summer, first Joanna and I, then Poll and I, had made a camp. It was a good place; the old bushes spread leggily around us and above us to make a safe, green arbour, and we had thought ourselves quite private there until one day, Mr Claud Connolly Fantom had disturbed us, his red face, topped by an old fishing hat, suddenly looming through a frame of dark leaves and mauve flower clusters. After a moment of mutual shock, he raised his hat, said, 'I beg your pardon, ladies,' and vanished. He never visited that part of the garden again, at least not while we were there, and, emboldened by what we took as official permission, we began to furnish our retreat. Through the hole in the fence, we lugged a couple of old canvas chairs, a piano stool, a strip of coconut matting, a Primus stove and some leaky saucepans. The stove was for the look of the thing; it was rusted solid and we cooked on a brick construction, using bundles of kindling filched from the coal shed. Our cooking was limited to our ingredients; last summer we had achieved satisfactory results with flour, water and icing sugar, twisting this mixture on peeled sticks and roasting it above the fire. When food ran out, as it did when Ellen cut off our supply line, we turned to improving our accommodation, adding a cushion or two and a few ornaments we hoped Ellen would not miss, and to making the stick dolls we needed to take the subordinate parts in our shows – the parts Poll, who should have taken them by rights, refused to play. At her age I had had to be the Peasant and the Bad Robot, but Poll ignored her duties as a younger sister: it was our fault, Ellen said, because we had always given in to her.

This morning I scrambled through the hole in the fence, noticing as I did so that it was a tighter squeeze than it used to be, and made automatically for the camp to check that everything was as we had left it. I picked up the Bad Robot who had fallen down, replaced his tin head with punched holes for eyes on his broom handle body, and leaned him against a fork of the rhododendron bush. Then I went on through the shrubbery, treading on dead leaves crisp with frost, to the circular lawn bordered with bamboo and pampas grass, and the back of Lock View.

The house was a monument to General Fantom's architectural tastes: large, solid, built of sickly, yellow brick, it had an uncompromising, institutional look. Its only ornament was an intrusive, blank-windowed tower, placed just right of centre and clothed with ivy that rustled like dry scales when the wind blew.

Poll and Mr Fantom were in the living room. I saw them through the window; Poll leaning against the wing chair in which he sat, smoking, his slippered feet propped up against the iron fender. His face was long and knobbly and mottled, with two fat pads of clear scarlet, one on each cheekbone; between them, his nose protruded, red and fleshy, with a divided blob at the tip. Grey eyebrows, large and stiff as toothbrushes, stuck out above his eyes which were light and watery; they regarded me blankly for a moment, then he took the pipe from his mouth and jerked the stem upwards, in recognition of my presence.

I went into the house by the back door and looked at the brass trays on carved, wooden legs and the fine, silk carpet at my feet; it was purple and crimson and gold and black, woven into a pattern so intricate that the eye tired, tracing it. Lock View was full of carpets, hung on the walls and laid on the old, cracked, brown linoleum of the passages. The doors fitted badly and sometimes when the wind was high, the carpets lifted on the floor. The house had a spicey smell, sweet and musty, which came from the joss sticks Mr Claud Fantom burned in his fireplace to cover up, so he told Poll, the smell of his sister's Abyssinian cat.

I could hear him through the half-open door of the living room, talking to Poll. His voice came out in little grunts and puffs of sound, like cannon fire. I fidgeted in the hall, unwilling to go into the room to fetch Poll out, and ashamed to admit I was unwilling: if Poll was not afraid of Mr Fantom, how could I be? To gain time, I pretended to be interested in the brass model of an elephant with a clock set into its belly that stood on a table under a glass dome. The

46

clock had stopped at ten inutes past four, and the glass
dome was dusty. When the British left India, Mr Fantom,
who had been in the Indian Civil Service, had left too, and
the brass elephant had been a farewell gift from his friend,
the Maharajah. The model was very carefully and wonderfully done and, although in a strange way I was aware that
the general effect was not of beauty but of ugliness and use-
lessness, I was beginning to be genuinely absorbed in the
tiny mahouts and the marvellous, stiff lacework on the top
of the elephant's howdah, when Poll came out of the room.

She was sighing and rolling her eyes like a middle-aged
woman expressing maternal exasperation. 'Always the same
old thing,' she muttered. 'They haven't brought his old
newspaper *again* and he wants *me* to fetch it.'

The newspaper in question was *The Times of India*. 'I'll
have to go up to the tower,' Poll sighed.

'There isn't time,' I hissed, one eye on the door.

Mr Claud Fantom's voice floated wrathfully through it.
'Cut along. Down to the dukka. Give 'em a piece of my
mind.'

'Hurry, then,' I said.

We trailed up the long stairs and along the corridor, past
the closed doors of the unused bedrooms and the open door
of the bathroom with its old geyscr and stained bath and
piece of string from which drooped Mr Fantom's under-
wear, limp and grey. A uniform chill hung over the house,
like the chill in a cellar or a cave.

At the end of the corridor was a narrow landing, lit by a
huge, stained-glass window. Either side of the landing was a
door; one led to the stair up to the tower, one to the part of
the house where Miss Fantom lived, Mr Claud Fantom's
sister, who was a recluse. Once, when I was in the garden, I
heard a woman's voice calling to the Abyssinian cat, a blue,
majestic beast who often sat on the back doorstep in the sun,
meditatively watching Mr Claud Fantom's chickens scratch
unproductively in the dry lawn, but I did not see Miss
Fantom herself. We had never seen her, but, unseen, she was
the more thought of. The windows of her rooms were

47

barred, a fact which had inspired me to spread around the rumour that she was dotty and her brother had locked her up like the mad woman in *Jane Eyre* but Boyd said this was not true: the bars were only there because her rooms had once been the nursery wing. I argued that she must be mad, otherwise she would not stay shut up there, never having visitors or going out, not even to the pictures; Boyd said that to cut yourself off from the world was not necessarily a sign of madness. I asked him what she looked like, hoping at least to hear that she was a dwarf or a cripple, but Boyd only said she had been very beautiful when she was young. Since he was clearly useless as a source of information, I had persuaded Poll to make enquiries from Mr Claud Fantom, but she could get nothing out of him, either, except, 'Can't stand the woman. Never could. Haven't spoken to her for years.'

'They write notes to each other,' Poll said suddenly. 'There's one there now.'

In silence, we looked at a folded, white square that fluttered a little in the draught that blew under the closed door.

'Should we take it down?'

Poll shook her head. 'He might think we'd read it. We could read it, it's not in an envelope.'

Her husky voice was far too loud. Mortified, I grabbed her hand. 'Come *on*.'

She came, with a longing, backward look at the piece of paper, and we climbed the narrow, bare stairs to the tower. Here were more carpets, rolled and tied with rope, tin trunks, a very large, teak elephant with a broken ivory tusk. In the corner there was a tall water tank and on top of the tank, yellowing back-numbers of *The Times of India* were piled high. Poll climbed on a trunk, reached for the top one and folded it neatly, creasing it with her thumb. 'We've got to wait a minute so he'll think I've been down to the shop and back.'

'Not for long, though. It's half-past eight. We've got to be back by ten to nine. Boyd said he'd drive us to school.'

We waited. A cistern emptied somewhere and the water tank gurgled. I looked at the newspaper Poll was holding.

48

'He must know it's not today's. The news is wrong, and the date.' It was on the tip of my tongue to point out that he was making a fool of her, but she shrugged her shoulders. 'He doesn't *read* it. He just liked to *have* it. And I fold the date page in,' she added, with a calm practicality that was smug and irritating to me, but natural to her. Once Poll had decided on a course of action she never itched and burned with doubts as I did: given a solution that worked, she never looked beyond it.

'I think we can go now,' she said, and started down the stairs as she did almost every day, to deliver *The Times of India* twenty years out of date to Mr Claud Fantom who had carried the white man's burden for most of his life and had not, in his mind, relinquished it.

Why he played his part in this ritual, I didn't know. It could not have been to amuse Poll: he was not a man given to humouring children. If he tolerated Poll, it was because he found her useful – she ran errands for him, fetched his tobacco, his groceries – not because she had found the warm spot in his crusty old heart. She was also, since she could not answer back, a good audience for vengeful diatribes against the Government who were a lot of communists who had 'sold England down the river,' and for long, nostalgic stories of his life in Bengal and his friendship with the Maharajah with whom he had shot tigers and played polo. The Maharajah was very rich; he had a palace and a private aeroplane. Poll did not altogether believe in him since she knew, from Miss Carter, that all black men were starving and had river blindness, but to please Mr Fantom, she pretended to. 'I expect he likes to have something nice to think about,' she said.

It is doubtful whether he thought of much else. He did what housework was done in Lock View, but the garden had gone to ruin. He had no friends in Monks Ford and only went out sometimes at dusk, striding along the tree-lined, suburban roads with his pale eyes fixed on distance. His only activity was the Chairmanship of the Royal Oriental

Society which met, monthly, in London. Once every four weeks, on a Monday morning, he took the train to town, returning the following morning with the red pads on his cheeks so hotted up by drink or excitement that they looked like twin boils about to burst.

They looked like boils now, when we reached the long landing, or maybe it was the light, falling through the red glass of the window. He was standing in front of Miss Fantom's door. The note had gone from the floor and her door was open and her Abyssinian cat sitting on the threshold, one elegant leg raised like a dancer's while he washed his bottom. Behind him was a long, empty passage, disappointingly like the rest of the house, the institution look only partly relieved by the colours of the carpets. I craned my neck to look; beside me, Poll slipped *The Times of India* behind her back. But he seemed not to notice her. He was looking at me and his light eyes were colder than ever.

He said, 'Get your father. My sister's ill. Quick-sharp now.'

Ellen took us to school that morning. We were late, but the odium we incurred on this account – lateness earned you a black mark for your house – was mitigated, for me, anyway, by the interesting rumours I was able to spread around in the dinner hour. (Living in a doctor's house had advantages for someone of my temperament: though Boyd never discussed his patients with us, we were often privy to excitements that gave us status.) By the time I came home in the afternoon I had started up various speculative hares that included a dramatic suicide and a mad Miss Fantom, foaming at the mouth.

At tea, the truth fell flatly on my ears. Poor Miss Fantom was not raving, nor had she slashed her wrists and died in a Roman manner. She was merely gravely ill. She had 'neglected herself' Ellen said, and a nurse had been installed to care for her until she was better.

After tea, Poll and I played Honeymoon Couples. This was a game Poll had lately become addicted to and in which, as usual, she played the star role: the bride, arrayed in an old nightgown of Ellen's, bangles, and the spangley crown that Mrs Wise, our daily help, had given Poll last Christmas. As it was a childish game and I was kindly indulging Poll in playing it, I did not mind the passive part of bridegroom; I lounged on the bed and thought my own thoughts while she arranged the wedding journey. We usually went to Herne Bay, but today, owing to a recent geography lesson, we were to visit the Heart of India. While I lay with my eyes closed, Poll gave a running commentary on the travelling difficulties which appeared to be considerable and entailed a great deal of shouting at porters and waiters. 'Come here, you stupid nit, put my case down . . . no, not *there*, that's my poor old husband's toe, pick it up at once, can't you see he's *ill?* Get him some brandy . . . quick-sharp now, or I'll give you a piece of mind.' Occasionally she asked me, tenderly, if I was feeling better now. I must buck up and soon we would be out of the nasty plane and I would be able to have a lovely ride on a camel. I pointed out that a camel was hardly a suitable conveyance for the ailing valetudinarian she appeared to have married, and that, anyway, there were no camels in India. She gave me a blue, piercing look and said, with a sarcastic edge that probably reflected Miss Carter's classroom manner, that if I had been paying attention I would have realized that the plane had lost its way and crashed, by mistake, into the Sahara. That was like Poll, to twist facts to suit her case. She was very feminine, Boyd said, but I called it dishonest: I liked even fantasies to have some rules. 'It couldn't have crashed in Africa. We could crash in India, if you like, and have a ride on an elephant,' I suggested.

She said, 'Mr Fantom used to ride on elephants. He used to hunt tigers on elephants in India.' She paused. 'Is she dead?'

'No. You heard what Ellen said, at tea time. She's just ill.'

'I expect she'll die, though. I expect *he'll* be glad if she does.'

'That's a horrible thing to say. Why, he's her brother. . . .'

'Doesn't mean he likes her. He says . . .'

'I know. But you're my sister, it's the same thing, even if

I didn't like you, I wouldn't want you to die.' She smirked, and I had an idle impulse to cruelty. 'Perhaps I would, though. Sometimes when you're horrid and bossy, I think I would be pleased.'

I rather hoped she would cry, so that I could have the pleasure of comforting and reassuring her, but she only said, placidly, 'You're only pretending. Mr Fantom's not. He says he can't stand Miss Fantom, he says she used to hide his gin bottle.'

'Perhaps he drank too much. I wouldn't be surprised, with that nose.'

Poll gasped. 'His nose! It's like a *bottom*.' The mention of this word sent her off into shrieks of demented laughter. I waited until the spasm was over and she was hiccuping, her face red and swollen. Then I said, 'Don't you go round telling people he drinks, though. You'll get into trouble. Or that stuff about him wishing his sister was dead. That's libel. You can get sent to prison.'

'*I* shan't,' she said, glaring. 'You're the one who tells stories, not me. . . .'

Chapter Five

I had an abcess under a back tooth. I was in such misery one night that Joanna, normally stoical about other people's pain, fetched Ellen and Boyd. They gave me aspirin and hot milk and I sat on Boyd's lap, my face buried in his dressing gown, until I went to sleep.

When I woke in the morning, I was back in bed and the pain had subsided to a bruised ache. Since I had a horror of the dentist, I pretended that the pain had gone altogether, but Boyd was not taken in: he telephoned the dentist and made a morning appointment.

Ellen could not go with me. 'It would be today of all days,' she cried, looking frantic as she always did when events seemed to conspire against her. Today, in fact, was the day that 'Jack's case,' as Aunt Hat called it, was to come up in court, and Ellen was to accompany her there.

Aunt Hat was not required to give evidence. The police had elected not to summon her and Mr Starling, our local solicitor whom Boyd had asked to act for Jack, had decided not to call her either. Mr Starling had come to see her; after half-an-hour in the dining room he had emerged looking tired and baffled. Ellen said she could have told him before he came that Aunt Hat could only be a liability. 'She's not dishonest,' she said, 'it's just that she knows you can't trust many people to interpret the truth fairly. So she's likely to adapt her narrative to her audience and this makes her awkward to rely on – if she thought the Judge had a nice, kind face she might suddenly decide he'd be bound to be good to Jack and come out with things the defence might not want her to. . . .'

'But Mr Starling wouldn't want her to tell lies,' I said, shocked.

Ellen hesitated. 'Well, no . . . but you see, it's his business to do the best he can. . . .' Then she ended the conversation by changing the subject. 'Oh, Kate, if I've told you once I've told you a hundred times, don't chew your *hair*.'

Aunt Hat was indignant, understandably I thought, at Mr Starling's refusal to let her 'speak up for Jack': she said, of course all those sort of people were the same, on the side of the Government. She flung herself into an orgy of planning the clothes she was to wear to court, planning in which we were all involved at one time or another, not to give her advice but as audience for her ruminative monologues. The only positive contribution was made by Ellen who, like Joanna, did not care to be made conspicuous in public: she steered Aunt Hat away from her best hat, a blue straw with roses and veil, and took her out to buy a neat black felt which made her look like a charwoman in mourning. Aunt Hat must have decided that this was not an appearance she cared to present, because after breakfast she came down dressed for the day, drenched in sweet scent and wearing the boater after all. I looked at Ellen's expression with a little glum amusement but not much, because my tooth had begun to hurt again.

Boyd said he thought it was time we went. He kissed Ellen and then Aunt Hat, through her blue veil which had little black stars on it, and she said, to me, 'Be brave, chickabiddy, here's something to cheer you up after.' She gave me half a crown and said Aunt Hat would be keeping her fingers crossed and thinking of me all the time.

Ellen said, 'Don't fuss her, goodness me, she's only going to have a tooth out,' but her face had softened and she added, 'Hattie, I think you were right after all. The boater does look nice.'

'Sure?' Aunt Hat touched the brim and looked at Ellen timidly. She said she had thought things were bad enough without looking as if you were going to a funeral. . . .

In the car the pain became terrible, like beating drums inside my head. It was so bad that I did not have the usual sinking feeling when I went into Mr Coombe's surgery and saw his gleaming, ghastly instruments laid out under the cold light; so bad that Boyd seemed to think there was no question of leaving me to face it by myself. He was there during the horrid business of breathing in the gas and he was there when I woke again, blood in my mouth, feeling sick. Mr Coombe held up my tooth with a little sack clinging to the root: he said that was the poison and if I asked him it was better out than in. I leaned forward, threw up bloodily into the basin Boyd was holding for me, and felt better.

When we got out into the street, I fingered Aunt Hat's half crown and said, 'Could we go to Jock's Parlour and have a Knickerbocker Glory?'

Boyd said he didn't think this was the most suitable occasion for for icecream, but perhaps we could go to Jock's and have something more harmless, like a cup of tea.

Even the tea proved too much; I had to go through the door at the back of the counter, through the kitchens and into the yard where there was a lavatory in an outhouse. When I came back, Boyd put his hand under my elbow, led me outside, helped me into the car and tucked a rug round my knees as if I were an old lady. We drove up the main street and stopped outside the converted house where our Mr Starling had his office on the first floor.

Boyd said, 'I'm afraid there isn't time to take you home. I've got an appointment and I'm late already.' He hesitated, looking at me. 'You'd better come in. Then someone can keep an eye on you.'

We climbed the cold stairs. I was going to ask Boyd why he wanted to see a solicitor. It couldn't be for Aunt Hat, because after today, she wouldn't need one any more. But there was no time. We had reached the office and were in the ante-room with its green-topped desk filling the tiny space and the bilious green walls and the white light and he was asking the secretary if Mr Starling was ready to see him and if she minded if I waited there, with her.

The secretary smelt of the peppermints she was sucking. The smell made me feel sick again but I couldn't escape from it because the room was so small that I had to sit facing her, on the opposite side of the desk and our knees almost touched underneath. She took no notice of me but tapped at her typewriter. She had white hands with long, beautiful, carmine nails, and a pale face with a superior expression: she looked like a pretty camel.

Boyd was in Mr Starling's office. We could hear their voices vibrating through the partition wall, though not what they said. After a little while, Mr Starling opened the door and said, 'I'd like the Fantom file, Miss Coombe, please.'

She got up. Her long nails clicked through brown files in the steel cabinet. I wondered if she was Miss Coombe the dentist's daughter and whether I should tell her that her father had just taken my tooth out, but she brushed past me with her eyes fixed on distance and I knew that she wouldn't be interested.

She went into Mr Starling's office, leaving the door open, and I heard Mr Starling say, 'It's a shocking business, Doctor Boyd, a shocking business. . . .'

Then Miss Coombe came out again, closing the door behind her, sat down, and began clicking at her machine again. She was remote and beautiful and busy, and I watched her enviously, sucking a strand of hair for comfort.

In the car, going home, I said 'Does Miss Fantom need a solicitor? She's not going to court, is she?'

'No.'

'Then why does she need one?'

'People do.'

'Why did Mr Starling say it was a shocking business?'

'Did he?'

'When Miss Coombe left the door open.'

'Miss Coombe?'

'The secretary.'

'Oh. Well, of course she's ill. . . .'

'That's not shocking. You don't need a solicitor when you're ill.' I craned forward to look into his face. 'Has she broken the law?'

'No.'

'You and Ellen are always saying we ought to be told what's going on, otherwise we might get the wrong idea about things.'

Boyd's mouth twitched. 'Miss Fantom needs a solicitor because her affairs are in a muddle. She doesn't understand money matters, wasn't brought up to it. The money's there, all right, but she's worried because she thinks she hasn't enough to pay the nurse. Worry's a bad thing when you're ill and I thought a chat with Mr Starling might put her mind at rest.'

'Why doesn't Mr Fantom pay the nurse? I mean, he's her brother, it's his business, when she's ill.'

'It seems he thinks he can't afford it either. People are sometimes very odd about money, Kate, you'll find that out.'

'Mr Fantom hasn't spoken to his sister for years. He told Poll.'

'Oh, there are a lot of things wrong in that house,' Boyd said.

I said severely, 'I don't see why you have to run round putting them right.' I repeated something I had heard Ellen say. 'You do too much for people and they take advantage.'

Boyd raised his eyebrows. We stopped outside our house. 'I feel sick again,' I said plaintively.

Boyd helped me upstairs and into bed. He took my temperature, frowned, went away and came back with two white pills and a glass of water. Then he said he had to go out now, but Mrs Wise was here and would look after me.

Mrs Wise came in to clean three days a week. I lay back against the pillows, anxious to look weak and pitiable, and she came to tidy up the room while she kept an eye on me.

I asked her in a faint voice where Boyd had gone and she said she had gone to see Miss Fanton, poor soul. I asked her if Miss Fantom was dying and she said we were all dying in a manner of speaking and I wasn't to worry my head. 'I daresay she'll go on better now she's having a bit of attention. Though it's not before time, if you ask me. Doctor asked me if I could spare her an hour or two and I went in yesterday. You never saw such a mess, dust everywhere and the cobwebs! You wouldn't think it to look at the house from the outside. Talk of a whited sepulchre. The nurse said it wasn't what she was used to and I can't say I blame her. Well, I did what I could, though not in *his* part of the house, no thank you! I went through when I had finished and he said if I wanted to be paid, I could go and ask Doctor Boyd. That riled me a bit, but I knew he and Doctor'd had words, so I kept my own council. But I ask you. His own house, his own sister!'

'It's a shocking business, isn't it?' I said cunningly.

She looked at me sharply, sighed, and said yes, indeed it was, the poor, poor soul. A few more questions, put with

57

careful innocence, and I had it. Not the truth, perhaps, but an approximation to it tempered by the heady indignation with which Mrs Wise, like Ellen, approached any situation in which a woman had been ill-used by a man.

It was not her brother's fault Miss Fantom was ill, but it was his neglect that had aggravated her condition. Quite simply, when she became too weak to boil eggs and make tea in the pantry in the nursery wing, he had not given her anything she could eat. To be fair to him – as Mrs Wise was not – he had probably not understood this: to a man with his iron digestion, someone who left untouched the good Indian curries he cooked for himself, was merely being awkward and faddy. When almost nothing was taken from the trays he grudgingly prepared and stuck outside her door, he took them away and ignored her. That morning, when Boyd finally saw her, she had only strength enough left to scrawl a note to her brother, push it under the door and crawl back to bed where he found her half-conscious: she had eaten nothing for days except a few sips of milk and a little bread.

'Why didn't she just ring up the shops and ask them to send her something?' I asked, and Mrs Wise shook her head in surprise at my innocence.

'There's no telephone in that house, he had it took out to save money. It seems he fancies he's poor. The lady too . . . she's taken what he's told her all these years and had no chance to learn different, what with not going out and no company, not even a radio. Couldn't afford batteries, he told her. I ask you! Him with a good pension and she . . . well, everyone knows the old General left her more than comfortable. Left her everything, and *he* wasn't poor, no, not by a long chalk let me tell you. Seems he didn't get on with his son . . . from what *I've* seen I can't say I blame him!'

It seemed I had been right, after all. Mr Fantom *had* shut up his sister, though not with bolts and bars. His way, though less spectacular, was worse, though I was too young to do more than dimly perceive this. It was also, as Boyd was to find, trickier to deal with.

58

After Mrs Wise had gone, I lay and reflected on how strange it was, that with parents like Boyd and Ellen who believed in being open with children, we should have to rely on other people for a proper account of what was really going on.

I slept. The light was on when I woke. Joanna was standing beside me with a cup of tea and a plate of thin bread and butter. I felt cross and hot. 'Where's Ellen? Is she back yet?'

'Downstairs with Aunt Hat. It's tea time. *That man* got eighteen months.'

I sat up at once. Joanna said, 'You're to stay in bed.'

'I've been in bed all day. I've missed *lunch*,' I protested indignantly, but I waited until she had gone before I got up and put on my dressing gown. I crept downstairs, on the alert for Joanna, but I could hear her voice answering Poll's in the kitchen.

I entered the living room prepared to remonstrate if I was sent back to bed, but Ellen only said, 'How are you, poor darling? Better?' She must have forgotten that Joanna had brought my tea upstairs because she poured me another cup and I went to sit beside Boyd, on the sofa.

Ellen looked pale; Aunt Hat rosy. She perched on the edge of her chair, still in her outdoor clothes, her flowered boater tilted sideways. There was a listening stillness about Ellen and Boyd which suggested that my entrance had interrupted a flow of talk. But not for long. Aunt Hat set down her cup, wiped her mouth daintily with a lace-bordered handkerchief, and said, 'I tell you again, I can't believe it, really I can't. If I hadn't heard with my own ears . . . oh, my poor Jack.' She looked directly at me and I held my breath but Ellen, leaning limply back in her chair, seemed to have forgotten I was in the room. 'You can't believe how he looked,' Aunt Hat said. 'I do believe if I'd met him in the street I'd have passed him by. I never saw anyone so changed. He'd always had a good, high colour but he looked pale as death up there in the dock and trapped . . . just like a poor animal. Whatever he'd done, you'd think you'd have felt pity. But not that judge, not he!' She gave a contemptuous snort and tossed her head so that her boater tilted even more drunkenly askew. 'I don't blame Dick. He said what he had to say, no more, no less . . . he had a nurse from the hospital with him and he spoke up beautifully, though he was in a wheelchair . . . but that judge! What a man! In my opinion he was jealous. Jack's a fine, big fellow even though he did look so broken down, and he was such a wizened little monkey, sitting there with his tongue going in and out, flick, flick, flick. . . . He said such dreadful things to Jack. Putting on he was shocked . . . as if he could be, sitting there in court and hearing all the dreadful things that happen day in, day out. . . . Enough to turn the milk of human kindness sour in any-one, I suppose, but you'd think he'd have had more imagina-tion, a man in his position. . . .'

'Perhaps he couldn't imagine himself . . .' Ellen began snappily, then she caught her breath and forced a smile. 'Hattie dear, have another cup of tea.'

'Well, just half, if the pot can stand it.' Aunt Hat looked at me, then suddenly smote herself on the chest with her clenched fist and cried, 'Oh . . . fancy me forgetting! How's your poor mouth, my lamb? Aunt Hat *was* thinking about you, she didn't forget . . . come here and let's see what she's got in her bag for you. . . .'

She opened her large, brown leather handbag and pro-duced a paper bag.

Ellen said, 'She stopped the taxi on the way to the station and went to the sweet shop specially.' She spoke as if there were something remarkable about this. Boyd stretched out his hand to her, smiling.

I thanked Aunt Hat for the sweets and took them to the kitchen to share with Poll and Joanna; when I came back, Aunt Hat was sitting silent, staring into the fire, and Ellen was saying, 'Go to bed my dear, you must be so tired. I'll bring you a hot-water bottle.'

Aunt Hat got slowly to her feet. 'I think I will get a little lie down if you don't mind.' She looked at me, rather vaguely. 'Oh, your Mummy and Auntie have had a day,' she said.

When she had gone, Boyd and Ellen stayed silent for a little, their linked hands resting on the fat arm of the sofa. Not wishing to bring myself to their attention, I slid to the floor and cautiously abstracted another sweet from the paper bag.

Ellen said softly, 'She told everyone . . . the policeman at the door . . . all the people sitting near us . . . that she couldn't believe it, it wasn't true . . . nothing was true. Jack had been a very good husband to her though any man is liable to be hasty at times. . . .'

There was an odd smile on her face as if she found this both funny and sad.

Boyd said, 'I expect in a day or two she'll be quite convinced Jack is the best and most amiable of men and the whole thing a dreadful miscarriage of justice.'

Joanna said, from the doorway, 'But that's not true, is it?'

No one answered her. Ellen seemed not to have heard her. She stood up. 'I'd better go and get her bottle,' she said, into the air, and went out, closing the door.

Joanna said, 'If Aunt Hat says that, she'll be lying, won't she?'

Boyd looked at her. 'Yes. But you mustn't blame her. She's only trying to protect herself . . . and in a sense, to protect us, too. She'd gone through a dreadful time and she can't bear us to be too unhappy on her account. She knows that what she says about her husband isn't true, but it's her way of telling us that she loves him and therefore what she suffered from him wasn't so terrible.'

'It's still a lie. And it's stupid as well, for her to pretend that he isn't the most horrible man.'

'Don't you ever pretend things are different from what they are?'

'No,' Joanna said sternly.

'Perhaps you don't need to.'

Joanna sat on the sofa and looked uncomfortable and stubborn at the same time. 'It's all very *well*,' she argued, 'I mean you say she only talks about him in that silly way to make us more comfortable, but in the end she'll come to believe it herself, won't she? And what'll that lead to?' She looked at Boyd challengingly. 'It'll mean that in the end she'll have convinced herself that nothing bad happened and when he comes out of prison, she'll do something really stupid, like going back to him and what'll her life be then?'

Boyd looked at her in a startled way. I thought he was going to be angry, but he only said, 'Yes, you're right. Lies are always dangerous. Particularly sentimental lies. I don't know why I tried to persuade you otherwise.' He sighed and rubbed at the side of his nose the way he did when he was tired or worried. 'But that doesn't mean you should condemn the people who tell them. They usually have a reason. Life's been a bitter pill for Aunt Hat, it's understandable she should prefer it with a sugar coating. . . .' He sighed again. 'She's very brave, you know. This has all been wretched for her, she's been ill, she's quite alone, she has no family, no money, nothing . . . and yet she never complains. . . .'

Joanna said slowly, 'Is she going to stay?'

'There's nowhere she can go. The house was rented and the rent hadn't been paid for months. Not since she went into hospital. And even if we helped her, she wouldn't want to go back there. People can be terrible, even when they mean to be kind.'

'I can see she wouldn't want to face her neighbours,' Joanna said in a stiff, cold voice. Then the blood came up into her face. 'It'll be the end of our private life.'

I thought this a feeble remark. It did not seem to me one was private at home, how could anyone be, in a family? Home was pleasant, but it was only one degree less public than the street outside: *I* was only private when I was away from the house, somewhere out of sight and sound like the camp under the tented laurels in the Fantom's garden.

But Joanna was only grouching about having me in her room. 'It's been bad enough these last weeks, but if it's going on and on . . .' She rolled her eyes heavenwards.

I opened my mouth to protest, but Boyd frowned at me to keep silent. He said, 'There's no reason why we can't put that right. Kate can move in with Poll.'

62

I was astounded. It seemed incredible that Boyd should be so considerate of Joanna, after *she* had been so mean about Aunt Hat. 'Poll grinds her teeth, it's like sleeping with an *engine*,' I cried, not because I minded this, but because it was unfair that my comfort should be so cavalierly ignored. But Boyd said, heartlessly, that he dared say I would get used to Poll's noises after a night or two, people could get used to anything.

'You sleep like the dead, anyway,' Joanna said.

Boyd cleared his throat loudly, and asked her if she would go and get Poll bathed, so he could read her a bedtime story before he went on his rounds. When Joanna had gone he held out one hand to me and patted his knee with the other. 'Stop looking like Saint Sebastian shot full of arrows and come here this minute,' he said in a commanding voice. I came, stiffly, and he laughed and pulled me on his lap and rubbed his bristles into my neck until I was helpless. Then he asked me how my mouth felt now and rocked me for a bit before he said, 'I'm sorry if you think I've been inconsiderate. But Joanna needs a room of her own. You've got a place you can go to be alone in, but she's got nowhere.'

I was surprised that he knew how I felt about the camp. Then it struck me that what he had said was true, not only of Joanna, but of most grown-ups. Some parents, I knew, locked doors to keep their children out, but Boyd and Ellen never did: they had nowhere they could go to be private. I said this and Boyd shifted in the chair to make us both more comfortable before he answered. He said I was quite right; growing up was a sad state of affairs that took some getting used to, and Joanna wasn't used to it yet. 'It takes time,' he said, and gave a little half-sigh which, for an absurd, fanciful moment, made me wonder whether he was used to it now.

I twisted up to look at him but all I could see were the hairy caverns of his nostrils and the red scratch marks under his chin where he had shaved in a hurry this morning before taking me to the dentist. The skin of his neck was rough, like a plucked fowl's. He was old, he had been grown-up for a long time; the disadvantages could hardly still worry him.

Relieved, I said, 'I don't expect Mr Fantom'll let us keep our camp, now you've had a row.' As soon as I had spoken I wondered if I was supposed to know this and held my breath, but he only said absently, 'Oh, I don't suppose he'll bother to take it out on you.'

We were quiet for a minute. I began to feel drowsy and might have slept if a coal had not fallen out of the grate on to the hearth. Boyd had to put me off his knee to replace it. Then he said suddenly, 'What do you do in your camp, Kate?'

It was the sort of prying question he almost never asked us and I was embarrassed. 'Oh, we just play games. I'm getting too old for it, really.'

He leaned forward to poke at the fire, though it didn't need it. He said, 'I used to play in that garden when I was quite a bit older than you. Of course it was bigger, then. I used to sit up in the cedar tree – the one that belongs to Miss Carter – and meditate on what profession I should honour. It was a matter of simple choice, you understand, no limitation of talent entered in. I wasn't much good at games, but up in that old tree, I knew I could climb Everest. . . .' I yawned. 'There was no end to the things I could do,' Boyd ended, rather lamely.

I said, 'What were you doing in the Fantom's garden? I mean you didn't live here; our house wasn't built then.'

'No. But Miss Fantom was a great friend of mine.

His tone implied that this was something I should have known. I answered a little indignantly, 'I thought she didn't have any friends. I mean she's a sort of old hermit. . . .'

'She wasn't always. Neither old, nor a hermit. They used to give croquet parties at Lock View.' He spoke with an irritable severity that startled me, but then, after a brief, frowning pause, suddenly relaxed and smiled, either because he realized his last remark must have sounded absurd out of the context of his memory, or at the memory itself. 'Oh, they were very grand affairs, Kate. The time I went, with my uncle, there was champagne and a butler to serve it and marvellous ices – not the kind *you* hanker after, but a special kind of water ice, made from blackcurrant leaves, I think.

. . . I remember I thought it all very grand, though I couldn't enjoy it at first – I was too scared of making a fool of myself at croquet. I was fourteen then, and still minded about being bad at games. But Miss Fantom took me on – she must have guessed how I felt because she said I must be her partner and we'd be bound to win, once we'd had a glass of champagne. It was the first time I'd met her and I didn't like to say I wasn't supposed to drink, but she must have known that, too, because she took me behind a clump of pampas grass, out of my uncle's sight, and told me to take it like medicine. It made me sneeze.' He smiled again, in an involuntary, reminiscent way. 'She was wearing a yellow dress,' he said.

'Did you win your game?' He was looking into the fire and didn't seem to have heard me, so I repeated the question, jogging his knee to make him pay attention.

'We did.' He looked as if this small triumph still pleased him. 'I had another glass of champagne afterwards and told her it was the first time I'd won a game in my life, the first time I'd ever been to a party and the first time I'd ever drunk alcohol. She said she hoped I'd come again and do it all for the second time. I said I hoped I would, too, but that it wasn't likely because my uncle had only accepted the invitation because he meant me to go into the army and he thought it would be a useful idea if I made a good impression on the General. I suppose I must have been drunk. . . . She asked me if I wanted to go into the army and when I said no, she said, 'Well, don't take any notice of the silly old buffer, then.' I remember I thought that a very dashing remark.' He paused. 'As a matter of fact, it was rather an important moment for me. It was the first time I'd really understood I didn't have to do what my uncle wanted . . . I told her so. I also told her that this was the best party I'd been to, in my whole life. She was kind enough not to remind me that I'd already told her it was the only one. She said she didn't usually enjoy parties, but she'd enjoyed this one, and she hoped I'd come to see her again. . . . I could come any time, either to talk to her if I was lonely, or just to be on my own in the garden. . . .'

'Did she think you were lonely, then?'

'Well, she knew my uncle didn't have a garden,' he said, and went on, rather quickly, to say that he and Miss Fantom had been good friends from that moment. For the rest of his schooldays, he had spent most of his holidays in and out of Lock View.'

'What did you do?'

'Nothing very exciting. There weren't any more parties, at least none I knew about, because the General got ill quite soon after and she'd never cared much for that sort of thing herself.' He looked at me, frowning a little as if wondering what would interest me. 'We talked and read . . . sometimes we went for bicycle rides. We used to cycle round the country looking for old churches and taking brass rubbings . . . we never found anything especially good, but we enjoyed looking. . . .'

For some reason I felt disapproving. 'She was pretty *old* to go bicycling about with a boy, wasn't she?'

'She was a good deal younger than I am now. About thirty, when I first met her. And I'm not confined to a wheel chair yet.'

'Well – you were only fourteen. So she was an awful lot older than you.'

'No more than an older sister. Or a young aunt.' He laughed suddenly as if this definition embarrassed him, clapped his hands on the arms of his chair with a great show of energy and said that Poll must be out of her bath by now, so he had better go and read to her.

Chapter Six

The weather changed. The Arctic wind blew January out and February dawned, mild and still. Though Aunt Hat still visited her stepson in hospital, Ellen no longer went with her: Dick was almost recovered now, and would soon be fit enough to rejoin his ship. There was calm at home and thin, sweet sunshine abroad.

I fell in love.

Gus Lightwater ran the Youth Fellowship at the church which we – not Ellen, but Joanna, Boyd and I – spasmodically attended. That winter I graduated from Sunday School, taken by the Vicar's wife, to the Fellowship which met on Tuesday evenings, in a room at the back of the church hall. There was an old piano, folding chairs, a high, black window curtained with fusty, dark material, and one hanging light. Though the window was never opened the room was always cold; on Fellowship evenings, Gus, which was what he chummily insisted we must call him, wore khaki mittens knitted by his mother. He was a stocky, athletic man with a moustache and a pipe which he carried straight as a weapon between his strong, white teeth, occasionally jerking it higher when he made a point. The only time I ever saw him without it was when he conducted the brief Tuesday service, a hymn, a prayer, and a straight talk on Life and God: we were Able Seamen in His ship. His images were frequently nautical, there was much talk of boxing the compass and steering by the Pole Star, though Gus had in fact, served in the Army: out of doors, he wore an old British warm, draped on his shoulders like a cloak. He lived with his parents in a neat, semi-detached house that had tubs of rhododendrons in the porch. That spring, when my love was at its height, I sometimes waited for his evening train and shadowed him home.

It was natural I should love him. There was no one else to love; though there were boys in the Fellowship, they were fourteen or fifteen, and ignored me. I told myself I preferred older men and, after the Fellowship hike, it was not an affectation, but the truth.

Half-term Saturday, we met outside the church, took a 'bus out of Monks Ford and walked a long way, ten miles or so. We must have crossed Epsom Downs, because I remember the race course and the huge, grey, deserted stands. We ate lunch in a barn, sitting on a pile of hay. The sun came through the open door, dust-motes floating in its beam, and we were warm; Gus pulled off his sweater and sat in a manly, open-necked shirt that showed black, curly hair at his neck. I sat beside him, eating the beetroot sandwiches of which I was particularly fond; I was the youngest and the newest member and, perhaps to bring me into the group, he began to tease me, calling me Katey-Did-Katey-Didn't. This attention both shamed and pleased me. When we had finished eating, Gus lit his pipe and said we would have fifteen minutes shut-eye before setting off home. He lay back, puffing at his pipe. Everyone became restless and there was some giggling and mild horse-play which Gus ignored. Then one of the bigger girls, a hefty wench with freckles and a redhead's pale, puffy skin, began to flick bread crusts at him, until he half rose, threatening her. She fled, giggling, and leaned in the doorway of the barn; the sun shone through her thin woollen skirt and showed the shape of her strong legs and the line of her knickers. I was mortally ashamed and stole a look at Gus to see if he had noticed, but he was resting on one elbow, his eyes half-closed. Daringly, I threw my last sandwich at him. It landed on his chest and, to my horror, it opened and the beetroot fell out. I stammered an apology, he opened his eyes, peered down at the stain on his shirt, and regarded me with mock dismay. Then he dropped his pipe, rolled over, and pushed me down in the hay. He tickled me in the armpits while everyone laughed. It was

68

the first time I had ever been so close to a man, other than Boyd, before. He was gently rough with me, his hands felt warm and firm through my jersey and he smelt of tobacco and sweat and dusty hay. I laughed hysterically, wriggling and throwing myself about. When he let me go, I sat up breathlessly, pulling down my skirt. 'You hurt me,' I said, pouting. He smiled and picked the hay stalks out of my hair, saying, 'Naughty girls must expect to be tickled.' The red head came back into the barn but I was pleased to see he took no notice of her, just looked at his watch and said if we wanted to get home tonight, we'd better get moving now.

The sun was going, orange jelly behind bare trees. The air had a winter chill. The group straggled out in twos and threes and I fell behind. I was tired and cold and my back had begun to ache. Tears pricked my eyeballs, and then Gus stopped to wait for me. He tucked my hand under his arm and we marched in step while he asked me about Joanna who had been a member of the Fellowship until this year. He said he was sorry she couldn't find time to come any more, he hoped it didn't mean she had given up going to church as well. I was depressed by the thought that he had only waited for me to talk about Joanna and said, crossly, that I wasn't sure that she believed in God any more. I hoped this would diminish his interest in her but it seemed to have the opposite effect: he began to question me about her interests, her friends. Did I know of anyone in particular who might have had an influence on her? I said that I believed her boy friend, Will Saxon, was an atheist, and then, since this seemed a way of attracting Gus's attention to myself, confessed that I had been having doubts, too.

'I'm not sure that it isn't really hypocrisy for me to come to the Fellowship,' I said solemnly, aware of my own falsity, but feeling expanded and uplifted by it. He smiled and said I must never feel that, even if one had temporarily lost Faith one must cling to the habit of expressing it, otherwise one was lost, adrift in a small, rudderless boat in an empty sea. The image made me tremble: I said, quite honestly now, that

69

sometimes I did feel very lonely and frightened. At once he was grave, his brown eyes searched mine through the growing dark, and his warm hand encircled my fingers. He began to talk about Doubt. I can't remember what he said, but I was happy because he was taking me seriously. My feet were hurting but I didn't care: I would have walked on knives to be beside him.

We came out of fields on to the road and marched, singing, 'One man went to mow,' to the 'bus stop. The 'bus came up out of the cold, country dark, like a lighted ship; we climbed on top and swayed home, singing.

Back in Monks Ford we separated. 'Good night all, good night, Gus.'

'Good night, Gus,' I said, and lingered.

He looked at me. 'No one going your way? Well – I'd better see you home.'

It seemed like an affirmation. 'Ooh, I'm *cold*.' I shivered coquettishly.

Gallant, he took off his anorak and spread it round my shoulders. Then he took my hands and rubbed them till the knuckles burned. He continued to hold my hand as we walked home, lightly swinging it between us as if he didn't mind the world seeing. I was light with joy and enchantment; I could have risen from the ground and rushed through the air like a bird.

'I don't want to go in,' I said as we approached our house. 'This has been the best day of my whole life.'

We stopped under a lamp. The yellow light spilled on his head, making his skin pale and smooth and shadowing his eyes. 'All good things come to an end,' he said, and smiled, sadly and beautifully.

'I don't *have* to go in, it's not late.' My heart thumped as I looked at his mouth. The upper lip was hidden by his moustache, but the bottom was soft and sweetly curved, like a girl's. Looking at it made me shudder.

He said nothing for a minute. Then he laughed. 'Get along with you, Katey-Did-Katey-Didn't.' As I turned, he walloped me lightly on the behind; when I turned at the gate, he was still standing under the lamp post, his pipe gritted between his teeth like a pointing gun, his hand raised in farewell.

I went in, humming. There was a mirror on the hallstand; I pushed the smelly raincoats aside and looked at myself. I was beautifully pale. I narrowed my eyes and smiled mysteriously.

'Is that you, Kate?' Aunt Hat came out of the kitchen in a flowered apron, her hands white with flour. 'Your Mummy and Daddy are at the pictures. Joanna's out with Will. Did you have a good time, Angel-pie?'

I turned to her. I seemed to be swelling with happiness, it was drumming in my ears. 'Oh . . .,' I said, and promptly fainted.

I had started my periods the year before. Ellen's attitude, that this was a humiliating disadvantage a girl must train herself to ignore, had not encouraged me to expect any special consideration. So I was startled, once I had recovered and explained what was wrong with me, by Aunt Hat's reaction which was curiously admiring as if I had attained some remarkable distinction by my own merit, and her romantic reference to the menstrual flow as the Curse of Eve. 'I'd never have thought it, you're so young.' I said, on the contrary, a lot of girls I knew had started when they were ten, people reached puberty much younger now. She gave a wondering sigh and said it seemed dreadful to her, children weren't children any more. She came into the bathroom with me and then insisted on tucking me up in her own bed so Poll would not disturb me in the night. She brought me hot milk and tiptoed round folding my clothes while I drank it, as if in a sick room. If Ellen had been around I would have been mortally ashamed at this fussing, but as it was, I lay back and enjoyed it. While she tiptoed, Aunt Hat talked. She said I must be careful when I was 'like that' and not get my feet wet or wash my hair. I knew this was old-fashioned advice and felt superior. Then, presumably because she knew I had been initiated into womanhood, she abandoned her previous reticence about her hysterectomy and the gynaecological troubles that had preceded it. 'It should have been done years ago but I put off going, you never know what the doctor's going to tell you, do you? Oh – the things women suffer in this life! Jack used to lose patience with me, but you can understand that; I mean you can't expect a man to know what it's like, dragging round with your insides falling out, can you?'

I didn't answer because I was thinking over the day and planning a letter to Gus. A beautiful letter, describing the hike and the emotions I had felt on seeing the bare trees and the early primroses – we had not actually seen any primroses but a little poetic licence was allowable – and mentioning my doubts about God. This would be difficult as I did not really have any, but there was a book Joanna had won as a Sunday School prize, *Letters to a Christian Child*, which might have some useful passages in it. I faced up to the fact that Gus would almost certainly think me too young to be taken out in the ordinary way, but if he knew I was in spiritual trouble, he might feel it his duty to ask me to tea. I could envisage no higher bliss and closed my eyes, the better to contemplate it.

Aunt Hat wished me good night in a hushed voice, kissed my cheek and crept from the room. I was glad she had gone and lay happily in the lovely dark, hugging my hot-water bottle and my memories.

When I woke, the sun was shining. The small room was filled with it and with the scent of Aunt Hat's powder. She must have only just got up; I moved my leg in the bed and felt her place, still warm. Her nightdress, made of pale pink stockinette with beige roses worked on the bust, was draped over the chair back; her curlers lay on the china tray on the dressing table, along with the little razor with which she shaved her corns. I stretched out, luxuriating in the sunny, Sunday warmth, and thought about Gus. I wondered what to wear to church this morning and whether Ellen would let me wear my last year's best summer dress. I had grown this winter but the dress had been bought full long and wearing it belted tight, with a pair of Joanna's high-heeled strap shoes – I could wedge the backs with cotton wool to keep them on – I might pass for fifteen. Gus was twenty-seven, but men often married younger girls to be a comfort to their declining years. Exhilarated, I got out of bed and went to the window to bathe myself in sun and hope.

I was uplifted by love: Miss Carter was made grotesque by it. In the garden – it was a sight to sink the spirits – she was talking across the privet hedge to Boyd. Trapped, poor man, he bent his head courteously towards her. She threw back her sad, horse face with a sparkling laugh as if someone had told her that vivacity transformed the plainest features. Disgusted, I opened the window and called out, 'Boyd, can I wear my summer dress?'

They looked up. Boyd laughed, shaking his head.

'In February. Oh, Kate,' Miss Carter cried hilariously. The sun flashed morse signals off her spectacles as she tossed her head.

I slammed the window shut. 'Cheek,' I said loudly, smiling through the glass. 'Silly interfering ugly bitch.' Miss Carter waved at me cheerily, to impress Boyd how good she was with children, and continued to mop and mow. Boyd was clearly attempting to beat a retreat; he had turned away slightly and I knew, by the enthusiastic way he nodded, that he was no longer listening. In response to his inattention, Miss Carter's gestures became wilder: she made swimming movements with her arms as if about to plunge after him, through the hedge.

I moved away from the window. 'In *February*. Oh, *Kate*,' I mimicked, scowling in the mirror. But Ellen would say the same, it was no use even asking her. I would just have to wear my school coat that was too short and showed my winter dress beneath the hem. Gus would not look at me twice. Heavy with misery, I flounced back on to the bed.

Aunt Hat got the backwash of my disappointment. She peeped round the door, stealthy, bright-eyed, like a mouse. 'How are you, sweetie? Aunt Hat was just wondering if you'd like your breakfast in bed.'

She was beaming with the anticipated pleasure of doing

73

something for me. I said crossly, 'No, I would *not*. I'm not an old woman,' and the smile went from her face like the light going out.

In the way of people who appear to ask nothing, Aunt Hat asked a lot from us. She was always wanting to bring us breakfast in bed, clean our shoes, dress Poll. Unaccustomed to these attentions, indeed embarrassed and surprised by them, we were often churlish. Ellen had taught us to be independent. It was partly circumstance, when Joanna and I were young and she was teaching, we had had, of necessity, to pull our weight, as she called it, but it was also a principle: Ellen believed that no human being should expect another to perform tedious, minor duties that they could well do for themselves. It worked both ways. She never asked us, as we had observed many mothers did, to 'just run upstairs' and fetch such and such a thing; in return, she assumed that no child, even one Poll's age, would expect someone else to polish their shoes, clean the bath after them, make their bed. Ellen would do anything for Aunt Hat, she had already done a great deal, except let her do what she really wanted which was to wait on us, hand and foot.

Disliking household jobs, Ellen was efficient at them: Aunt Hat who loved to potter with a duster and a distracted air of busy-ness, was not. Ellen cooked well, considering it her duty to give us good, balanced meals: Aunt Hat cooked superbly and indigestibly and made a muddle in the kitchen. Taking refuge in Aunt Hat's recent illness, Ellen insisted that she needed rest. She took to lighting the sitting-room fire earlier than usual and persuading Aunt Hat to sit beside it. Unused to resting – or to reading or any other activity which might have made resting more tolerable – Aunt Hat sat as on a bed of nails, watching, lynx-eyed for the opportunity to perform some minor service. We were used, when we came down to breakfast, to fetching whatever had been cooked from the hot plate. Aunt Hat, who after the first days of breakfast in bed was always down early so as not to give trouble, would leap up as we entered and fetch it for us.

74

Once she realized this irritated Ellen she desisted, but with difficulty: when we appeared in the dining room she would half rise from her seat, glance nervously at Ellen and sink back with a sigh.

What she was not allowed to do openly, she did by stealth; creeping out before supper was properly finished to begin washing the dishes; seizing the opportunity when Ellen was shopping to turn out rooms, attack cobwebs, clean paint. And whatever you were doing she was always there, humbly and apologetically offering to do it for you.

She talked all the time. Once we were used to this, her conversation became no more of a nuisance than the radio which she turned on for company whenever she was alone, haphazardly tuned: we would often find her, sitting in the dark to save electricity, apparently listening to a talk in a foreign language.

Ellen's affection for Aunt Hat was greater than the annoyance Hat caused her. She was often sharp and tight-lipped but always penitent after. As for us, it was pleasant to have a grown-up around who was so completely partisan. Ellen was critical, you could never do anything well enough for Ellen, and Boyd, though he was the rock our lives were built on, was not exactly lavish with praise. Aunt Hat thought we were wonderful. She had never seen such girls, so talented, so pretty. Our lives became punctuated by her admiring cries. She seemed to think it remarkable that we could read and write, let alone learn French verbs and do Greek. She knew, without seeing any of our friends, that we were cleverer and more beautiful than any of them. When Joanna was upset because she had done badly in a class test, Aunt Hat said there must have been dirty work at the cross roads. 'I know these teachers. A lot of sour old maids. They're always down on the pretty ones and try to take them down a peg when they can.'

Joanna was not altogether pleased by this argument as she liked to think she was a teacher's pet, but, thinking it over, she decided that there might be something in it.

'Miss Spalding's had an awful down on me lately, I think

it's unfair,' she complained to Ellen and added, with apparently irrelevant malice, that the girl who had come top was plain and spotty.

Ellen was ironing. She tested the iron against her cheek and set it aside to cool. She said, was there any evidence to suggest Miss Spalding had falsified Joanna's results?

Joanna said, indignantly, that Miss Spalding had been 'funny' ever since she saw her and Will coming out of Jock's Parlour one afternoon. 'I expect she's jealous, silly old thing,' she said, preening in the kitchen mirror.

Ellen raised her eyebrows and asked, in a light, incredulous voice, if Joanna really thought that Miss Spalding, a dignified lady of some fifty summers, had her eye on Will?

Joanna's ears reddened. She said no, not exactly, but Ellen knew what she meant.

'More likely, isn't it, that you've not been working hard enough?'

Joanna said resentfully, 'Aunt Hat says she's never seen a girl work as hard as I do.'

'Aunt Hat thinks you're perfect, of course.'

Ellen spoke in a mild, friendly way that Joanna chose to think deceptive. She addressed the wall behind Ellen's head in passionate, meaningful tones. 'It's rather nice, *I* think, to have *someone* around who sticks up for you and doesn't always think everything is your fault.'

'I happen to think it's wrong to tell people what they want to hear, just to please them.'

Ellen's voice held the cold, special anger that she and Joanna often aroused in each other. Joanna's look reflected it back.

'That's not fair. As if Aunt Hat was just sucking up . . .'

Put in the wrong, Ellen began to stammer. 'N-no, that's n-not what I . . . I mean she b-believes what she says. She believes everyone she loved is p-perfect and she wants everything to be perfect *for* them. It's a m-mistake.' She collected herself and smiled rigidly at Joanna. 'Love isn't much good without sense. A mistake that comes from the heart is none the less a mistake for all that.'

'Pardon *me*,' Joanna said heavily, 'but it seems a very nice kind of mistake.' She gasped, as if suddenly suffocating, and went precipitately from the room.

Ellen looked sadly at the closed door, then, nervously, at me. I felt she would rather I were not there, but could not see how to go. Joanna's misery made me miserable. Though I had often hated her viciously, had sometimes punched and kicked her in a holy ecstasy of rage, that was between ourselves: when she was attacked by someone else, I ached internally. The instinctive love of the flesh was still strong between us, stronger, perhaps, on my side than hers: I sensed that, having a naturally lower opinion of herself, she bore criticism less well than I.

The kitchen smelt of airing clothes, stale and damp. It was the Saturday after the Fellowship hike. I sat with my feet hooked on the rung of the chair, my heart squeezed tight against the table, and allowed myself to think about Gus. To heighten the sweetness of this indulgence, I had rationed myself to three periods of thinking about him: when I woke in the morning, before I went to sleep at night, and one other time during the day. This morning, in bed, I had developed a brilliant proof of the existence of God: if people like us could be found, living on other planets, it would be a sure sign that He had made us in His own image. I had planned to bring this up at the next Fellowship meeting but now, feeling heavy and sad, I knew I would not dare. Instead, I comforted myself by thinking about after we were married, ironing his shirts and getting his meals, just the two of us in a small, cosy house somewhere. I would be waiting when he came home out of the rain, his hair sleeked and his pipe turned upside down to stop it going out. After supper we would sit by the fire, in the same armchair, and talk – though apart from God and occasional soulful monologues about Nature from me, I could not find any suitable conversation for us. Though I concentrated hard, Gus remained silent and more shadowy than usual. Worse, I felt silly, as if I had been caught talking to him out loud. A tight shame gripped my throat and I had to break it by doing something – anything – in a hurry. I pushed the chair back, scraping the legs on the linoleum with a noise that set my teeth on edge.

I was at the door when Ellen stopped me. 'Kate. Was I unkind to Joanna?'

I was startled. 'Oh, I dunno, she's awfully cocky sometimes,' I mumbled, not sure what was expected of me: Ellen so rarely appealed to us for comfort. Perhaps for this reason her humble, searching expression went to my head. I said the first thing that came. 'You're sometimes a bit unkind to Aunt Hat, though.'

'In what way?'

She was folding Poll's school blouse as if she had nothing but its neatness on her mind, turning the sleeves in and dabbing at the collar points to make them lie flat. The heat of the iron had made the veins stand out on the backs of her hands and they looked swollen and clumsy. She was standing lopsided, the way she often did when tired, her left hip jutting bonily through her loose, tweed skirt. There was a ladder in her stocking.

Quite suddenly she looked awkwardly pathetic in the way a big, thin woman can easily do, but I had never noticed before. As I looked at her, surprised by this revelation, that strange inversion took place in which the child becomes the parent: I was made old and strong by her frailty. I felt burningly sorry because she looked so tired and shabby and, at the same time, pity excited me and gave me a feeling of power. It was my duty to tell her what she had done wrong: wasn't it Ellen herself who had taught us that to criticize was a natural function of love? She always dropped, hawk-like, on the smallest faults in our characters and, though we squirmed, we never doubted that she believed it to be for our own good. Who is to tell you these things if your mother doesn't?: who is to tell *her* these things, if her children don't?

'You won't let her do things. She wants to help and you won't let her. Like this afternoon. She wanted to do the ironing for you, to stop you wearing yourself out, and you wouldn't let her. She looked awfully miserable when she went out for her walk. She wants to pay you back for having her to stay and you won't let her do a thing. It's selfish, really. And look how you talked about her just now! As if you didn't really *like* her. It's not fair, behind her back. . . .'

'Don't wave your arms about like that, you remind me of Hitler,' Ellen said. She looked at me sadly. 'You're partly right. I should let her do more. But she's not always sensible, she still isn't strong and she must take things more easily than she wants to. And so much of the time I'm afraid she will spoil the three of you. . . .' She sighed. 'But you mustn't ever think I don't like Aunt Hat. Whatever I say . . . she's one of the best friends I've ever had. Almost the only one, really. I had no friends at all, when I was young.'

'You must have had friends at school.' Since I was seeing Ellen for the first time as a human being with failings I could understand, I was condescending: like Joanna, she was laying it on, for effect.

She glanced at me as if something in my tone surprised her, then shook her head. 'I wasn't allowed friends. My father . . . oh, Kate, dear, you can't possibly understand. You don't know what my childhood was like.'

'You've never told us,' I said huffily. All I knew about my maternal grandparents was that they had been killed in an air raid on London. 'You never tell us anything,' I said.

Ellen sat down suddenly, as if her knees had given way. She leaned her elbows on the table. 'It didn't seem . . . oh, don't scowl like that! The only reason I didn't tell you was that there wasn't really, anything interesting to tell.'

'I'd find it interesting.'

She looked at me. 'Well . . . the reason I didn't have friends was that my parents were religious. Not in any way you'd understand, thank heaven. But because of their religion I wasn't allowed to mix with other girls except as I had to, at school, or do any of the things girls do . . . go to cinemas, parties, use lipstick. . . .'

'Sounds potty to me.' Wasn't this just the old, grown-up ploy of pretending things were easier for us than it had been for them?

Two red spots appeared on Ellen's cheeks and her eyes

snapped. 'Kate, you don't know you're born!' She was forcing herself to speak softly to show she wasn't angry with me, but if she hadn't been I don't think she would have gone on. 'Let me tell you something, my girl. One of the girls in my class once gave me some cosmetic samples. She'd sent up a coupon out of a magazine. My father burned them . . . he picked them out of my drawer with a pair of tongs. Then he scrubbed my face with disinfectant. He said I'd been sent by the Devil to punish him.'

'That's a wicked thing to say!' It seemed so terrible to me that I couldn't believe it.

Ellen wasn't looking at me. 'He often said it. When I married an actor, he was sure of it. I'd met him when I was away, in my first job. My father wouldn't have me in the house again. Mother came to see me once, when you and Joanna were babies, and he found out and made her eat her meals in the kitchen for six months. He wouldn't speak to her. For six whole months she had to carry his meals into the dining room and wait without speaking until he had finished. She wrote and told me. She said my father was right, she had sinned and had to be punished. She told me I was never to write to her again. That was the last I heard. A neighbour wrote, after the raid.'

She sat silent for a minute. Then she looked at me. 'Don't look like that, Kate. For heaven's sake. Or I'll wish I hadn't told you.'

She was wishing it already. Her hands, clasped on the table in front of her, were trembling. 'Oh . . .' I moaned, and went to sit on her lap, something I had not done for a long time. I cried into her neck until I felt better. She fished out her handkerchief and blew my nose and said briskly, 'Now, you. That's enough, forget it. Don't make a production out of it, whatever you do. It was something that happened to another person, a long time ago. But you can see why I didn't have friends at school. I was ashamed, that was the chief thing. Aunt Hat . . . well . . . she was the first person I could relax and be silly with.'

Suddenly she smiled, easily and naturally. 'Oh . . . but we

were silly! We read beauty hints and did exercises to prevent double chins. Once we did them on the 'bus . . . do you remember the old 'bus into Bishop's Castle, the way they used to pack in the people with the chickens and the geese? Well, one day we did the chin exercise, sitting in the back with our shopping baskets. Like this. . . .'

She pushed me off her lap, tautened her neck muscles and twisted her head sharply from side to side, like a hen watching tennis, and said loudly, 'Y-east, Y-east . . .'

I thought they must have looked a proper pair of fools. But I could see that, trying to cheer me up, she had cheered herself up too. So I laughed because she did.

'Whatever did the other people think, in the 'bus?'

'That was the funny thing. No one took any notice.' She stood up, twisting her skirt straight. 'I'd better get on with the ironing.'

I frowned, 'But you quarrelled with Aunt Hat sometimes, when we lived in the country.'

'Quarrel? Me and Aunt Hat? Never, Kate . . .'

Her little laugh, as if I were mad – or spiteful – to suggest such a thing, made me stubborn. 'You did once.'

'Oh, Kate . . . you were only a baby!'

'I remember, though. That time we stayed with her and you came back when we were in bed.'

'You have a remarkable memory, Kate. I'm sure I can't . . .'

'But you had an awful *row*.'

She shook her head. The skin under her eyes had turned pinky-purple, the colour of a foxglove.

'*Why* did you quarrel?' I insisted.

She turned away, reached for the iron, switched it on and stationed herself behind the board as if facing into a wind. 'If you must know, Aunt Hat had given me some bad advice. But I was wrong to be angry with her. It was my own fault for taking it.'

'Why did you, then?' I longed to ask her what the advice was about, but didn't dare.

She half-smiled. 'Aunt Hat has some very romantic

81

notions. That means she doesn't always see things as they are, but as how she would like them to be. How it would be nice if they *were*. So it means her judgement isn't always sound.'

I said, impatient because she hadn't answered my question, 'If you think she's silly, why did you listen to her, then?'

'I don't think she's silly. It's just that she . . . thinks with her heart.' She spat on the iron, to test it, and then hesitated, frowning, while the spit sizzled. 'People like that can be very persuasive. They make you feel so . . . cold and hard. Even when cold and hard is the sensible thing to be.' She looked at me with a perplexed expression. 'It's hard to explain.'

I thought I understood. 'Joanna said she was silly about Jack. The way she kept saying he hadn't really meant to hurt her or Dick. Well, it would be nice if that was true, so you'd feel awfully mean telling her it wasn't, wouldn't you?'

Ellen nodded. She seemed fascinated. Encouraged, I proceeded with my analysis. 'But if she goes on telling herself he isn't a horrible man, she'll come to think he really isn't, and it'll end up with her going back to him, won't it. . . .'

'*Kate* . . .' Ellen's voice was loud and startled. For no reason that I could see, she suddenly turned that ugly, foxglove colour and began thumping away with the iron, mouth pursed, eyes lowered.

I could think of no reason for her embarrassment except a dreadful one. I said, horrified, 'You don't want her to go back to her awful husband, do you? Just so that you don't have to be bothered with her any more?'

Ellen put the iron down and stared at me. 'Oh, Kate, how *could* you . . . that would be the most dreadful thing . . .' The flesh round her mouth seemed to wobble, loose and formless, the way it does when people are in very great distress. 'I p-pray every night . . .' she said.

Chapter Seven

For a few hours I was raised to the heights of filial piety. I saw Ellen as a frail, gallant figure, a combination of David Copperfield and Elizabeth Barrett Browning: since parental tyranny of the kind she described was as far outside my own experience as thumb screws and the rack, I had to turn to literature. Now I knew how Ellen had suffered, I would make it up to her. It would be nice to be able to do this in some heroic way, like rescuing her from a burning building or saving her life with a transfusion of my own blood, but all I could do, immediately, was to fetch her a footstool as she sat darning after tea and shush Poll when she got excited over the game of Snap I was playing with her. 'You'll get on Ellen's nerves, bellowing like that,' I said severely.

Ellen said, 'I'm not in my dotage yet,' and looked as if something was amusing her as she swung her legs athletically off the footstool and got down on the floor to join our game. She had done her hair and changed out of her skirt and jersey into a new dress of a lovely green colour that made her skin look pearly. Boyd had been appointed to a part-time consultancy at the local hospital and they were going out tonight to celebrate at Joanna's suggestion: she had said Ellen and Boyd owed it to us not to let themselves get too old and stodgy.

Ellen shouted 'Snap,' louder than Poll and said, 'Come on, Kate, play properly, you're not trying.' She grinned at me, and I had a moment of cheated discontent: how could she look so cheerful after the dreadful things she had told me?

I had kept them to myself. I longed to tell Joanna but she was in no mood to be told. Before tea we had walked down town to get a new nib for her pen. It was dark and blowy and exhilarating; I pulled the band from my hair and let it stream, wet as a mermaid's across my face. While Joanna chose her nib, covering paper with neat, spidery writing, I leaned over the display counter and, secretly, regarded my reflection in the chromium fittings. I looked like a beautiful waif. I saw myself, running through the rain away from my cruel father and mother, running forlornly with the rain on my face and nowhere to go. Perhaps not running, though: if I were leaving home, I would have a suitcase to carry. I would walk, very slowly up the street, carrying my heavy suitcase and saying a sad, lingering good-bye to the shops and the places I knew. It would be strange, seeing everything for the last time. People would look at me curiously as I waited by the 'bus stop in the rain, my thin, film star's face pale in the lamp light. So young, so sad, so beautiful. A lump came into my throat.

Joanna said, 'Come *on*.' She hustled me out of the shop, muttering wrathfully, 'You look like a raving loony, suppose we met someone, what *are* you thinking about?'

I thought: why didn't Ellen run away, and the lump in my throat grew big and hard as a golf ball. I liked feeling sad but this was different. I wanted to tell Joanna about Ellen, but what she had said about not making a production of it, inhibited me: my mouth felt stuck up with glue. I sought for some good, cool, opening remark to begin telling her, just the plain facts, no elaboration, no drama, but then I saw something across the road that stopped me: Will Saxon going into the Odeon with a girl. I couldn't see her face but she had a very smart back view, a waisted coat and high-heeled, strap shoes.

Joanna was staring, her head thrust forward. Her cheeks fell into little pouches, her mouth half open. She started to walk fast.

I ran beside her. 'I thought you were going out this evening?'

She said quickly, 'I didn't say so. Actually . . . as a matter of *fact*, Will rang up this morning and said he couldn't.'

84

That was a lie: I had been in all day and no one had telephoned except patients. 'Did he say why?' I asked innocently.

She didn't answer. Slinking along close to the shop fronts as if she were playing at being a spy, she was watching her dark, transparent reflection in the windows. She said, in a strangled voice, 'She was wearing a hat. She must be years older than Will.'

'Age doesn't make any difference,' I said, tenderly thinking of Gus.

'Shut up, what do you know?' she said in a bitter voice. She jerked the belt of her raincoat tight and grunted with despair as she saw the sack-like effect in the chemist's window.

'Will's too young for you, anyway,' I comforted her. 'Girls mature more quickly than boys, it's a known fact. So perhaps it's best, really. It would be awful if you found some nice, older man and had to give him up because of Will.'

She wheeled round and dug her fingers into my upper arm. 'If you say another word, I'll kill you.'

She let me go and marched ahead all the way home. Offended, I thought of bitter things to say that would expose her before the world as an ungrateful fraud. When we got in, tea was ready. Joanna said, 'I don't want any, thank you. I've got a lot of work to do.'

Aunt Hat said, 'Don't you feel well, pet?' She examined Joanna anxiously and then smiled. 'Come on, lovey, just a little cup of tea and a nice piece of cake. There'll be plenty of time to titivate afterwards.'

'Titivate?' Joanna said slowly as if this was some strange foreign word she had not heard before. 'Titivate? What for?'

Aunt Hat smiled archly and mysteriously and I felt my ears go red. Of course she knew Joanna should be going out with Will. We had planned a session of planchette this evening: we could only play when Joanna was not there because she thought the supernatural common.

'I'm not going out anywhere if that's what you mean,' Joanna said. I admired the calm way she spoke: in her place I would have died of shame. All my bad feelings turned to tender pride. 'Tonight or any other night,' she said, looking cool and composed as marble. 'Time's running short. I have my work to think of.'

The dignified gentleness with which she closed the door, reproached us all.

'Oh, dear,' Aunt Hat said. 'Oh, dear. Hattie, you clumsy gawp, shoving your great foot in.' Suddenly, she raised her right hand and gave her left a stinging slap.

'I daresay I should have done if you hadn't,' Ellen said. 'I suppose she's quarrelled with Will. Do you know anything, Kate?'

A mouthful of bread and jam saved me from replying. I shrugged my shoulders.

'Oh, well . . . I'm not altogether sorry. It won't hurt her to do a bit of extra work.' Ellen looked at Aunt Hat whose expression was doleful – to her mind, there was no sadder thing than a lover's quarrel – and added, bracingly, 'She'll have plenty of time for that sort of thing later on.'

Knowing what I knew, this familiarly irritating remark developed poignancy: when Ellen was Joanna's age, the future must have been her only comfort. She had not lost the habit of enjoying herself, as Joanna sometimes said, she had never had the chance to acquire it. Watching her drink her tea, I saw her, not as she was this minute, but as she had been at other times, pictures swirling and crossing in my mind. Frosty school mornings and Ellen stirring porridge, Poll perched on her hip and fretting; her profile as she bent over the table to help with a difficult arithmetic problem; stuffy evenings, long ago in the flat, and her screwed up, contriving look as she worked out if she could afford some extra thing we had asked for. And other memories, not placed in time, of Ellen in the middle of the night; lifting Poll from her soaking bed and crooning to her, drawing curtains to keep the lamp light out, or the moon; the look of her red thin hand, holding out a willow pattern cup full of water. Remembrances swirled thick and sad as autumn leaves, all coloured by pitying fervour.

'Ellen,' I said, 'shall I cut you a piece of cake?'

86

While we played Snap, Aunt Hat washed up. When Ellen had said she could do this, Aunt Hat had gone pink with pleasure as if she had just been given a lovely present. It was easy to make her happy. We could hear her singing in the kitchen, *Wish me luck as you wave me goodbye*, her voice quavering on the high notes. I was proud that Ellen had taken my advice and, to please her, played Snap properly, as she had told me. I won one game after another until Poll grew bored and began to ask riddles instead of watching the cards. 'What did the sock say to the foot?'

'I've got you covered,' Ellen said. Poll pouted because she had wanted to give the answer herself, and stuck her thumb in her mouth.

'Someone's ready for beddy-byes,' Aunt Hat said, coming into the room, and, in case we had missed the point, 'I think a Certain Party is ready for Bedfordshire.'

'I'm not tired,' Poll said, though her eyes were turning up. 'I haven't had my supper.'

'What d'you want, then?' Ellen stood up, stretching till her joints cracked, and yawning at herself in the mirror over the fireplace.

'Water in my blue mug and a suggestive biscuit,' Poll said, deliberately making the babyish mistake that had once made everyone laugh, in order to coax Ellen's attention back to her.

But Ellen was looking at the clock. 'He's late, he said six at the latest.'

'What can have happened?' Aunt Hat, whose mind lurched naturally towards disaster, looked apprehensive: I knew that within a space of time so small as to be almost immeasurable, she had buried Boyd, comforted Ellen, rearranged the house to take in lodgers and worked her fingers to the bone to help support us.

'Nothing. The usual things. Goodness, Hattie' – Ellen, who knew Aunt Hat's tendencies as well as I did, looked at her impatiently – 'you know doctors can never make arrangements.'

'Oh, dear. Well . . . we won't start worrying just yet,' Aunt

Hat said, managing to imply that in five minutes or so it would be permissible to imagine all kinds of horror.

Ellen smiled, but only briefly. She began to tidy the room, shaking cushions irritably: the evening out meant more to her than she cared to show. Aunt Hat tiptoed across to Poll who turned awkward, scowling at the suggestion that she should be a good girl and come upstairs with Aunt Hat who was going to look after her this evening and would bring her a nice little supper in bed. Poll lay unmoving on the floor. 'Get up at once,' Ellen was forced to say finally, 'I'm ashamed of you, you're not a baby.'

'I are,' Poll said in a strange, lispy voice. 'I's an icky baba.' She threw Ellen a look of reproach. 'Icky baba wanna bicki,' she whined, jerking herself up and down as Aunt Hat bent over her with flustered cries that were meant to soothe but only made it impossible for Poll to abandon her performance with dignity. She could only throw herself heart and soul into her nauseating impersonation, kicking her legs and mouthing baby talk. 'Leave her, Hattie,' Ellen warned, but Aunt Hat ignored her. Red weals flushed her forehead beneath the curls as she struggled to pick Poll up, beseeching her to come on and be sensible, be a sweet, darling angel, did she really want to be a naughty girl and spoil poor Mummy's evening? Short of pulling Aunt Hat away physically, Ellen could do nothing but hover impatiently. Poll could do nothing either. By now she was too deeply committed to her own, dreadful creation, to break away from it. At last she burst into tears, taking refuge, as Boyd's entrance into the room distracted Aunt Hat's attention, against Ellen's shoulder. 'Tears before nightfall,' Ellen said, smiling angrily at Boyd. He held out his arms for Poll but Ellen shook her head. 'Bed,' she said, and carried her from the room.

Aunt Hat collapsed into a chair. Her hands fell into her lap and lay palm upwards in a gesture of inert despair. 'My fault . . . oh, what a useless old fool!'

Boyd looked at me, eyebrows raised. 'Just Poll playing up,' I said.

Aunt Hat made it seem worse than that. 'A useless old

woman,' she mourned, 'no good to anyone . . . can't even get
a child to bed when her Mummy's going out . . . oh, I feel so
dreadful, spoiling everything for both of you . . .'

I felt terribly sorry. I knew how hard it was, when you
tried to do something for somebody, to have it go wrong.
But Boyd did not look particularly sorry, just thoughtful,
rubbing the side of his nose with his forefinger as he looked
at her. Finally, he said, 'Have a drink, Hattie.'

'Well, I won't say no. Oh, not as much as *that*,' she protested, looking at the whisky he handed her as if it were a
cup of hemlock. But she drank it quite quickly. 'What must
you think of me,' she said, and repeated several times how
sorry she was and how dreadful she felt. While she recited
her inadequacies, Boyd's gaze roamed the room in a puzzled
way as if he felt a lot had gone on here that he didn't know
about. When Ellen came back he got up quickly and smiled.

'She's out,' Ellen said. 'Dead till morning, I hope. An act
like that must be as tiring as playing King Lear three times
a night.'

Aunt Hat sighed. 'The poor moppet. Oh, Ellen, I . . .'

Boyd cut her short in a way that seemed to me unkind.
'I'm sorry I was late, Ellen. . . .'

'Aunt Hat was ever so worried about you,' I told him
reproachfully and though he said he was sorry about that
too, saw him smile at Ellen privately. That surprised me
because Boyd had often told us that it was bad manners to
exchange private jokes and smiles in front of other people
because it made them feel left out, and, on the whole, he was
a man who practised what he preached. Ellen smiled back
but she looked tired and resigned. She glanced towards Aunt
Hat and said, 'I'm not sure . . . should we . . .' but Boyd took
her arm and propelled her firmly from the room. I heard him
murmuring in the hall and then Ellen's sudden laugh, like the
laugh of a young, young woman, and I was glad they were
going to enjoy themselves. Ellen had had such a sad, dull life.

We played planchette after all, because Joanna did not
come down for supper. Aunt Hat took it up on a tray and

89

came down distressed. 'She'll wear herself out, slaving away night after night. Her poor face looks so pale. Still, I suppose it's a help to have something to lose yourself in, if you've quarrelled with your sweetheart.' Deep sigh. 'Oh, I know what she's going through, there's nothing Aunt Hat doesn't know about the ups and downs of love.'

I encouraged her to talk about love and marriage. It was a subject that was uppermost in my mind at that moment and was always uppermost in Aunt Hat's, in spite of the fact that none of her marriages had been happy. Dick's father, killed at Dunkirk, had been a drunk, and the one before that, Mr Carter, had been disturbed in his mind. 'It was the full moon always set him off, it ran in his family, dear, in the male line. Not that he was violent, he never laid a finger on me, not like Jack. Mr Carter was gentle as a rabbit, poor man. And sad. Sometimes that was a hardship for me, I was a fun-loving girl, I always liked what my Mam used to call a bit of crack. She was an Irishwoman from Cork. But Mr Carter couldn't help it, he had this worry, you see. It was always on his mind all the month through that he never knew what he did when the moon was full. 'It's a burden on my soul,' he used to say, though he wasn't a religious man in a church-going way. But he was as good a Christian as any-one, he read the Bible every night. He had a nice speaking voice.'

'What did he do when the moon was full?' I asked, before Aunt Hat got too far away from the point.

'Nothing, until that last time. He used to get out of bed . . . oh, I used to draw the curtains tight and pray for cloud, but it never made any difference. He got up and wandered about in his night shirt. Sometimes he went down to the cow sheds – he was a cowman, you know, and we had a farm cottage – but more often he just stayed indoors, creeping about with a candle and staring. Your poor Aunt Hat used to wake up and find him leaning over the bed and staring with this sad look on his face and the candle tipping . . . once he dripped hot wax on my face. You could speak to him but he didn't hear, it was like speaking to the dead. Lucky he was a very light-made, runty man, even so it used to take me an hour to get him back to bed. He was frozen by then, his poor legs and his poor feet so cold. I used to rub them to get the blood going and that seemed to bring him round. He'd start to cry like a baby. 'Lord,' he said sometimes, 'let this cup pass from me.' He often spoke of being dead and out of this wicked world, but I thought it was just morbid talk. I worried about him hurting himself, falling downstairs or into the pond in the yard, but never about that. So I wasn't prepared. That night when I woke up and he wasn't there and I went downstairs and pushed against the kitchen door, I thought it had just jammed. It was a rotten old cottage and the farmer never repaired anything. But when I gave it a good shove and it still didn't move, I knew something was wrong. I had to go out the front and look through the kitchen window and I saw him, hanging from the ham hook. It's hard to believe but the first thing I thought, the very first thing, was that he looked like a fowl, hanging there with his skinny legs dangling. I ran next door and they thought I'd gone off my head, because I couldn't speak for laughing. It's funny the way things take you. They helped me get him down and he was a terrible weight, though he'd gone down to nothing in the last months. My neighbour said it was a shame I slept so heavy, I might have heard something and saved him. But, you know, Kate, I couldn't agree. Terrible as it sounds. I could only remember him crying and crying and his poor, cold feet as he said, 'Let this cup pass from me.'

'It was a merciful release,' I said.

Aunt Hat nodded. 'He looked just like a little boy in his coffin, a bit shrunken, but peaceful.'

I paused for a respectful moment before I asked, 'Did you love him very much? Was he your true love?' I felt that Aunt Hat, with her experience, could provide me with a yard-stick against which I could measure my love for Gus.

'True love is hard to find,' Aunt Hat said. She was wearing a flouncy blouse, pinned at the neck with one of her many brooches. This one was two silver hearts, joined by the pin.

While I laid out the cardboard letters for planchette, she fingered it, and mused. 'Sometimes I think of one man and think I would have loved him more than the others, but I never saw him alive. It was just before Mr Carter passed over. There was a knock on the door and I hurried to take off my apron, but by the time I opened up, he was dead. He had fallen dead on the doorstep. It was heart, the doctor said when he came, but it was all they ever found out about him. He had nothing on him to say who he was. We didn't even know why he'd come to the door, perhaps to ask the way, or for a drink of water if he was feeling bad. He'd walked some way from the look of his shoes, but he wasn't a tramp. He was nicely dressed and his nails were nice and he was well-shaved. My neighbour ran for the doctor while I laid him flat and bathed his face. . . . I couldn't believe he was dead, though my neighbour said he was, and she'd been a nurse in a fever hospital. He was about my age which was twenty-six then, and beautiful looking. You won't believe me, but as I knelt there beside him, I had the feeling I'd known him all my life. When the doctor came and said he was dead, I cried out as if he'd been my own dear husband. Just once, then I was quiet. I sat on a chair in my kitchen, not able to move hand or foot, and felt as if I was suffocating. The doctor said it was the shock, and my neighbour pushed my head between my knees, but it was more than that. It was more as if there was an extra eye inside my head that had opened all of a sudden, and seen something new. I loved that man without ever knowing him or speaking one word. And when no one turned up for him and they never found out his name, it made him seem closer. I thought about him day and night for a while and ever since, when things have been bad or sorrowful, I find myself thinking about him and how happy we might have been together, happier than any two people in the world. . . .'

Her voice stopped in the fading, unwinding way of a singer ending a sad song.

'What did he look like?' I whispered.

'Black hair and very blue eyes, a nice looking man. He

was. . . . ' She stopped, her mouth relaxed and quiet, then smiled.

'Was what?'

But she didn't answer. She said, 'It seems terrible to think he might have had a wife and children and they cared so little about him that they didn't even enquire. . . .' Her eyes filled and she sat quiet for a moment. Then she said briskly, 'Well, what about this game of planchette?'

I said the letters were ready and turned out the light so there was just one table lamp. We set the tumbler upside down in the middle of the circle of letters and while we sat silent, with our forefingers resting gently on the smooth bottom of the glass, waiting for the spirit to move, I thought of Aunt Hat's dead love. I had a shivery feeling that if I glanced sideways I would see him out of the corner of my eye, lying dead on the doorstep with his blue eyes open. Perhaps because I was thinking of this the planchette didn't work very well: you were supposed to make your mind a blank. I asked the usual question, who I should marry, and the glass slid slowly over to G and then to U and then to S, but after that the answers were only gibberish. Finally, Aunt Hat let her finger fall and said, 'We're not in the mood to-night. You have to be in the mood.'

I thought she probably wanted to be left alone to think about her life which, though romantic, had really been much sadder than Ellen's.

I looked in on Joanna before I went to bed. She was still sitting at her desk, hunched in a blanket. One cheek was pale and the other flaming red as if she had toothache. She had been writing a letter which she covered up with a fold of the blanket when I came in. I guessed it was to Will. Her slanted look was hostile and cold and I knew she was afraid I would start talking about him.

I told her what Ellen had told me about her early life. Sorrow made me feel sweet and good. I said that of course Ellen had told me in confidence and perhaps it was wrong of me to tell Joanna in a way, but then, in another way, perhaps it was right. Perhaps it was best we should both know, because now we could understand her better and make allowances.

While I talked, Joanna made dents in her pale cheek with a pencil point.

She said, 'Oh, I knew all that. Ellen told me ages ago.'

I was thunderstruck. 'Why didn't you tell me?'

'You know what you are.' My fists clenched at the familiar insult and she smiled secretly. 'As a matter of *fact*, I advised Ellen not to tell you. I told her I thought it might turn you against religion.'

Her voice, ice-cool and superior, tolled a knell in my head. I saw now how things were in our family. I was the despised, the left out one. Ellen discussed me with Joanna behind my back; together they conspired to keep things from me. Ellen had only told me what she had because she had been spurred into it by my disbelieving rudeness. It had been a punishment, not a confidence; only Joanna, her favourite, was worth confiding in.

My stomach shrivelled. I said, 'Thank you for telling me, even though I know you only did it to make me suffer. I shan't have to bother to be sorry for you ever again. I was awfully sorry for you about Will but I'm not now, I'm glad for his sake. He's lucky not to be in love with such a low, treacherous, disloyal person. I expect you'll be sorry one day when you're alone in your lonely old age, but it'll be too late.' I paused. Joanna seemed to be struggling for breath. 'I daresay I shall be a little bit sorry for you then,' I said, relenting.

She blew out her cheeks and burst into laughter. It was partly affected, partly real.

'Blast and damn you, you horrible fat *cow*,' I shrieked, and ran from the room.

I banged her door, then mine. I tore off my clothes and flung into bed, burrowing under the clothes. Sometimes when I cried, I looked in the mirror to pity myself, but now I only wanted to hide. I felt sick and empty and mean and unloved and my skin shrank from the touch of the bed-

94

clothes as if I had been burned raw. After a little, I pushed the sheet back from my face and whimpered, hoping that Poll would wake up and come in with me for comfort. Even if she wet the bed, it would be better than being alone. But she didn't wake, just muttered and ground her teeth.

Aunt Hat came in, gently opening the door and stealing across the room.

'Is anything wrong, love?' Her voice was anxious and she smelt of lilies of the valley. I was too ashamed to tell her what was the matter, so I said nothing was. She bent to kiss me and, though she must have felt my face wet, she said nothing.

I loved her for that tactfulness and when she had gone I lay and thought how different she was from Ellen and Joanna. *She* didn't think I was low and detestable, she didn't despise me: she talked to me like a friend and told me her intimate memories and thoughts.

'Aunt Hat is my only friend,' I said into the darkness. They were mournful, beautiful words, and though they made me cry afresh, I wept comforting tears.

Chapter Eight

Holding Miss Carter's hand, Aunt Hat was saying, 'You have a pronounced mons veneris, that means you are a very loving person by nature.'

They were sitting on the sofa, this Sunday morning, coffee cups on the table before them. What Joanna and I had feared had come to pass: Miss Carter had taken to dropping in. Her excuse was not Ellen, but Aunt Hat. Innocent and friendly as a robin, she had responded to Miss Carter's overtures across the hedge and accepted her first invitation to tea with a flustered pleasure that seemed ludicrous to us, since we had only experienced contemptuous boredom in Miss Carter's company. I thought Ellen should warn Aunt Hat – it would come better from her than from me – but she told me not to be silly and unkind: it was unlikely that Aunt Hat would feel as we did and, anyway, it was nice for her to make a friend. Aunt Hat was probably a little lonely, Ellen said.

I received this, first with amazement – how could Aunt Hat be lonely when she had us? – and then with sadness: poor Aunt Hat, could she not see she was being used? I thought Miss Carter devilish cunning and could not conceive that there might be real pleasure on her side too, though admittedly, as the friendship prospered, there seemed to be. 'They are like two girls together,' I heard Ellen say to Boyd, and this was true: they sat together hour after hour, comforted by little snacks, sweet drinks, gossip of a low-voiced speculative kind, horoscopes, the reading of hands . . .

But this was not an occupation Miss Carter cared to be caught indulging in. When she saw me, she withdrew her hand from Aunt Hat's grasp and blushed like a plum.

'Your Auntie and I have been playing party games,' she said.

'You have a very interesting hand, Ethel,' Aunt Hat said. 'The right so very different from the left. It always is, of course, the left is what you are born with and the right is what you make, though I suppose this is the other way round in left-handed persons, but in your case the change is exceptionally strongly marked. The heart line, for instance. The left hand is rather weak, but the right is very deep and strong. I would say you were a teeny bit fickle as a young girl' – she laughed, admonishing and arch – 'but that you have changed considerably. I would say you were now an unusually faithful type.'

Though pleased, Miss Carter laughed dismissingly. 'And what is Katey doing this morning?'

'I'm going to church.' This was an unfortunate admission

because Miss Carter was going too. She said we would be company for each other, wouldn't we? There was no polite answer to this question, so I remained silent while she explained she had only just popped in for a minute to return a recipe Aunt Hat had given her, for honey cake: she had not meant to stay. 'But your naughty Aunt tempted me and I fell,' she said merrily, rising and fussily adjusting her feathered felt hat and her stole of marten's fur: the little, dead heads dangled before and behind and made her look like a gibbet. 'Not that it wasn't very nice, to rest my weary bones a-while,' she said, smiling at Aunt Hat. 'Thank you for the coffee, dear.'

'You're very welcome,' Aunt Hat said. 'Kate, love, your hem's coming down. I'll put a stitch in for you.'

I said happily, 'It'll make me late. You go on, Miss Carter, don't wait for me.'

But she said, oh no, she would wait, it wouldn't take long, would it? Aunt Hat sealed my fate by saying that perhaps a safety pin would do – just for *once*, she murmured, falsely implying that she did not usually employ such sluttish methods. While she pinned, I reflected gloomily on the ordeal before me. Not many of my friends went to church, but some did. Gus did. My blood ran cold. Appearing in public with Miss Carter, I would rightly be an object for derision and contempt.

Humiliation made me fidget. 'Keep still, my duck,' Aunt Hat said, and rising, spilled the pins.

I helped her collect them. Waiting by the door, Miss Carter did nothing until Boyd came in, when she swooped down upon one we had missed. 'See a pin and pick it up, all the day you'll have good luck,' she cried, waving it triumphantly in his face. I knew she had been prodded into activity by his step in the hall and was astonished, as I always was when I caught a grown-up employing the kind of subterfuge we children used.

Boyd smiled politely. She wriggled her shoulders beneath her dreadful fur, and lowered her voice. 'Doctor Boyd, I've been meaning to ask you, how is poor Miss Fantom?'

Boyd said she was better, he was glad to say.

Miss Carter's eyes rolled sideways. 'Of course, one doesn't want to pry, but she is such a near neighbour and one can't help hearing things. One knows the position. So sad. Naturally, if there is anything I can do . . .'

Boyd murmured that she was very kind. I said we would be awfully late for church if we didn't hurry, and he smiled at me.

'I think your Aunt is such a charming person,' Miss Carter said, and looked pleased, as if it was kind of her to say this. 'So cheerful, always. One admires her for it.' She sighed, elongating her jaw. 'It is so terrible about her husband.'

I wondered what Aunt Hat had told her. Not the truth, of course. She would never take anyone outside the family into her confidence. Perhaps she had told Miss Carter Jack was seriously ill, perhaps, even that he was dead? Not knowing, all I could do was trot beside Miss Carter and make loud, puffing noises, in the hope she would think I was too out of breath to reply.

Luckily, by the time we got to church, they were singing the processional hymn and no one saw us enter. We slipped into a pew. Miss Carter knelt devoutly, rose, opened her hymn book and lifted her face to sing.

She sang like a shaken saw. I was convinced that heads were turning. Tense with shame, I kept my lowered eyes on my hymn book, miserably aware that beside me Miss Carter was quivering while she sang, shaking her whole body as her voice soared tremulously high. FORWARD into B-attle, GOES the Church of God, BROTHERS we are treading, WHERE the Saints have trod . . . I banished the temptation to ask God to strike her dumb and, more charitably, prayed for the hymn to end. When it did, I fumbled for the hassock and sank on to it with gratitude. Miss Carter's eyes were closed; a suppliant murmur came from her lips. I looked across the aisle and saw, with a thump of happiness, Gus sitting with his mother. Above his dark jacket a sliver of shirt collar showed dazzling white against his neck which

98

was wonderfully and smoothly tanned. His fair head was slightly bowed and resting on the fingertips of one hand, an attitude which seemed to me both reverent and sophisticated. When the praying was finished, he remained in that position a fraction longer than other people: most of the congregation, shuffling hassocks and clearing their throats, had slid their bottoms back on to the seats by the time Gus raised his head, turned towards me, and smiled.

His smile was broad and open, as if it were quite natural and proper to smile in church; it was part of the same graceful assurance with which he stayed kneeling longer than anyone else and then re-seated himself with one easy, accomplished movement. Dizzy with love and admiration, I watched his profile as he lifted it towards the pulpit, and then, suddenly afraid that Miss Carter would notice the direction of my gaze, stared beyond him, at the big, brass plaque in honour of General Claud Archer Fantom.

Below this plaque there was a smaller, prettier one to his wife, a scroll of speckled marble unfurled by two angels. Her name was Concordia Jane; she had been born in 1872, had married the General in 1889 and had died ten years later, having borne him nine children of which seven had died in infancy. Beneath this lamentable account, the General had caused to be inscribed Good Works Were Her Life. Whenever I looked at this plaque I had a general feeling of awe and sadness and a specific feeling of gratitude for my own luck: my mother was now fourteen years older than Jane had been when she died.

There had been a time when I had dreaded her death. She had once said, when Poll was little and ill with her colic, *that child will be the death of me*, a chance remark that had taken root and grown into a fear that was nourished by a natural taste for death-bed scenes in the Victorian children's novels Joanna sometimes read aloud at bedtime. Though the tears I shed over these fictionalised accounts sometimes comforted me, real fear remained. On those mornings when Ellen had slept badly and her face had a pink and ragged look, it was especially bad. It became a tightness knotted inside me so that I could not eat, not even drink a glass of milk. One morning she shouted, 'Eat, eat . . .' and tried to ram porridge into my mouth. I retched and cried and she suddenly smote her forehead with the heel of her hand and said, with bitter anger, 'Oh, how can you be like this, haven't I enough to worry me?' On that occasion fear gave way to indignation: how could Ellen be so unkind when I was worrying about *her*? It was not until recently that I had realized my fears had not been wholly for Ellen: when she married Boyd they had begun to lessen slowly. Almost unadmitted, there had come the feeling that if she died now there would be someone to take care of me.

Almost unadmitted, but a source of shame. When I looked at the plaque to Concordia Jane, I knew my present fear was only fear remembered, a pale shadow of what I had once felt. This filled me with a sudden, superstitious dread: suppose, because I no longer worried about her death, she were to die? The Lord Thy God is a Jealous God. I closed my eyes and tried, frantically, to think of something I could offer in return for Ellen's safety. To promise merely to be good was too difficult, as well as too vague: to make the bargain effective, it was necessary to offer some solid sacrifice. 'Please let her go on living for years and years, if You do, I won't look at Gus again in church or speak to him at all today. Unless he speaks to me,' I added, cautiously.

This arrangement accomplished, I began to feel more comfortable, though my neck soon began to ache from staring rigidly ahead. An itch began behind my knee but I dared not scratch it, in case, shifting my position, I inadvertently glanced across the aisle. Usually I enjoyed being in church and might even have gone if I had not expected to see Gus there; church, like the camp in the Fantom's garden, was a good place to be private in, you could think there. But today it wasn't easy to think. Beside me, Miss Carter fidgeted and fingered her gloves and the marten's heads on her stole, while a series of grimaces contorted her face: her eyes narrowed and then widened as if with innocent surprise, her lips pursed out and receded while she nodded and frowned, approving or contradicting the points made in the sermon. Even when she prayed, her presence distracted me. Her air was so elaborately devotional that it would have been a shame to have missed the opportunity of marking it for reproduction later.

Throughout the service I was comfortably absorbed in committing her peculiarities to memory, but by the end, I had had enough. My lips moved to the words of the final hymn, but inwardly I was planning how to escape her.

It wasn't difficult. I merely rose from my knees before the coughing and rustling that preceded the general exodus, and, wearing the abstracted smile of someone not really conscious of her surroundings, hurried down the aisle to the small exit by the vestry door. Here I could lurk among the weed-grown graves until the congregation had dispersed to Sunday lunch: in case any stray members should stroll round the side of the church and wonder what I was doing there, I pretended to be absorbed in reading the tombstones. The gravel crunched behind me and I concentrated hard. Henrietta Castle, who fell asleep in the Lord in the year 1901. Blessed Be Thy Ways.

'Katey-Did,' Gus said, and my skin prickled.

I turned awkwardly. Gus and his mother were smiling at me.

'Old tombstones are fascinating, aren't they?' Gus said kindly.

Crossing my fingers, I reminded God, in case it should slip His notice, that I had not arranged this meeting.

'Yes, they are, aren't they?' I gabbled fervently.

Gus did not answer, only smiled, and this embarrassed me.

I said, 'It gives one a feeling of awe, to think of those dead and gone.'

Gus's mother looked surprised, but friendly. A tiny woman in a brown coat, she made me feel overgrown and clumsy.

Gus said, 'Mother, this is Kate Boyd. One of our Fellowship.'

'I'm really pleased to meet you, dear,' she said, and held out her hand.

I took it, and then began to worry. Nervous tension had made me sweat and the tight armholes of my coat made matters worse. I was terrified in case I was smelling.

'Isn't it dreadfully *hot*?' I said, as an explanatory diversion, and fanned myself with my prayer book.

Mrs Lightwater looked reasonably bewildered: the day, though bright, was cold for March.

She laughed, rather nervously, 'Well, I wouldn't . . .'

'It was pretty warm in church,' Gus said gallantly. 'It's thirsty work, praying. Perhaps Kate could do with a little liquid refreshment.'

His mother's face cleared. 'Why, of course. . . . Won't you come home with us, dear, and have something . . . lemonade and biscuits?'

Her enthusiasm for this project grew visibly as she spoke of it. 'It would be so nice, we do like to get to know Gus's young friends. As long as your mother won't worry, of course. We won't keep you long.'

Perversely, this long-dreamed-of invitation brought me nothing but shame and horror. Though in imagination I had conversed fluently, stunning Gus's family with my wisdom and wit – 'That girl is remarkably mature,' his mother said when I left, 'a really lovely, unusual person, you are very lucky, Son' – in reality, I could see only abject social failure ahead of me. There were so many terrible hurdles. I would have to take off my coat and there was a grease mark down the front of my dress. What would I talk about? How bored they would be! Suppose I needed to go to the lavatory? My misery was increased by the fear that Gus's mother might think I had fished for the invitation by saying how hot I was. Perhaps, even now, behind that lined and gentle brow, was the thought: *this dreadful girl is forcing herself upon us, she is running after Gus.*

'Oh, I can't do *that*,' I said, agony coming out as bad-mannered abruptness. Ashamed, almost in tears, I added, 'I have to help my mother with the lunch.'

Rude, a coward, and now a liar, too!

Mrs Lightwater said, 'What a shame. Another time, then,' and smiled as if it was not important.

'See you on Tuesday, Kate,' Gus said. For a moment, his eyes looked gravely and encouragingly into mine, then he took his mother's arm and led her down the path to the lychgate. Through misted eyes I saw the courteous way he ushered her ahead of him, his fair head inclined to hear something she was saying. He laughed as the gate hinges creaked behind them, and it was as if my shame had been proclaimed from the roof tops.

I wanted to tear up grass with my hands, stuff earth in my mouth. Oh, to disappear, not to *be* . . . 'Please God,' I moaned, 'don't let him know how much I mind and I'll . . .' I remembered my other bargain and it came briefly into my mind that I had sensibly avoided a temptation that had been deliberately sent to make me break my part of it, but I did not, in my heart, believe this. That was only a game, fearfully half-believed, played out of lingering superstition like saying 'Touch wood, no returns,' when you saw the back of an ambulance. No – I had merely panicked. I hated myself for my cowardice, my treacherous incompetence, and ran home, swollen with misery – swollen is, I think, an exact word: my limbs felt like over-stuffed bolsters, my cheeks puffed out hard and lumpy, like potatoes.

Apples is what Aunt Hat called them. 'Rosy as apples,' she said fondly, as I entered the kitchen. 'That's what I like to see. Nice pink cheeks. It shows you've got a good grip on life.'

'Or a temperature,' Joanna said, and eyed me more closely than I cared for.

'I've been running,' I mumbled.

'Oh, it's nice to be young,' Aunt Hat said.

Chapter Nine

I went to the camp to be alone for a little, but Poll and Walter were there, sitting side by side in two old crates from the greengrocer's. Their voices, rising and falling in affected cadences, stopped when they saw me: their faces became blank. I was too miserable to be indignant that Poll had not asked my permission to take Walter there. 'Are you being King and Queen?' I asked stupidly.

They looked at each other in a secret, side-long way.

I smiled brightly. 'You ought to sit *on* your thrones, not inside them.'

Walter stared at me. He popped his grubby thumb into his mouth while he waited for me to go away.

Poll heaved a deep sigh. She said, very reluctantly, 'They're boats. We're crossing the Atlantic Ocean.'

I saw now that they each held a piece of splintery wood and knew that there were two perfectly clear sections in their minds: one in which they were rowing two boats across a dangerous sea, and another in which they knew they were sitting in vegetable crates with inch-wide openings between the boards.

I saw, also, that I was the intruder, not Walter.

It filled me with anger and sorrow. I said to Walter, 'If you suck your thumb with those warts, you'll get warts all over your insides.'

He removed his thumb and blinked. 'They're goin' 'way. I rubbed snails on e'm.'

'*Snails* are no good,' Poll said bossily. 'You want *beans*. Rub the warts with the whitey part and wet them with spit, first thing in the morning.'

'That's a lot of silly nonsense,' I said, though I had

believed it until now. 'And if those were real boats, you'd drown. The water would come in through the sides.'

My eyes began to burn and I went away. I could hear them giggling as I squeezed through the fence. I ran to hide in the outside lavatory and sat on the seat and cried.

After lunch Boyd said he must go and see Miss Fantom. Oh, *must* you?' Ellen said, and then gave an awkward little laugh, almost as if she wished she hadn't spoken.

Boyd didn't answer but he kissed her before he left, as if he were going on a journey.

He left his bag behind and Ellen sent me after him. 'You can slip through the back,' she said. She was lying with her feet up, exhausted by the strain of Sunday lunch.

'Can't Poll?'

'I'm cutting out families.' Poll sat cross-legged, surrounded by jaggedly cut magazines, scissors flying round a baby.

'That's not important.'

'It is to me.' Poll refused to meet my eyes. She knew how things were between us.

'Oh, don't *argue*,' Ellen cried, in a voice that could hardly have been more frantic if we had been slitting each other's throats with knives.

'My God, I'm not arguing,' I said. 'It's just that it's always me who does things around here.'

'Don't talk like that, lovey.' Aunt Hat smiled anxiously at me and then, in a sad attempt to improve the situation, 'Is that a little black dog I see on your shoulder?'

I left the room in disgust.

'Put on your coat,' Ellen called after me.

Coatless, I went into the garden. There was a crocus poking up in the rockery by the back door and, a surer sign of spring, fathers digging in the neat line of gardens. The sky was a torpid, Sunday grey. Miss Carter was planting roses; her glasses were spattered with wet peat and round her head she wore a scarf painted with hunting scenes. As I passed she waved a cheery hand.

I went through the fence and stopped for a minute in the

camp. I had hoped for comfort but found none: the camp was just a clump of rhododendrons with a load of old junk in the middle.

I left it, heavy-hearted, and walked on. The back door of Lock View was open. I had not been in the house since the morning Miss Fantom had been taken ill. It smelt different from the way it had smelt that day: the smell of old carpets and dust was still there, but it was overlaid by the smell of polish and disinfectant. I remembered that after Mrs Wise had refused to 'oblige' any more because, she complained, Mr Fantom was rude to her and had been hitting the bottle, Boyd had arranged that Mrs Tanner, Walter's mother, should go and clean once a week. He said it fretted Miss Fantom to think of the house running down. He did not mention what Mr Fantom thought.

The brass elephant's case had been dusted and the clock in its belly set going: the house was so quiet that I could hear it ticking through the glass.

The quiet made me nervous. Mr Fantom's sitting-room door was closed. I thought of him suddenly opening it and standing there, nine feet tall, his eyes hot as embers with rage. I dwelt on this picture deliberately, partly out of superstition – if you fix your mind on a thing it won't happen – and partly because I found the sensation it produced enjoyable in a dreadful way. After a minute or two I had worked myself up into such a state that if he had opened the door, I think I would have fainted.

But the house remained quiet. I climbed the stairs slowly and reached the landing without incident, except for one creaking stair. My pulse slowed down. I crossed the landing. I had reached the place where we had seen Miss Fantom's note fluttering in the draught and was reaching out for the handle of the closed door when Mr Fantom spoke.

'Walking in without a by-your-leave,' he said.

I had time to think that it was all my own fault; that he had caught me because I had stopped being frightened of him, and to vow never to be so foolish again, before I turned.

106

He must have just walked out of the bathroom. In one hand he held a glass of fizzing Alka-Seltzer, and with the other he was fastening his flies. Embarrassed, not because I minded, but because he might think I did, I raised my eyes to his face. He was not as terrible as I had imagined, but he was terrible enough: his eyes, under those bristling moustaches, cold as winter, the red patches on his cheeks, fiery as chilblains.

'I brought this . . .' I said faintly. Incapable of further explanation, I held up Boyd's bag.

'Ah – I understand. The doctor must have his medicaments. Naturally, his requirements take precedence over any other consideration. Don't feel you owe me any courtesy, ma'am!' He bowed with mock obsequiousness. 'I am of no account in this house. Walk in . . . walk in any time you please. Do what you like. Roll out the red carpet. Bring in the whole neighbourhood. Have a party. Burn the place down.' He gestured grandly with the glass of Seltzer and it slopped over, fizzing on the carpet.

'I'm s-sorry. I only wanted . . .'

'To kick me in the teeth. To humiliate me. That is what your father is doing, naturally the child follows the parent's example. I don't blame you. You see me for the poor thing I am. Am I master in my own house or am I not? I am not. It is your sister this, your sister that. No thought for her unfortunate brother. The whole purpose is to humiliate and ruin me. Money is spent like water. Nurses. Women to clean. And worse to come. My sister, that bitch, that sourpuss, must have a companion. Cannot be left alone once the nurse has gone. That is what your father says.'

Too fascinated to be frightened now, I was only repelled by the sourness of his breath as he advanced on me.

'Oh, she's under his thumb, all right. What does she want with a companion? She has that stinking cat. Talks to it . . . when did she last throw a kind word at me? Her only brother, her only kin! Not that I would want it, not from that old bitch, that spoilsport. I tell you, I've had no life with her. After a career in which I was highly respected, highly respected by influential people, people in high places, I come down to this! A lackey in the house. Her house. My only function to cook meals she threw back in my face. Notes on the tray. She would like a boiled egg, a glass of milk. Please. Soft-syruping me, always the lady. But my cooking disgusted her, that was the implication. She was too fine to eat what I ate, her brother, that coarse pig, that drunken sot. Now it turns out I ill-treated her. Women in the house like rabbits, looking at me reproachfully. The house is filthy, she tells them. Filthy! Was I trained as a house boy? For years I never lifted a cup from the table, never picked up my own clothes from the floor. I wasn't too proud to learn. I've been on my hands and knees in that kitchen. But it wasn't good enough for her. She wants polish, Vim, radios, dainty food, regardless of cost. Oh – she's got the bit between her teeth all right, now she's got backing. Solicitors, doctors, telling her I'm the nigger in the woodpile. Your father, telling her she must have what she wants, she's not to worry about money, not to worry about me. . . . *You* don't worry about me, do you?'

The question startled me. Until then I had felt myself safe. His gun-fire monologue had not been directed at me but at some unseen opponent.

I said, 'I'm sorry.' I was sorry. In some way his outcast condition seemed to reflect my own. I went on, 'It's a real shame Miss Fantom doesn't appreciate what you've done for her. Especially when you've had to do housework and things you've never done before. My father says retirement comes awfully hard on men sometimes. I'm . . . well . . . I'm sorry.'

He rapped out, 'I don't want your pity, young lady,' in a tone of voice that made me swear, inwardly, that he would never have it. His face was all red now, red as a boiled prawn's, except for the divided blob at the end of his nose which was a pinched, yellowish colour. 'Nor your father's comments. I've had a bellyful of them already. Who does he think he is, God Almighty?'

I said stiffly, 'Please don't talk about my father like that.

He only wants Miss Fantom to be looked after. Sick people need special food and things like that.'

He gave a short, barking laugh. He drained the last of the Alka-Seltzer and tossed the glass on to the floor. It was made of some sort of plastic, and bounced.

'You don't need to tell me what your father wants.' His teeth were still bared in laughter. I knew they were false because they were so white and even. 'She's worth something, the old cow. I imagine he knows that.'

I was shaking from head to foot. Even my teeth were chattering so the words would hardly come out. 'You're horrible,' I said, 'a horrible, mean, beastly old man. To say a thing like that just shows you up for what you are.'

I turned my back on him, sweat starting up along my hair line. Knees quaking, I marched up to Miss Fantom's door. I knocked, skinning my knuckles. After a hundred years, the door opened and the nurse stood there. Speechless, I held out Boyd's bag and she smiled and said, 'What a shame, your Dadda's gone.'

She was quite old, but pretty, with dark hair curling under her white cap. She glanced along the passage where Mr Claud Fantom was standing, staring at us. He hiccuped suddenly and, with what seemed to me miraculous understanding of my predicament, she took my arm and said, 'Come this way, dear.'

Her apron crackled as she drew me into Miss Fantom's part of the house. Warm air struck me, and a smell that was a compound of Dettol and soap and the paraffin stoves, of which there were four, placed at intervals along the broad, dark passage. As she closed the door behind us, I gathered my wits sufficiently to hope that I might catch a glimpse of Miss Fantom herself, but all the doors were closed. The walls of the corridor were covered with chcocolate-brown, bubbly paper; the only light came from the round paraffin stoves which flung a yellow daisy pattern on the gravy-coloured ceiling, and from a small window at the end, above a narrow stair.

This stairway, the treads covered with dark-brown linoleum, led down to a ground floor kitchen that looked out on to the back lawn. Everything was brown here, too, except for the black boiler, whispering in an alcove. The Abyssinian cat sat before it on a rug, upright, but dreaming with its eyes closed.

Nurse said, 'You mustn't mind Mr Fantom. A lot of gentlemen take a drop too much from time to time. I'm accustomed to it, because my old Dad was the same.'

'I wasn't frightened,' I said.

'No? That's a good thing, then. Mr Fantom's bark's worse than his bite, of course. All the same, another time I should slip in this way. Your Dadda does. Least said, soonest mended. Never trouble trouble till trouble troubles you,' she remarked gaily, and winked at me.

She was so nice, I wanted to say something polite. 'How is Miss Fantom?'

'Oh, going on famously, dear,' she said, telling me nothing in the bright way of nurses. 'The doctor's visits do cheer us up, we're always very chatty. Talk – you'd be surprised! It's not nursing she needs really, so much as someone to talk to. I only hope your Dadda will be able to fix something up before I go. I should hate to think of her being left alone.'

Her cheerful smile and clean, bright skin shone like lamplight in the drab security of this house. I should hate to be left alone here, I thought, and asked, 'When are you going?'

'Next week. I've got a confinement. Doctor's begged me to stay, but babies won't wait on other people's convenience, you know.'

She winked again and opened the kitchen door for me. Outside, the day was not darkening so much as blanching: the light seemed to be draining out of the sky, leaving it flat and cold.

'Did you want anything? I mean, was it a nuisance my being late with the bag?' I asked, and she shook her head.

'Bless you, no. We only wanted some sleeping pills and I daresay Doctor'll drop them in later on. It'll be another little treat for us to look forward to, though where your Dadda finds the time, I don't know. Oh,' she said, suddenly expansive, 'I've seen some good doctors in my time, but your Dadda's one in a million, I don't care who hears me say it.'

I ran home, swelling with pride. Before me rose a series of inspiring pictures: Boyd, bending over sick beds in sad, sepia-coloured dwellings, healing with a touch, a smile; placing a child in its mother's arms and receiving her speechless gratitude with the words, 'I think we can hope now'; Boyd, worn-faced and robed in surgeon's white, passing through hospital wards where dying soldiers lay. The hospital ward bore a close resemblance to a picture in one of my history books of Florence Nightingale at Scutari. I had no time to invent a more likely background for my pious visions because when I entered the sitting-room, Aunt Hat was there with Miss Carter.

She was sitting on the floor in front of the fire still wearing the scarf painted with hunting scenes, but she had taken off her gardening shoes. Her feet, in thick, splashed stockings, looked ugly and lumpy and I was astonished when she stretched them out in front of her and said, with an awful coquetry, 'Just look at me, what a way to go visiting! What a sight to frighten the crows!'

I could hardly say yes, and honesty forbade me to say no, so I stayed silent. She wriggled her toes, laughing gaily, and it came to me that she thought there was something rather appealing in a gamine way about her dishevelled appearance. Some of my disgust must have shown in my face because Miss Carter suddenly withdrew her feet from under her spread-out skirt, and, putting up her hands to tuck away strands of hair under her scarf, began to explain that she had been slaving away in the garden ever since we came back from church, not even stopping for lunch. It was silly but she was like that, she said, simpering, once she had started a thing she had to go on and on until she had finished it, but today she really felt that she had overdone it a bit and that she must have a little sit down and a chat before putting herself to right. 'So I thought just for today you would all have to take me as I am,' she said with a despairing brightness that even I could see as pathetic, though at that moment, her pathos only increased my dislike of her.

I asked where everyone was. Aunt Hat said Boyd was upstairs, writing letters in the bedroom. Ellen had gone for a walk with Poll. They had only just gone this minute, what a pity I had missed them.

'And where has Katey been?' Miss Carter said, arching her neck and giving me one of her wild, jaw-wrenching smiles.

Since I could not ignore her question – it is impossible for children to be as rude as they would like – I told her about my abortive errand, managing to speak pleasantly though my thoughts were murderous. I knew quite well – or thought I knew quite well – what had happened. Ellen rarely went for walks and Boyd always did his paper work on a leather blotter balanced on the arm of the chair, quite undisturbed by what was going on around him: when Poll and I were smaller, we had played round his feet like puppies. Of course Miss Carter had driven them out; they had fled from her hideous presence! Though I knew that, in fact, my parents would never be so unkind, I enjoyed the feeling of burning indignation that rose up in me as I thought of them, banished from their own fireside the one afternoon in the week when they were able to sit and be lazy together.

'Poor Boyd, he must be awfully cold in his room!' I remarked with a heavy-handed, mock innocence that made Aunt Hat look at me sharply.

She said, at once, 'I'll make a cup of tea, Ethel, I daresay you can do with it,' and then, looking at me with unhappiness and reproach, 'Kate will look after you for a minute.'

I saw that I had embarrassed Aunt Hat and was more astonished than sorry. Since I thought of her as one of our family, I could not really believe that she did not feel about Miss Carter as we did. When she had gone, I sat down on the edge of a chair and regarded our neighbour unblinkingly.

She said, 'You know, Kate, I didn't really drive your father out of the room.'

This direct attack was unexpected. I had meant my remark to strike home but, in the cowardly way of most children when they insult grown-ups, I had hoped Miss Carter would think my rudeness unintentional, and so not take me up on it.

But she had taken me up. I did not know how to answer her and in my confusion thought of the plan Joanna and I had conceived to put Miss Carter off Boyd. Though we had giggled over it often, we had never really intended to put it into action, it was too outrageous, but in this moment it seemed the only way – short of sudden death – out of a hideous situation, the only way to divert Miss Carter's attention. I say 'thought' and 'seemed' but I didn't really reflect upon it: the idea simply rose up in the empty panic of my mind and I seized upon it.

'Oh, dear,' I said. I clapped my hand over my mouth and looked at her over my spread fingers, wide-eyed with consternation. 'Please – oh, please, Miss Carter, *don't* tell Boyd what I said. I shall get into such terrible trouble.'

She looked mildly mystified. 'Of course not, dear. Though I'm sure he wouldn't be angry.' She tilted her head on one side and said playfully, 'But just for the record, dear, your Papa was on his way upstairs when I popped in – we met in the hall, actually – and he told me to go in by the fire and warm myself up and he'd be down the minute he finished his letters.'

I had to go on now. I wanted to go on. Not to hurt her – though I suppose I must have known I would – but because I had to know how she would react. My curiosity was too strong, too basic, to make any pain I might cause her more than incidental in my mind. I was filled with a wild, unthinking excitement.

'Oh, he's awfully *polite*. To people's faces, that is. It makes it awfully difficult for us, sometimes. You see, we know how he really feels about visitors. He's ever so nice in front of them, it's only afterwards that he takes it out on us. He . . .' I faltered, not with dramatic intention, but it was difficult to think what Boyd might do or say afterwards: he was not an easy man to present as a monster. 'The trouble is, he's a dreadful misogynist,' I said.

She was smiling. 'Do you know what that means, Kate?'

'A man who hates women.' This was easier; suddenly I felt as cheerful as a comedian who is being fed the right lines. 'I mean, he doesn't hate my mother, or Aunt Hat, but he can't stand other women. He can't even stand being in the same room with them sometimes, it's like a person hating cats. He doesn't mind so much if they're really pretty' – it struck me that Miss Carter might, incredibly, have illusions about her own physical attractions, so I hastily qualified this – 'or if they're really *young*. I mean he can just put up with some of Joanna's friends as long as they're not too plain, but mostly he just hates all women over about twenty.'

Miss Carter was looking at me with a peculiar expression which I identified as horror.

'I expect it's being a doctor,' I said, 'and having to look after sick women. They get so many disgusting diseases when they get old, things wrong with their insides, that sort of thing, that I suppose he can't help thinking about it when he looks at them.' I paused effectively. 'Like St. Paul,' I whispered, 'he thinks women are *unclean*.'

A crimson tide crept up Miss Carter's neck. She drew a long, quivering breath and opened her mouth.

I said quickly, 'Oh, of course it doesn't *show*. But then no one can tell what a person's like, outside their families, can they?'

There was a discouraging gleam in Miss Carter's eye. 'Kate,' she said vigorously, 'you are a naughty girl. I am very shocked. I'm not at all sure that I oughtn't to tell your parents what you have been telling me. Really, I've never heard . . .' She went on, working herself up, the round, indignant phrases, *such disgraceful behaviour*, *never in all my life*, rolling richly off her tongue while she stretched her neck and rolled her eyes and I sat still, swallowing hard until the water came into mine. When it was welling up properly, I put up the back of my hand to call attention to my tearful state and Miss Carter said, rather nervously – I suppose she was afraid someone might come in and ask why I was crying: it was a difficult position for her – 'Well, Kate, that's all . . . just say you're sorry and dry your eyes and we won't say any more about it. All right?'

I gave a tiny, breathy sigh and said, 'I'm sorry. But I wasn't telling lies . . .' and then let my lip quiver the way I had often practised in the mirror. Miss Carter's face remained pink but I could see, as her eyes searched my face, that a faint doubt was growing. Inspiration seized me. From time to time, various people had said that Ellen was lucky in marrying a man who was so good to her children. This was an attitude we found extremely peculiar but now I could see how to put it to use.

'It's awful for my mother, she can't have any women friends in case he takes against them and she can't really say anything. I mean she can't complain because she has to be grateful to him for looking after all of us.'

'Kate, that's ridiculous,' Miss Carter said, but her voice had altered. She did not believe me but she was, basically, an honest woman who tried to be fair: once doubt had arisen, she had to admit it. So when she spoke she was not so much attacking me, as trying to convince herself I was lying. 'Of course it isn't true. Everyone knows your father is one of the kindest of men. His reputation – well if I hadn't heard from other people, there is an example on our own doorstep. Look how marvellous he has been to poor Miss Fantom . . .'

I heard the thud and chink which meant Aunt Hat was pushing the tea trolley down the hall. I was beginning to feel the first prick of shame: I was also desperately anxious to have the last word.

'Oh, he's only after her money,' I said.

Chapter Ten

There followed a time in which I was ugly and lonely, an
outlaw. Poll no longer wanted me now she had Walter who
came to play most days after school. Joanna withdrew into
her role of dedicated student: over-acting as usual, she rarely
spoke to me and answered my questions absently, as if she
had been called back from a long distance. At meals she ate
little, posing silently with an expression intended to convey
that her mind was on other things than food. It looked to
me as if she were merely suppressing a desire to be sick, but
Ellen was angry when I said so and sent me out of the room.

Fear of Miss Carter consumed all my attention: for some
days I was convinced that exposure was imminent. I dreaded
every step on the path, every ring at the door. One morning,
Boyd and I met her in the street. My heart pounded and her
boney face seemed to swim through a red haze. Boyd smiled
and spoke to her pleasantly but she passed by with a brief
nod and a darting, acid glance. I thought her spiteful dis-
trust written clear – and therefore my own shame – but
Boyd's face showed no more than a mild surprise as if, to
him, she had only appeared pre-occupied, a busy neighbour
who had barely noticed his polite good morning. Instead of
making me feel safer, her obvious desire to avoid him – and
this meeting was not the only evidence, she had called no
more gay greetings over the garden hedge – impaled me on
a new and sharper fear: she had already told Aunt Hat who
had told Ellen and Boyd, and they had decided, for the
moment, to say nothing to me! They were waiting until my
conscience spoke up! This was not really likely but guilt made
me half-believe it. Certainly, it seemed that they had begun
to look at me in a sad, reproachful way. Some evenings, when
we were sitting quiet, I became certain that one of them was

going to say something: I would stare at the swimming words of my book while my heart quivered and almost stopped. I was sure that they talked about me when I was out of the room: at night, listening to their voices murmuring on downstairs, I lay awake and writhed.

At school, someone wrote *Kate Boyd loved Gus Lightwater* on the lavatory wall. It could only have been one girl, Jane Owen, my best friend. I took all the things she had ever given me, the case of coloured pens, the yellow pencil sharpener in the shape of an ostrich, the beautiful shell, the chambered nautilus her Uncle had brought back from New Guinea, put them in her desk before morning prayers and, after that, cut her dead.

Friendless, I took up with two girls, Eve and Coralie, I had hitherto despised. They were overgrown, ruddy girls, dark-haired and busty as Italian matrons, always bottom of the class, always giggling in corners and looking up *womb* and *whore* in the dictionary. I won their attention by expounding my knowledge of sex which, on the theoretical side, was far superior to theirs. Though they giggled and eyed each other when I used the word penis, I put up with this silliness for the sake of their company. We formed a secret society, the Three Grey Sisters, and met every lunchtime, in the ditch that ran along the end of the playing field. I drew up the rules, writing them out in red ink on three sheets of paper torn from my English exercise book and, good-natured and giggling, Eve and Coralie agreed to keep them.

It was the only initiative I was able to take. They were kind, placid girls, apparently yielding as cushions, but they had a firm core of solid resistance to any external influence. I knew that if I tried to change them in any way they would cease to bother me and my isolation – for Jane, once rebuffed, could not be won back yet – would be shamefully apparent to everyone. I needed them. They did not need me. All I could do, therefore, was to play along and share their interests.

At this time, their chief interest was birth control. The reason for this was not practical – they were not *that* mature

– but fortuitous: on the way to school every morning they passed a newly opened shop that sold contraceptives. There was nothing in the window except a syringe and a display of literature in clinical-looking covers: Coralie said she thought one of the books had diagrams inside. It seemed that for some time they had been daring each other to go into this shop: once, Coralie had dressed up in her older sister's coat and shoes, but had lost her nerve on the threshold. I asked what they wanted to do, buy a book? My question made them explode with laughter and exchange one of those peculiar, meaningful glances that I had come to dread because it set me down as an outsider. Finally, I discovered that neither of them knew what a contraceptive appliance looked like.

'Do you know, Kate?'

I had to admit that I didn't.

'I bet Jane Owen knows,' Eve said, with a look at Coralie.

'Don't mention that bitch to me,' I raged.

'Sorry.' Eve's smile was cheerful, but insincere.

'I thought you knew everything,' Coralie said.

This exchange was as near unkindness as either of them would ever come, and it was an omen. My only use to them was as a source of information: if I failed to supply it, they would grow bored with me.

I said that if they really wanted to know about contraceptives, they should ask their parents.

This produced more laughter of the shocked, sideways-glancing kind, and I saw they thought the suggestion mad or indecent, probably both. Their reaction shook me. They might lack technical knowledge but in matters of opinion both girls seemed to me much more competent and assured than I was. Besides, they were two and I was one. Perhaps they were right in thinking it was disgusting to talk to one's parents about such things: though I couldn't quite persuade myself that it was, I knew, from that moment, that I would find it impossible to ask Ellen or Boyd what we wanted to know.

But I had to suggest something. My mouth went dry. 'I

expect your parents use them,' I faltered. 'I mean, you could look.'

As soon as I had spoken I felt sick with apprehension. This was a terrible idea, much worse than simply asking for enlightenment. They were bound to despise me, cast me out. I hardly dared look at them.

'My Mum and Dad go to the pictures, Thursday,' Eve said thoughtfully.

'There's always my sister,' Coralie said, and laughed.

My pieced-together recollection of Coralie and Eve is of two rather heavy girls, stolid and sly, and yet I have a quite different pictorial memory of Coralie at that moment when she laughed suddenly, a proper laugh, not a snigger: her eyes danced with light and she looked quite astonishingly mischievous and pretty.

'But your sister isn't married,' I said, and there was more laughter of the same happy, delighted kind.

'I don't suppose she goes out with her chap just for the pleasure of his conversation,' Coralie said, wiping her eyes.

And it was from Coralie's sister's drawer that the more interesting item was purloined. Perhaps it was the next day, perhaps a couple of days later, that we foregathered in the ditch; I can only remember that it was bitterly cold and that snow had begun to flurry in the wind. Pinched and shivering, three little girls crouched to examine a limp french letter and Coralie's sister's rubber diaphragm. It seemed an extraordinary object and Boyd's instruction in anatomy had not been extensive enough to suggest how it might be used. I did say that the female parts must be fairly elastic, or babies would never get born, and Eve and Coralie nodded gloomily. 'Oh, I think it's a horrible idea,' Eve said suddenly, and prodded at the thing with a twig. 'And anyway, you don't know how it works, do you, Clever Dick?'

Stung, I picked up the other exhibit and said, well, at least we knew how *this* functioned, didn't we? And then, taking their silence as a desire for instruction, explained that the male member became tunescent.

'I don't like dirty talk,' Eve said, astonishingly. She stumbled to her feet and stood, staring over my head. Her face was very flushed. 'I'm going in, I'm starved cold,' she said, and ran off across the playing field.

'She's crying,' Coralie announced. She got to her feet, miserable herself. 'I better go too.'

I caught the belt of her school coat as she turned away. 'Hey, what about these *things*?'

Coralie twisted her coat out of my grasp but remained beside me, her eyes on the ground.

'You'll have to put them back, won't you?'

She shook her head violently. Like Eve, she had gone berry red.

'Your *sister's*, anyway. I mean . . .' The difference between the two appliances was embarrassingly clear to me. 'I mean, what'll she *say*?'

Coralie swallowed hard. 'She won't say anything. She daren't. I mean, it stands to reason! She'll be scared I'll tell Mum!' Reassured by this comfortable assessment of the situation, she bridled virtuously. 'Our Mum 'ud give her *hell*. . . .'

'But we can't leave them here,' I wailed hopelessly.

Looking at me, she seemed to hesitate. Then, to my horror, she shrugged her shoulders. 'I reckon getting rid of them's *your* worry. It was you asked us to get them for you, wasn't it?'

There followed the most agonized afternoon of my life. The walls of our classroom were cream and butcher blue; the inkwells in our scratched desks veined with cracks and full of sludge. Outside, the snow now fell in earnest; indoors, the lights were on. Added to the usual educational smells of ink and chalk was a whiff of dog-fish from the biology lab. next door. While Miss Price wrote algebraic formulae on the board, my neighbour sniffed and pinched her nose, little finger elegantly crooked. When I took no notice of this performance, she opened her desk and took out a bottle of Woolworth perfume, waving it in front of her like smelling salts. I was stiff with fear that Miss Price would turn round suddenly: I could not afford, this afternoon, to be in the vicinity of anyone likely to attract the attention of authority.

I was in a state of terror bordering on imbecility. I thought of flinging myself on the floor in a mock epileptic fit, running away, putting an end to my life. But I was fixed to my chair with iron bands. When I looked at my desk, my forehead went cold and clammy. Miss Price's eyes were blue and penetrating: they could look through the lid of my desk and see what was hidden in the paper bag which, this morning, had innocently contained two wholemeal biscuits. Any moment she would leap upon me with flashing eyes and cries of scorn.

Unbelieveably, she did not. Nor did Miss Beresford who taught us history, or Miss Lark, the solicitor's sister, who taught us French. Unbelieveably, the afternoon ended. A blonde prefect stalked the corridor, clanging the brass-tongued bell. We rose behind our desks. '*Au revoir*, Mademoiselle Lark,' we chanted and she answered, as always, '*Au rrrrrrrr-evoir*. Use your *tongues*, girls.' Noise broke out as soon as she closed the door, laughter, scraping chairs, banging desk lids. Feverishly, I opened my desk and crammed the paper bag into my satchel. I knew, without looking, that Eve and Coralie were watching me and nudging each other.

I did not wait for Joanna. I stopped one of her class in the corridor. 'Tell her to fetch our sister,' I said. 'Tell her I'm going straight home.'

Our school was on the far side of the railway line from our house. The snow was falling lazily as I crossed the foot-bridge. Usually I enjoyed snow, tasting the flakes on my tongue and thinking about being Scott of the Antarctic or Captain Oates, but not today. In a white, sick dream, I thudded down the steps of the footbridge and walked stiffly along the cinder path between the allotments. The snow was settling: on a waste patch at the end of the path some little ones, Poll's age, were rolling a snowball. It was gritted with dirt and had grown almost too big for their small arms to push. A dog barked round them, kicking up feathery plumes. There was a dip at one side of the patch, filled with scrubby bushes, old cans, rubbish, but there were too many people about to hide anything there. The satchel burned my shoulder blades. I walked on, through the back streets that bordered on the railway line. This was a poor neighbourhood, like a maze: alleys and streets of small, crowded houses with front rooms opening directly on to the street and plaster Alsatian dogs on the window sills. I ran down an alley where there were no houses, only yards and the back of shops and dustbins. A man came out of a yard, pushing a bicycle. He was wearing a long, black coat and a black hat; his blackness, like a hooded crow's, frightened me. I ran off, whistling loudly, towards the safe, yellow lights of the street. Behind me, his bicycle swished softly through the snow, a soft, mothy sound that stopped me whistling and made me run faster. He caught up with me as I came to the end of the alley and swerved past into the street, the black skirts of his long coat flying.

This street was one I didn't know. The lamps and the lights shining out of small shops, made purple and green colours on the snow. I walked slowly because running and being frightened had given me a stitch; my chest hurt with every breath. In the end I had to stop for a minute outside a fruit shop where an old man in green mittens was serving a woman in a brown coat and there were mounds of oranges glowing in the window. They made my mouth water. Before Aunt Hat came, Poll and I had not enjoyed oranges, the peeling was so much trouble and the juice ran into the cuts on our fingers and made them sting, but she had taught us how to eat them with a hole cut in the top, sucking the juice through a lump of sugar. I was looking at the oranges and thinking that Aunt Hat had taught us a lot of small, pleasant things, like putting castor sugar on lettuce and slivers of butter into boiled eggs, when the woman in the brown coat turned to come out of the shop and I saw it was Gus's mother, Mrs Lightwater.

I ran off at once, heart pounding, and came at the end of the street to the small square where the church stood. I went in through the lych-gate. The churchyard was empty and the
122

snow had mounded up over the tombs, so that they looked like people sleeping. I had to take off my gloves to unfasten my satchel and when I buried the brown paper bag in one of the mounds, the snow stung hot on my fingers. They tingled as I pulled on my scratchy school gloves and the tears burned on my cheeks as I ran home.

As soon as I got inside the front door, I burst out crying. I had not intended to, but once I had started and Ellen and Aunt Hat were in the hall, it was impossible to stop.

'What is it? Are you hurt?' Ellen said, over and over again in the cross voice that meant she was frightened, and this made me cry louder because I could think of no answer to make. Then Aunt Hat said, 'Has something scared you, lovie?' and I saw what to say.

'A man followed me,' I gulped, 'he chased me down an alley.'

'Oh, *no*,' Aunt Hat cried. 'Oh, my darling, oh, Ellen . . .' and burst at once into the torrent of self-accusation with which she greeted almost every calamity: it was *her* fault, she should have come to meet us from school, she had thought about it earlier when the snow started and it got so dark but then she had turned lazy – oh, she would never forgive herself. . . .

'*Nothing* is your fault, Hattie,' Ellen said, and, taking me by the shoulders, pushed me gently into the kitchen and shut the door. She went to the sink; there was the clang of plumbing as the tap was turned on and she gave me a cup of water. 'Drink it right down,' she commanded.

It is impossible to continue crying while you are drinking a cup of cold water. When it was empty Ellen took it from me, set it on the table and said, 'Now, Kate. What happened, exactly?'

'A man followed me,' I said. 'He chased me down this alley . . .'

'Yes. And then? Did he . . . speak to you?'

Her manner was sharp with fear, but I did not recognize the fear, only the sharpness. I was afraid she knew I was lying, and trembled: Ellen was not unsympathetic, but she liked her sympathy to have a worthy object and a liar was not that. And, as I longed for sympathy, it was impossible to retract my lie. So I burst out that I had gone down this alley and this man had been there, standing in my way and showing himself. This was something that had happened quite recently to a girl in our school when she was going home through the park: the incident had been the subject of a lecture at morning prayers, a warning so politely worded that none of us younger ones would have known what it was about if the girl herself had not spread the story proudly around. I said that he had tried to stop me but that I had dodged round him and run so fast that even though he got on his bicycle, I was safe in the street before he caught me up. 'He didn't hurt me, I was frightened, that's all.' I began to howl again, from shame.

Ellen patted me awkwardly and dried my eyes. I had the strange feeling that she was terribly embarrassed. I was handed over to Aunt Hat for tea and kindness, and, when he came in, to Boyd. I sat cradled on his lap while he explained that there were some unhappy men who got pleasure out of exposing themselves in public and that, although I must be sensible and keep out of their way and always tell my parents or my teacher about them, I must remember that they were not wicked men, just rather unfortunate and sad. I lay there, listening to his voice, and, my ear being pressed against his shirt front, to the crackle of his breathing, and thought how odd it was that a simple thing like wanting to be friends with two other girls in my class, could have such unpredictable consequences.

Not undesirable consequences, though, since the effect had been to restore me to general favour: ever since tea, when Aunt Hat had let me sit closer to the fire than we were normally allowed to in case we scorched our legs, I had been fussed over and made much of. Even Joanna, awed by my experience, had promised to finish her homework quickly and play backgammon with me, later this evening. I had begun to feel, comfortably, that everything was really working out rather well, when Boyd's voice changed. He prised my chin loose from his chest, made me sit upright on his knee and said he wanted me to tell him exactly where all this had happened and what the man had looked like. Mistaking my horrified stare for distress, he went on, very gently, to say that he didn't want to upset me but that I must be sensible: I wouldn't want other girls to be frightened as I had been, would I? I sat, scratching a whitening spot on my uniform skirt with my fingernail while his kind voice explained that he would have to inform the police and it was almost certain that they would want to talk to me, but that I mustn't worry, because he was sure everyone would be kind and try not to embarrass me.

I felt utterly trapped. I had put this terrible machinery into operation by my own disastrous folly, and there was no stopping it now. Except by admitting the truth. I don't know at what point I realized I could do this. If Ellen had been there, I don't think I could have done: it was not her anger that I feared but her disappointment, that most fearful of adult weapons. But Boyd expected less from us than she did: his kindness was not limited by fears of being 'soft' and so irretrievably ruining our characters. Boyd would not think it necessary for my own good to stop being sorry for me because I had lied: he would be sorry for me because I had needed to lie.

And so it turned out. 'You silly one,' he said gently when I had stumbled through my miserable confession: there had been a man in the alley, but he had done nothing, I had pretended that what had happened to the girl at school had happened to me. He rocked me silently while I cried against his shoulder, feeling empty and wretched because I had judged his attitude correctly; it was depressing to discover how easy it was to tell half-truths and get away with it. It was even easy to answer the inevitable question, 'But *why* darling? Why should you make up this stupid story? And what in heaven's name were you so upset about?'

'Because no one loves me in this house, no one takes any notice of me,' I wailed, and went on to enumerate silly instances of uncaring behaviour, deliberately exaggerating my childishness in order to give weight to this weak excuse and prevent further questioning. My motives were not entirely selfish. My own shame was uppermost, of course, but beneath it was the certainty that if the truth came out, Boyd would be deeply hurt. Not by my precocious curiosity – that my good parent would welcome – but because I had not asked him, or Ellen, what I wanted to know. Both of them took their parenthood very seriously in the modern manner: if we behaved badly, they searched their own consciences far more vigorously than they punished us. Ellen might be more ready to condemn our faults than Boyd, but in important matters they worked together, like two horses in double harness. They would not blame me for being furtive but themselves for having failed to create an atmosphere in which we could come to them with anything that worried us.

It seems to me that we often went to a deal of trouble to allow Ellen and Boyd to keep this, and other, illusions. For example, Joanna had learned very young from the blunt statements of the cowman on the farm how babies were conceived, but she had blandly pretended ignorance so that Ellen could enlighten her. We acknowledged that by loving us and minding so about our upbringing, our parents had put themselves in our power and we tried, honourably, to avoid taking advantage of their weak position. We did not often lie directly: the most we did was to blur and gloss the truth a little in order to accommodate it to their sensitive perspective. Now, because I knew it would distress Boyd to hear that anything he or Ellen had done had made me feel unloved, I laid, cunningly, all my misery at my sister's door. 'Poll doesn't want to play with me, Joanna won't talk to me any more,' I moaned, making it easy for Boyd to comfort me. Joanna was grown-up now, Poll still a baby; I was bound, at the moment, to find I did not quite fit with either of them.

But Boyd was not stupid. 'Now, what *else* is the matter?' he asked, smiling as he took out his handkerchief and held it for me to blow my nose. His kindly-severe look was one I recognized: he had determined to get to the bottom of this matter. 'I don't believe you can have got yourself into such a fuss just because of Joanna and Poll,' he said.

My heart sank. Oh, if it were only possible to tell him the whole truth, from the beginning! For a moment I was furious with Boyd for driving me into this ramshackle edifice of lies, forcing me to pile one rotten piece of timber upon another until the whole shoddy thing fell down. It was cruel, he was putting more upon me than I could manage. Then both self-pity and rage were gone and I felt weary and stale. It was no good. Lying was no good. It was too much trouble. It wasn't, as Aunt Hat said, *what a tangled web we weave*: weaving implied deliberate, directed effort. It was more like pouring water aimlessly and endlessly into a bucket with a hole in the bottom; there was never any end to it, never any finish.

And, all the time, Boyd's gentle, remorseless voice was encouraging me. Was I in trouble? Had something happened at school? Much better to tell him. He couldn't promise to put whatever it was right – he was always honest and careful – but he could promise not to be angry if it was something awful and do his best. . . .

'Jane Owen,' I began, and stopped. Impossible to tell what *she* had done; I would rather be thought sinful than so pathetically sinned-against.

'What has Jane Owen done, darling?'

I was finished. Nothing remained, nothing. I was hopeless and helpless. What could Jane Owen have done that was terrible enough to convince Boyd, to make him put a stop to this torment? What would *he* think terrible enough?

Then, miraculously – it *was* like a miracle because it jumped at me ready-made out of a conversation I had overheard Aunt Hat begin with Ellen several days before – the solution came to me: a solution which I knew Boyd would accept without at all understanding why he would accept it, merely aware, in a flash of perception that had nothing to do with knowledge or reason, that he would. 'Oh, Jane's a beast, she goes on teasing me,' I said. 'She goes on teasing

127

me about my father. She says it's damn silly that none of us knows anything about him.'

An obscure guilt must have crept in, or I would not have said 'damn'. But my conscious emotion was relief. Boyd's troubled face told me that my ordeal was over. His arms were round me, his hand soothingly on the back of my head, my cheek was pressed comfortably against the patch on his shirt that was still damp with my earlier tears.

Chapter Eleven

The conversation was one I had simply recorded and filed away. It had not worried me.

If Aunt Hat was partisan about us; about Ellen and Boyd, she was reverent. We were often told how good Ellen was, how kind, how beautiful she had been when Aunt Hat first knew her, how beautiful she was still although she looked tired sometimes. This was balm to me since I feared outsiders did not appreciate Ellen: she was so often shabby and had a nervous habit, when she met people in the street, of blinking her eyes rapidly and tightening the muscles of her face and neck in a way that made her look much older than she was.

Boyd, because he was a man and Aunt Hat had never expected kindness from men, came in for even higher praise. 'That man is an angel from heaven,' she said to me. 'When I think of all the things he has done for me from first to last!' She gave a deep, contemplative sigh. 'When I think he took the trouble to come all that way, just to visit me in hospital!' This seemed the least of the things Boyd had done and I said, rather grumpily, that it wasn't much that I could see, why shouldn't he visit her? 'It was a lot to your Aunt Hat, dear,' she said reprovingly. 'Oh, I don't suppose you can understand, you're only a kiddie, but he did a lot for me, a doctor's not like just any visitor. Up to the time he came I was just any slum woman who'd been beaten up by her old man. It had been dearie this and dearie that. But when *he* came to see me, that made the nurses sit up, I can tell you. Your Aunt Hat was Mrs Hussey after that, twopence to speak to her!' She chuckled for a minute over the memory of this small triumph and then gave another of those long, contented sighs which punctuated her speech whenever she was summing up a situation. 'Well, Kate love, no one can say Aunt Hat isn't grateful,' she said.

Indeed, no one would wish to. But her constant adulation sometimes wearied Ellen and on this occasion she was weary already: Poll had had one of her nights of bed-wetting and bad dreams, and Ellen and Boyd had taken it in turn to sit up with her. The fact that Boyd shared this parental burden provoked one of Aunt Hat's admiring outbursts while Ellen was getting breakfast, hurriedly and late, and I was cleaning my shoes out of her sight on the kitchen step. Oh, Ellen was lucky, Aunt Hat said, not many men, in her experience, would help their wives with the children the way Boyd did.

Ellen answered, mildly, that nowadays fathers did more than they used, and Aunt Hat said in her considering voice, 'But you're extra lucky, dear. Under the circumstances. I've known many stepfathers mean well to begin with but lose interest. Not Boyd, though. Oh, he's a man in a million, I can tell you!'

Aunt Hat's praise might please us, but it embarrassed Ellen and I could see why. Aunt Hat was one of those people who are not false, but sound so. Her expressions often had a tinny, platitudinous ring, but this was only because she was so completely unselfconscious that she simply used whatever words lay nearest to hand. 'Like his own they are to him, like his own dear flesh and blood,' she said, and, though I could imagine the tearful sigh and the little curl-bobbing shake of the head that would accompany these words and made her seem like a third-rate actress, I also knew that she meant them quite honestly and simply. Ellen knew it too, I'm sure, but she was tired, in a scratchy mood, and heard only the falsity, the oily over-praise.

She said something, I couldn't hear what it was, but her voice was sharp, and for once Aunt Hat answered her sharply, 'There's no call to take me up for saying what's true. I daresay gratitude's old-fashioned nowadays, but you can take my word for it there's a lot of poor women who'd go down on their bended knees for a slice of your good luck. You're edgy, Ellen. Oh, I know you had a bad time with your first husband, it was really an unfortunate experience, but there's no reason why you should be edgy now. It quite shocks me, sometimes, the off-hand way you treat Boyd. You should study him more. He's been good to you and your girls. I can't see the harm in admitting it, I really can't.'

Like most mild people when they force themselves to speak out, she had said too much: she must have realized this at once because her voice faltered. 'Oh, Ellen dear, you know I didn't mean to upset you. You know I don't mean half I say.'

Ellen said grimly, 'You haven't upset me. But gratitude's a – a *humiliating* thing in a marriage. And I don't think you should refer to the children's father as an unfortunate experience.'

She was making a verbal point, as people did in anger. I knew it would be a bad thing for me to be caught listening, so I went into the outside lavatory and pulled the chain before I came back into the kitchen.

I had never thought much about my father. Joanna said I wasn't of an age to, yet; she had never bothered thinking about him until she was thirteen or so. And, of course, if I had wanted to think about him I had nothing to go on; I had absolutely no memory of him, no more memory than Poll who had never seen him and whom he had never seen, because when I was born it was war time and Ellen was living in the country while he went travelling with his ENSA company. Joanna said she thought he had come once or twice to the cottage in the beginning, but I had been too small to remember, only a baby. My father had not gone out of my life, he had, quite simply, never existed in it. I never even missed the idea of him, since, as most fathers were away from home at that time, his absence was not remarkable, nor remarked upon. As far as I was concerned, then, Boyd had not taken his place because there was no place to take. The role Boyd played was entirely his own, more so, perhaps because we never called him Daddy: when Poll was small, she used to amuse a certain type of grown-up by pitying children who had only a father. Where, she would ask them, was their Boyd? What Joanna remembered and felt – or what she pretended to remember and feel – was completely outside my experience.

So, saying what I did to Boyd, was really the worst lie I told that day, worst because cruellest, though to do myself justice it was not meant to be cruel: I was young enough, still, to think of him as someone who could not be hurt. And then, having told this lie I had to go on, driven by the kind of fearful compulsion that makes you put your finger in a candle flame: it was as if there was something I wanted to know though I did not know what and would hate it when I did. I said, backing away, as I would have backed away from that lit candle, 'I mean, I don't even know what he looked like' – another lie, because even a twelve-year old, looking at Poll, could have had a good guess at that – 'it's just silly. I mean what would you feel like?'

Boyd made a little, rasping sound, like an old man with a tickle in his throat. 'What do you want to know?'

'Oh, what there *is* to know. Jane says,' – I was quoting Joanna – 'that most mothers would have pictures of him to show their children or they'd talk about him sometimes.'

Boyd hesitated. Then he said regretfully – and this was a thing he would regret, but, if as well as protecting us he wanted to protect Ellen, what else could he do? – I shouldn't ask Ellen. It might make her unhappy talking about him. You wouldn't want that, would you?'

My mind flew to a different interpretation from the one he intended, the one that had been clear in Aunt Hat's speech though I had not consciously understood it at the time nor thought about it after, except in the blank, idle way you reflect on something about which you can come to no conclusion. Like, how can you *know* the refrigerator light goes off when you shut the door, or, if you woke up at the right moment, could you catch yourself dreaming?

'Was he . . . bad to Ellen?' I asked.

Boyd made that throaty sound again and I wondered if he were getting a cold, but he looked all right. I said, clarifying my question, 'I mean, did he knock her about like Aunt Hat's Jack?'

Boyd said quickly, 'Oh, no, of course not,' sounding relieved, which was natural: it would have been awful to think of Ellen being knocked unconscious.

Well, that was all right. I felt we were coming to the end of this conversation and turned to something more interesting. 'Poll's friend Walter – *his* father knocks his mother about. Poll said poor Mrs Tanner's face was all stuck up with Elastoplast and Walter said he hit her with a chisel. He knocks Walter about, too.'

'Er – h'rm,' Boyd said and looked at me in an abstracted way which didn't mean – as it would have meant if I had been talking to Ellen – that he had not been listening to me, but that what I had said was a side-issue and there were more important things to talk about now. Or so he thought. Boyd had fewer failings than most grown-ups but he did have that particularly boring one of worrying a subject to death which puts most children off asking questions at all: you want to know something simple, such as why did Mrs White have three sets of twins, and you get trapped by a tedious monologue about genes and ovaries which goes on long after you have lost interest and want to know something else, like how long could you train yourself to breathe under water? So Boyd went on, talking about my father and saying he understood he had been very handsome and charming and that we must be very proud of him because he had been a very promising young actor, and, as he talked, I had to clench my teeth to stop myself yawning. Then he hesitated a minute before saying that he supposed, if I really wanted to know what he looked like, I could ask Aunt Hat who had met him once or twice. 'But keep it under *your* hat,' he said, grinning suddenly at this silly joke that was more likely to amuse Poll than me. He tipped me off his lap and I collapsed on the rug, groaning, because my legs had had gone to sleep. He got down and rubbed them to bring the blood back and then looked at me with a mock-fierce expression. 'If you don't, you might find me handy with a chisel, like Walter's father,' he said.

I suffered no punishment for that wicked day. What Boyd said to Ellen, I never knew; perhaps, like us, he modified the truth a little to suit her vision of things. Whatever it was, she was nice to me. She came up after I had gone to bed and brought me a dusty little velvet bag, drawn up at the neck with a silk cord, that she had found in her work basket. She said that her mother had given it to her when she was a little girl to keep her thimble and darning materials in, but that she thought I might like to have it for marbles. I had given up marbles sometime before but the present encouraged me to dig them out from the abandoned rubble at the bottom of the toy cupboard. I had eleven marbles of different sizes: one was chipped. I can't remember what they looked like, only how they felt through the cat-like softness of the velvet bag; I knew each one with my finger-tips, as I knew the kitchen chair by the scratch of the broken cane under my bare thighs and my grazed knees by the tacky pull of the hole in the horrible black stockings we wore in winter. Those marbles, as far as I can remember, were the last things I knew intimately by feel: perhaps it is a sense only blind people keep, once childhood has gone.

The velvet bag drew me back for a spell to infancy. I gave up Eve and Coralie and their pre-occupations, and began polishing up my collection of last autumn's chestnuts with Kiwi boot polish. Or perhaps it was nothing to do with the velvet bag at all, but a half-conscious retreat from knowledge I was not ready for. What went on, what had gone on, I would have to know some time but I didn't want to know now: I was back-pedalling, retracting what I already knew and, at the same time, affecting an innocence I no longer possessed in order to learn more.

Because, although it was Joanna who asked Aunt Hat, it was me who prodded her into it by saying, casually, that if she wanted to know what our father had looked like – innocently pretending that I thought it was all she wanted to know – she could ask Aunt Hat, who had seen him. Whether Joanna raised the matter with Aunt Hat before or after she took on the job of looking after Miss Fantom, I can't remember; perhaps I never knew. (*That* was simply something that happened off-stage, behind my back: by the time I heard of it, the arrangement was settled and approved from every angle. It would be such a help to Miss Fantom, poor soul, it would give Aunt Hat something to do, and, also, get her out of Ellen's hair, I suppose, though this was naturally never mentioned: on the contrary, much was made of the fact that Aunt Hat would still spend a lot of time with us because a local woman, a retired nurse, was to look after the old lady during the day and Aunt Hat's duties were only to begin in the late afternoon. She would give Miss Fantom her last meal, spend the evening with her, and sleep the night at Lock View.)

When Joanna spoke to Aunt Hat, then, I don't know, nor how she phrased her first question: I only know that I was there too, in the kitchen where we were all washing up together, and that Aunt Hat was evasive at first. 'Oh, I can't tell you anything, dear, I only saw him once,' she murmured and bent her head over the sink. The back of her neck was flushed. Joanna coaxed her a little – not much, because Aunt Hat never needed much coaxing to talk – and in the end she sighed, straightened her back, wiped her hands on her apron and said, in a low voice, with one eye on the door,

'Well, he was a fine-looking man, dear.' She screwed up her eyes like a child might do to remember. 'Tall, not *too* tall, you know, and slim. What I would call a graceful man. He had a very fine complexion, like a girl, though he wasn't girlish. Dark hair and blue eyes . . . lovely blue eyes. . . .'

I thought, confusedly, of Aunt Hat's love, who had fallen dead at her door.

Joanna said impatiently, 'But what was he *like*?' and Aunt Hat looked flustered.

'Oh, I don't know, I'm sure, who can tell what a person's like?' she said, and then, reproachfully, 'I shouldn't really talk to you, you shouldn't ask me.'

'Who can I ask, then?' Joanna's face was suddenly convulsed with bitterness. 'Ellen never says a thing. I've a right to know. Wouldn't you say a person had the right to know about their own father?'

She was half-shouting and Aunt Hat looked nervously at the door. 'Ssh, dear. Little pitchers have big ears. . . .'

'Poll won't hear. Aunt Hat, what was he *like*?' Joanna asked again, in a voice that suddenly made me wish I wasn't there but safe playing Ludo by the fire with Poll, or, even, not playing anything but just sitting, knowing that Poll was there doing whatever she was doing, comfortably and dependably unaware of anything outside the fixed circle of her own existence; unaware that the lives that touched hers had other lives radiating from their fixed centre, and that those lives had other lives, circle upon circle, moving away into distance . . .

Aunt Hat's pretty hands smoothed the front of her apron in a helpless gesture. 'Well . . . of course, any woman needs a home for her children. And acting's not a steady profession, he couldn't be expected to send her money regular, but he never sent it when he had it, apparently, which wasn't right. Though who am I to judge? Your mother wasn't happy with him, he wasn't good to her, but who's to say he was altogether at fault in the beginning? Mind you, I believe your mother, she's a good woman, not the sort to run away for nothing, but things must have been hard for him too, though I didn't see that till the end. Oh . . . I blamed myself then, but at the time I just wanted to help put things right for her, it seemed so sad that a young woman should have to struggle on alone, but of course that was wrong. . . . I should have held my tongue and said nothing. She'd left him and that was that . . . her business . . . I should have left well alone instead of rushing in where angels fear to tread. The trouble was, when he came down to see her, I couldn't help thinking what a lovely looking couple they made and he had such a nice way with him . . . before he went away he came to see me and said, 'Hattie, be a brick and drop me a word from time to time, I'd like to know how she gets on – and my babies.' He looked so sad as he went away, looking up at the window to see if she was looking out, but she wasn't. . . .'

It was so sad, the tears prickled my eyes.

'What d'you mean, *she'd left him*?' Joanna said. 'If you only saw my father at the cottage – that was long before Poll was born.'

'Yes . . . yes, that's true'. Aunt Hat's eyes roamed miserably from Joanna to me. 'I persuaded her to go back to him . . . oh, it was all my fault.' She shook her head slowly and her hands fluttered up and down her apron. When she spoke again, her voice had changed. 'We ought to get on and wash the dishes. What'll Ellen say if she comes back and finds all this how-de-you-do?'

Joanna said, 'I despise, I utterly and completely look down upon the sort of person who starts telling you a thing and then leaves off in the middle.'

She was much taller than Aunt Hat who stood before her looking small and hunted. She was much stronger, too. Ellen was strong in the same way: when either of them wanted something badly, they were people to be afraid of.

'Well, it isn't suitable,' Aunt Hat said helplessly. 'Talking to you . . .'

'Life isn't suitable,' Joanna said. 'But we have to live it. Ellen had left my father and you persuaded her to go back to him and then she got pregnant, is that it?'

'I thought I was doing right at the time,' Aunt Hat said. 'Oh – it was a terrible mistake. . . .'

My heart thumped. *A mistake that comes from the heart is still a mistake.* . . . That's what Ellen had said.

'A terrible mistake,' Aunt Hat repeated. 'But I wasn't to know, was I?'

She was pleading with us. I said, to comfort her, 'I don't see it was such a bad mistake. I mean, if she hadn't gone back to live with my father, she wouldn't have got Poll, would she?'

They both looked at me as I made this sensible statement, but their eyes were unseeing as glass.

Joanna said, 'So Ellen left him just because she wanted security? A nice home and a nice husband, coming home regularly every night and bringing his pay packet on Friday?'

Her voice was contemptuous, but it seemed to me there was nothing very wrong in wanting this.

'You make her sound . . . oh, dear, she's not like that, not *that* terrible sort of woman. For the right man, your mother would have worked her fingers to the bone. . . .'

'Why did she leave him, then?' Joanna asked, more gently, but desperately.

'Dear, I can't . . .' Aunt Hat wrung her hands, literally: they hung limp from her wrists like dishcloths and she twisted her fingers as if trying to squeeze out water.

'I expect I can think much worse things than you are likely to tell me,' Joanna said.

'She . . . she didn't love him as . . . as a *husband*,' Aunt Hat stammered, and, for no reason that I could see, Joanna blushed scarlet. Aunt Hat blushed too; they both looked as if they had been sitting in front of a hot fire. 'But I wasn't to know, was I?' she cried. 'If I had, I'd never have said a word . . . that must be a terrible thing in a marriage, worse than poverty and neglect and hard words, and not his fault, nor hers, either. . . . But she didn't tell me, she was too shy, I suppose, and ashamed to speak of such things . . . *that* was the terrible way she'd been brought up, the poor, poor girl, she thought it was right to suffer. . . . So she didn't tell me, she just sat quiet while I said foolish things, though I didn't think they were foolish at the time, I just wanted things to be nice for her. I said they were both so young, she ought to give their marriage another chance. I don't know why she listened to me . . . the only thing I can think is that she has that sort of terrible conscience that makes her feel she's doing wrong, even when she's doing right. Oh . . . she has such a conscience, your poor mother . . . she wanted to leave him, you see, and because it was what she wanted, she was afraid it must be wilful and wrong. . . .' Aunt Hat's voice quavered. 'Oh, my dears, if I'd known the truth, I'd not have said one word to send her back to him, but as God's my witness, I didn't know till afterwards, when she came home. *That* was terrible. She stood at one side of the room and I stood at the other and she threw words at me like knives. Just like knives. I felt I was being pinned against the wall. *Well I did what you told me*, she said, *and I hope you're pleased. It's finished at last – he's had enough this time and I'm left with this baby. And I can't stay here in case he changes his mind and comes after me . . . it would kill me if he touched me again, you've ruined my life, all our lives, Hattie.* . . . I can't tell you how I felt. The look on her poor face – I shall remember it to my dying day! Oh, you can't know how dreadful I felt when she looked at me like that, I loved her so,' Aunt Hat said, so softly and piteously that I was sorry for her, though I could see, even in my bemused state, that she was more absorbed in the pain she had suffered than in my mother's pain. 'I shall never forgive myself, never,' she went on. 'Though your mother forgave me . . . oh, she is *good*, Joanna . . . when I came to see you in that horrible flat she never said a word of reproach to me, not one, but I looked round and I said to myself, Hattie, this is all your doing, and I tried to give her a bit of money . . . I'd have given her the clothes off my back if she'd have taken them . . . but she wouldn't take a penny, not a penny . . .' Aunt Hat groaned and sank suddenly on to a chair, tears starting in her eyes.

Joanna said in a bewildered voice, 'Do you mean my

father just went off and left her, left all of us. Do you mean to say he never knew about *Poll*?'

Aunt Hat mopped her eyes. 'No, he never knew he had another dear little girl, Aunt Hat's often thought of that,' she said, with the satisfied sigh with which she always contemplated the beautiful, enriching sadness of life, and, hearing that sigh I knew – though I could not have put it into words then – that she had retreated on to that plane, not so much of fantasy as of fictionalised truth, from which she found it comfortable to survey the world. It was not sad that my father had not known Poll was born, how could it be sad, since he never knew? The sadness was only a pleasant feeling in Aunt Hat's mind.

It seemed to me very strange that Joanna, who was so sensible, did not understand this, and, indeed, seemed more upset by it than by anything that had gone before. She said in a choked voice, 'Oh, it's awful, I can't bear to think of him not knowing, not just about Poll but about all of us, wondering how we are and what we're doing, do you suppose he . . .'

'Hush. Don't cry, my love, my precious,' Aunt Hat said, crying herself as she stood up to comfort Joanna who bent over her, weeping, and swaying like a young tree.

I heard the front door open, and Ellen's voice. Aunt Hat said quickly, 'Dry your eyes, my darling, don't let poor Mummy see you like this,' and went out – she was never at a loss in this sort of situation – to intercept Ellen in the hall.

Joanna struggled with her tears, hooting into her handkerchief. I said, to help her compose herself, 'Well, it's all over now, isn't it?' words that grown-ups often used stupidly, to comfort us, but which, in this case, seemed reasonable enough.

Though in the past few seconds I had realized that my father was not dead as I had believed – not because anyone had told me so but because death had always seemed the natural explanation of his absence – the discovery was interesting, not traumatic. Alive or dead made no difference: he had no place in my life, nor, I thought impatiently, in

139

Joanna's. It was plain silly, I thought, with a kind of rage that had something to do with tiredness and something to do with fear, plain silly to cry over what her father might feel when she didn't know what he felt and never could know. As plain silly as crying over some sadness in a book. My mind began to ache suddenly, the way the body aches with two much exercise.

'Oh, do give *over*,' I cried frantically. 'For Pete's sake, there's been enough old talk and nonsense around here.'

'Leave me alone,' she said.

Chapter Twelve

One of the advantages of Boyd and Ellen as modern parents was that when we behaved badly, treats often came our way. I don't remember when I first became aware of this relation of cause and effect but I think I knew, when Boyd took me on his rounds that spring, that this special favour was directly traceable to my orgy of lying.

Going on the rounds with Boyd was a great treat, better than the cinema or the Zoo. We especially liked visiting the old people, Boyd's chronic cases, partly because they seemed to enjoy it as much as we did, and partly because there were so many interesting eccentrics among them: Boyd said this was because people often got spicier as they got older. There was one very spicey old gentleman I remember: the only part of his conversation I really understood was the phrase, 'If the young lady will pardon me,' which always heralded a flood of interesting obscenities. One elderly lady kept rabbits hopping loose indoors; another, alligators. They were liable to crawl into the sitting room while you were sipping your rhubarb wine, and lay their cold jaws on your foot.

There were two kinds of people in Monks Ford; the commuters on the new housing estates and the locals who lived there so long that they all looked a little alike. There was frequently a resemblance to be observed between families as wide apart as the Hedges on the caravan site and the Carlings in East Street. Anyone who was kipper-footed – who walked with their toes ten-to-two – was bound to be related in some degree to Edgar Carling who owned a chain of steam bakeries and was reputed to be a millionaire, though seeing him, in worn carpet slippers and a striped, collarless shirt, it was hard to believe it. Edgar was eighty-nine; he kept an iron hand on the control of his bakeries as he did on the lives of the unmarried three of his six sons who still lived with him above his shop in East Street and for whom he prepared, rumour said, senna tea every Sunday morning of their lives: Edgar believed that his own remarkable good health was due to a regular weekly turn-out. The boys, as he called them, were forty-five, forty-nine, and fifty-eight, and were allowed out to visit the Golden Harp for two hours every night from eight to ten o'clock. The spectacle of Edgar, standing at the door of his shop at five minutes to ten, fob watch in hand, was so common that it was only remarked upon by newcomers, the middle-class commuting population who told their friends that Monks Ford was not a suburb but a real old town with a great many quaint characters, treating Edgar as a tourist attraction like the lady in Railway Cottages who had embraced Islam in her later years and turned to Mecca from her garden, in full view of the newly electrified line.

Apart from the Fantoms and the Carlings, the older inhabitants were poorer than the new arrivals. Monks Ford was not attractive enough to have kept its richer sons who had moved away, before and after the war, either to 'real' country or back into London. The ones who were left stayed out of poverty or inertia – the one bred the other, Boyd said – and lived, either above their shops, in down-at-heel, condemned cottages, or on the caravan site.

Having been poor ourselves, we did not fall into the trap

141

of thinking poverty fun, but it was impossible not to feel, sometimes, that the children on the caravan site led more congenial lives than we did, and certainly more congenial lives than the children in the bungalow developments who, though they rode their gleaming bicycles up and down the pavements, were not allowed out of sight of the picture windows. They were not allowed to play near the river like the caravan children, nor to roam the streets after dark, nor to steal lumber from the derelict houses near the dental factory. We were allowed less freedom than the one group and more than the other: we had to earn the right to play by the river by swimming two lengths of the local baths, and, though the condemned houses were officially out of bounds, when Poll came home filthy, with splinters in her hands and ripped clothes, her appearance was not often commented on. Once when Ellen did protest, Boyd said there were several kinds of poverty, and not being allowed to get dirty or tear your clothes occasionally, was one kind there was no need for us to have to endure.

But though there had been times when I envied the caravan children, Walter Tanner's family could arouse envy in no one. They lived at the 'dirty' end of the site, at the bottom of the sloping field: in wet weather they were mud-bound. Some of the caravans were comfortable and had electricity laid on but theirs was not even an old, run-down caravan, but a rusty, single-decker bus. Poll thought it marvellous but I was old enough to see that it was really a wretched place; some of the windows were broken and the children's bunks, lining one side, were covered with an indescribable collection of filthy, grey, army blankets, old clothes, ripped gum boots, cornflake packets, sticky sweets, half-eaten biscuits. I never knew exactly how many children there were. The time I went there with Boyd there were four, excluding Walter who was spending the Saturday with Poll: three little ones and a girl my own age in a woman's cut-down dress and gum boots. She had straight hair scraped back from a high, mild forehead with a jewelled plastic band, a runny nose and red eyes. Mrs Tanner had a thin, kind, fretful face: as soon as she saw me she reached for a tin with pink roses on the lid and gave me a chocolate biscuit. This was her instinctive reaction as soon as she saw any child: the faces of her own three babies were caked with dried chocolate mixed with dirt and the slime from their noses.

Boyd went inside the bus and I stayed with Walter's sister who had been told to mind the little ones. For the most part she just sat on the step and watched them apathetically, but now and again she would suddenly rush forward and slap or shake one of them, an operation they endured philosophically, barely bothering to cry: irrational violence must have been a natural hazard of their lives. I picked up the smallest child who seemed in imminent danger of cutting his mouth to pieces on a jagged tin but this attention did make him cry, and, as he smelt horrible, I was glad to put him down again.

To make conversation, I said to Walter's sister that I hoped her mother wasn't very ill.

'She's bin in 'orspital,' she said. 'She fell for a baby but she went into 'orspital and the doctor took it out of her.'

'Was it a boy or a girl?' I asked, thinking she meant her mother had had a Caesarian, and wondering where the new baby was, but she stared at me blankly, and giggled. 'You don' know much, do you?' she said contemptuously and then darted at one of the babies who was laboriously piling one flat stone on top of another, up-ended him, banged him smartly on his sopping bottom and set him down again. He let out a half-hearted wail and went back to his stones.

Back in the car, I asked Boyd what had happened to the baby and he said there wasn't one: Mrs Tanner had had an abortion.

'Was she too sick to have the baby?'

'Not exactly,' Boyd said, 'but she'd got enough to cope with, don't you think?'

'I don't know.' I felt, suddenly, rather queer.

Boyd sighed and went on to explain that Walter's mother was very poor and would now be poorer because Walter's father had gone away, no one knew where. She would get National Assistance but it was barely enough and, though she had been able to earn a little extra, cleaning for Miss Fantom, that was all she could manage to do because of the babies she already had. 'Poor woman, she has enough to bear,' Boyd said.

I saw this was true, but it seemed to me terrible. It was as if the baby had been waiting somewhere – outside a gate, or a door – and Walter's mother had said, 'No, you can't come in, I've got enough babies, I've got enough to worry me,' and it had to stay outside, in the dark and the cold. Suppose anyone's mother could say that, suppose Ellen had said it, about Poll? Suppose she had said, 'I've got enough to cope with now my husand has gone away. Joanna and Kate are enough for me.' My stomach began churning and I burst out passionately that it was a dreadful thing to do, a terrible thing, how could anyone know what the poor baby felt about it?

Boyd heard me out patiently and then said that a great many people felt as I did, felt it so strongly that there was a law forbidding abortion except for certain medical reasons, but that he did not think it a good law. A great many people, he said, good people who would not willingly hurt anyone, would feel that Mrs Tanner should have been made to have her baby, because it would not actually kill her to have it, but they wouldn't really think about what it would mean to her, or to the baby, or to her other children. I said it was awful, like murder, and Boyd said no, I could take his word for *that*, though it was a natural, emotional reaction to think so. But I must teach myself to think as well as feel. Of course in one way it was wrong to prevent a child being born, but in another – and *he* thought in this particular case – it was right.

'But it can't be both,' I said, suddenly feeling stiffly hostile. 'A thing's got to be either right or wrong.'

'Only in arithmetic,' Boyd said, and went on to say that this was the trouble with most people, they wanted a straight, comfortable answer to all their questions, yes or no, and this was the reason why they thought as little as possible and

144

took the first answer that came, because thinking made them uncomfortable: the more you thought, the more you realized there was no right, true answer to anything. All you could ever do was to think round each individual question and through it, and try to get an answer as near right as you could make it.

'Truth often sits on the fence,' he said. 'The trouble is that we have to get down on one side or the other.' Then he looked at me sideways. 'If you get stuck, talk to some sensible person, but don't rely on their answers altogether.'

But I was thinking about Poll and, as I couldn't talk to him about that I sat quiet, feeling hurt and unanswered and puzzling over all the things that were beginning to worry me that year: why I was who I was and why Poll was who she was and why other people, all the other people in the turning world, were who *they* were, questions that were sometimes comfortable and idle, to be pondered lazily on long, flowering afternoons, and sometimes painfully alarming so that I had to squeeze my eyelids shut or sing under my breath to take my mind off them.

We visited Miss Fantom. My heart thumped as we climbed the back stair but she was not sinister or frightening, just a slender, silvery woman sitting in a high-backed chair, wearing a straight, long wrap of pale, green silk and smiling as she held out her hand to me. It was cool and light. She wore a gold signet ring on one finger, a man's ring that made her hand look tiny. 'You must be the pretty one,' she said.

'Oh, no, I'm Kate,' I said, looking at her in surprise because she was not what I had imagined. She had high, arched brows above eyes that were startlingly dark in the pallor of her delicate face, and soft hair looped down the sides of her cheeks before being caught back in a bun: a pre-Raphaelite style that would have looked strange if she had been wearing ordinary clothes. It was impossible to envisage her riding a bicycle.

She laughed gently. 'She should make a good marriage, Arthur,' she said.

This astounding remark was the only notice she took of me, except to tell Boyd to give me a book of Steinberg drawings to look at, and to motion me to a chair.

I was glad to be told where to sit because the room was so crowded with tiny tables each bearing its load of alabaster figures, silver shoes, jade, china ornaments, that it made me nervous. I was not clumsy, but in this kind of room I sprouted extra hands and feet. I sat still on a low chair and turned the pages while she and Boyd talked.

Since their talk was not about people, it did not interest me. I can only remember the sound of her voice which was cool and imperiously incisive – it might have made me pity Mr Claud Fantom if I had thought about it – and that while she talked I had the feeling that she was slowly unwinding something rather delicate, like a ball of silken string. She made Boyd laugh and after a while he joined in, talking, and their voices were like two bells, one deep and resonant, one high and clear and sweet, sounding on while the spring sun slanted low through the barred window and shone directly into my eyes, so that when I looked up I couldn't see Boyd or Miss Fantom, only two dark shapes edged with light.

'Thank you for coming, Arthur,' Miss Fantom said when he got up to go. 'You do me so much good.'

I had never heard him called Arthur before, and it seemed to turn him into someone quite different.

'You do me good,' he said. He lifted his arms wide and stretched and yawned lazily, like a boy.

'You work too hard, Arthur,' Miss Fantom said. 'Do you enjoy it? Measles and old women. Oh, I know you don't complain, but I could have wished for something different for you. Is it wrong of me to say that? You had so much energy, so many ideas.'

' A long time ago,' Boyd said affectionately. 'You narrow down as you get older.'

Her voice sharpened. 'You're not old, Arthur. Don't sound resigned, I don't like to hear it. You used to expect so much from life.'

Boyd laughed in a surprised, slightly awkward way.

She went on, 'Do you remember? We had tea under the cedar tree. I used to get the maid to make raspberry splits, that was what you liked best. We used to talk – my, how we talked! People used to think it odd, but I thought *they* were odd. As if people of different ages could have nothing to say to each other! Claud used to call you my protégée. He was always a fool. I was much more selfish than that. Oh – I enjoyed those afternoons so much! The things you were going to do, the plans you made!'

Boyd was watching her with an indeterminate expression. 'What was he going to do?' I asked, eager to hear about Boyd as a boy.

She gave a start of surprise as if she had forgotten I was there, only the start was a little too deliberate, had a stagey-ness about it that puzzled me. She turned to me with an eager, wide-eyed look. 'So many things, Kate. Some were just boyish and bragging' – her voice had a scolding edge mixed with pleasure – 'and some were real, or could have been. Certainly I always thought Arthur would do something exceptional. He was a very exceptional boy, even my father thought so. "There's a lot of potential in Arthur," he used to say. That made me very proud. You see, Kate, women of my generation had so little chance to do things themselves and, though I wasn't old, I was old enough to be on the shelf, as we said then, so I treasured Arthur. I treasured him because I hoped he would do all the things my son might have done. And he could have, you know. I wasn't sure what he would do, but I was sure it would be something out of the ordinary. I never thought – well – when he decided just to settle down quietly in Monks Ford, it was quite the last thing I expected.' She gave an artificial sigh. 'Though I suppose, given a ready-made family, there was nothing else the poor man could do, was there?'

Her manner was vivacious, but the undertone of reproof sounded clear. Suddenly I understood that she wanted me to know of her vexation at Boyd's marriage, though this was something she would not wish – dare to let? – Boyd know. That she had managed this I saw – Boyd's expression was one of affection mingled with a mild embarrassment – and I realized something for the first time: that a woman can convey to another woman however young, age being of no account in this, only sex, how she really thinks and feels without any man present being aware of it. It is not that women are more sensitive than men, sensitivity hardly enters into it, only this extra sense which is as peculiar to women as a bat's hearing to a bat.

So Boyd heard nothing except the privileged scolding of an old woman who was fond of him, but I caught the cold, sharp edge of her anger and knew that she blamed us, Ellen, my sisters and I, for having dragged Boyd down, and that she intended me to know it. Exactly what damage we were supposed to have done Boyd, I couldn't have said, but I felt that her anger was in some way related to Ellen's disappointment when we came near bottom of the class instead of top.

'Oh, I'm not an ambitious man,' Boyd said, smiling, and I was suddenly irritated by his stupidity because it was not his ambition that mattered but hers, as it was not ours but Ellen's. That was the limit of my understanding, further I couldn't go, wasn't old enough to. Children are well acquainted with most sins but only in their simplest forms and as they can be related to their own experience: that an old woman could be jealous was as far beyond my comprehension as an old man's lust. Though I knew there was something here that stopped me cold, I couldn't put a name to it.

'Not ambitious, Arthur?' Miss Fantom said. 'Oh, my dear – don't you remember all those letters you wrote me? Marvellous letters. You could have been a writer, I always thought.' She made an impatient gesture with her little hand. 'Though why do I run on? What value is an old woman's opinion, after all?'

'I always valued it,' Boyd said.

'You did once.'

'I still do,' he assured her. Then, clearing his throat, he asked how Aunt Hat was managing.

Miss Fantom said they got on famously. Aunt Hat was such a nice soul, she even got on with Claud. 'And that is

148

something I would never have thought possible! It seems that Mrs Hussey has a number of unexpected opinions. Apparently, like Claud, she disapproves of the Monarchy. Has she told you how she was nearly run down by the royal carriage, near Sandringham?'

'Several times,' Boyd said, and grinned in a way I didn't like.

'That's a good story, Aunt Hat always tells good stories. It's mean to laugh at her, it's *foul*.' I stopped, my ears ringing with my own loud voice. Boyd frowned at me, both cross and surprised, because it was usually Poll or Joanna who burst out rudely in company, not me, but Miss Fantom said, 'She's a good, loyal child, Arthur,' and smiled at me with a surface pleasantness that didn't take me in for a moment.

It took Boyd in, though. He looked fatuously pleased by what he took to be her approval of me. I could not understand how he could be so blind.

I said, as we walked home, 'She doesn't like us.' It was a statement meant as a question.

But he didn't enlighten me. He only said, 'Of course she liked you. She wasn't being unkind about Aunt Hat, you know, only making a joke, and you were really rather rude, but I think she understood.'

'I didn't mean she didn't like me. Not just me. Us. Ellen and . . . oh, all of us. I mean,' I went on, making allowance for his masculine obtuseness, 'she's never wanted to meet any of us, all the time we've been living here. Don't you think that's funny?'

'Not in the least. Miss Fantom's not gone out, or met anyone, for years. So don't talk nonsense, Kate. Please.'

He spoke with an unfair brusqueness that concealed, I think, a certain guilt. He knew – must have known – what I did not learn until later, that although Miss Fantom had not, since her father's death, been a very sociable woman – the croquet parties had been in *his* day – it was not until Boyd married and came to Monks Ford that she had become a complete recluse.

Ellen must have known this too, but if she was hurt she never showed it. Or almost never. I remember that one day Aunt Hat had made an arch, joking remark about the amount of time Boyd spent with Miss Fantom, and Ellen answered her with rather too much vehemence.

'Don't be daft, Hat, how could I be jealous of a sick woman? It's right he should be good to her, look how good she was to *him*? All those terrible years he spent with his uncle! If it hadn't been for her, he would have been desperately lonely. And it wasn't just time she gave him, though perhaps in a way that was more important than anything else, but she paid for his medical training too. His uncle refused to do a thing for him, once he'd left school, he was a stingy brute. Oh – she helped him in every way, gave him books, helped him to think, he says a boy couldn't have had a better friend. After all, Hat, how many young women – and she *was* young then – would give up so much time to a boy?'

'It's been known.' Aunt Hat's expression was rather more reserved than usual. 'Mind you, I've nothing against her really, speak as you find, *I* say, and she's been pleasant enough to me, though her poor brother tells a different story. But I'd have thought with her it had always been Number One first and foremost. Clever she may be, unselfish, no! A nice woman wouldn't take up a man's time the way she does, when she knows he's got a wife and family. I'm surprised *he* doesn't see it.'

'Oh, everyone has their blind spot,' Ellen said.

I could not accept it so lightly. It seemed to me that it was monstrously unfair of Boyd to spend so much time with – and apparently enjoy the company of – someone who disliked us. Nor could I forgive Boyd for being unaware of that dislike, for having, as Ellen said, a blind spot. For the first time in my life, I saw him as something less than perfect and, as a result, began to be critical of everything he said and did, or had said or done.

I told Aunt Hat about Mrs Tanner's abortion. This had honestly upset and troubled me but I was also, in a sense, using it as a vehicle to express my resentment against Boyd.

Aunt Hat's reaction was disappointing. She was not indignant about the baby; she merely said it was a lucky thing for Walter's mother that she had had Boyd to turn to. 'There's not many like him, who'd help a poor woman in her trouble, I can tell you.'

'But it's illegal,' I cried impressively.

Aunt Hat shrugged. 'Better done in a good, clean hospital than in some filthy back room. . . .' She stopped, and suddenly the indignation I had hoped to rouse against my poor stepfather, was turned on me. 'You shouldn't be talking about such things, a child like you. Goodness me, is there anything you don't know?'

'Very little,' I answered coldly, and swept from the room.

I met Gus on Monday afternoon on the way home from the swimming bath. Since I hoped to get into the school relay team this summer, I had been practising hard all winter and the exercise had developed my chest: I looked at myself in the changing-room mirror after my bathe, and was delighted to see that I stuck out splendidly, side view. When I dressed, I left off my brassiere and vest and wore nothing but my sweater over my nakedness. The effect was as startling as I had hoped, and I went into the street proudly conscious of it.

Gus was coming out of the station. 'Hullo, Gus,' I called gaily. He had been less in my thoughts lately, and so I was able to greet him without embarrassment.

'Well, Katey-Did.' He stopped, smiling. For an instant, his eyes fell to my breasts and then lifted hastily to my face. He jerked his pipe stem upwards in his mouth. It struck me suddenly that this movement had a sexual connotation and I went red.

'I've been swimming,' I said, talking desperately to avert attention from my colour. 'I swam seven lengths this afternoon, though I'm a sprinter, actually, not long distance. I might make the relay team this year.'

'Lucky you.' He gave a mock sigh.

'What have you been doing?' I asked, though I knew he had just come off the evening train from London.

'The usual. Sweaty grind in the old city.' His voice changed. 'You look fresh as the spring,' he said.

This remark seemed to embarrass *him*: we walked on, not looking at each other, our cheeks rosy. As we reached the arcade of little shops beyond the station, he said, 'What about a cuppa?', took my arm and turned me into a café.

The tea was hot and strong. We sipped it and smiled at each other. I could think of nothing to talk to him about and he seemed to find some difficulty too. He asked me how Joanna was and whether the rest of my family was well; after that he fell silent. From time to time, his eyes fell on my breasts as if drawn by a magnet and then jerked away. The chilly evening air had hardened my nipples and they stuck out like nuts through the thin wool of my sweater. I began to be ashamed and hugged my damp, rolled towel to my chest until the cold seeped through to my skin.

Suddenly Gus said, 'Don't do that, you'll get rheumatism.' He leaned across the table and removed the towel. 'Haven't you got a coat?'

I shook my head. 'I wish I had. I'm cold.' I added, daringly, 'I forgot to put my bra' on, and my vest.'

He looked at the wall above my head. 'Perhaps you'd better go to the cloakroom and put them on,' he suggested gently.

There was a mirror in the Ladies and I saw what I looked like. My ears burned with shame. I dressed, unsure whether to be grateful to Gus or to hate him. One minute I thought he was the most chivalrous man in the world, the next I loathed him for treating me like a child. When I crept out, he was standing by the door of the café, smiling. He opened it with a flourish, saying, 'Home, James, and don't spare the horses.'

He came part of the way with me and I thought of the evening he had walked down my road, holding my hand. I looked at him but one hand was holding the bowl of his

152

pipe and the other, the one next to me, was in his trouser pocket. There was the width of the pavement between us. He asked me about my swimming, and about school, as if he thought these were the only things likely to interest me. I resented that, and answered in sullen monosyllables until he looked at me and said, 'What's the matter, Katey-Did?'

'Nothing.' This did not seem a very interesting answer, so I embellished it with a deep sigh and a little, sad shrug of my shoulders. 'Nothing – and everything,' I said in a melancholy voice.

He took his hand out of his pocket and gripped my arm lightly above the elbow. 'Come on, you can tell old Gus.'

There was a look of kindly boredom on his face as if he wasn't, really, expecting much in the way of worries from a child like me. Because of that look, and because of the mortifying incident in the café, I told him about Mrs Tanner.

I began by saying, 'I'm afraid my father has done something terribly wrong,' and went on, working myself up into a fine old state about the sin of taking an innocent life. I knew, with the horrible, clear cunning of childhood, that the things I was saying were things I might well be expected to feel by any kindly adult who was concerned for the tender susceptibilities of childhood, but, by the end, though I was still keeping an eye on Gus to see how he was taking it, I had convinced myself that I was really suffering moral torment: there was a lump in my throat and my knees were shaking.

Gus heard me out gravely, sucking his empty pipe, not letting go my arm. He said, 'Do you really believe it's wrong, Kate, to save a woman's life?' He went on without waiting for my answer, saying that we, as members of the Anglican Church did not subscribe to the Catholic point of view, so I could put that sort of theological argument out of my head. Then, veering off into botany, he said that he, personally, believed that it was right, when necessary, to cut off a branch so that the tree might live.

'But she wouldn't have died. My father just did it because it would have been hard for her to manage with another baby. Just for her *convenience*. And that's against the law,' I cried, with adventitious, sanctimonious bitterness.

'A good doctor must do what his conscience tells him,' Gus said. 'I think you can be sure your father did what he thought right. My advice to you is to stop thinking about it.' He hesitated. 'I don't suppose you'll like my telling you that you're not really old enough to understand a situation like this.'

'I understand perfectly well,' I said, bridling.

'Do you?' He looked at me doubtfully. Suddenly he grew rather red. 'I'm very much afraid you've been having a good time, working yourself up into a nice, enjoyable state of moral indignation.'

This truth hurt me deeply, and I began to cry. At once he put his arm round my shoulder and drew me into the privacy of an empty bus shelter where he made comforting, clucking noises and tried, ineffectively, to mop my face with his handkerchief. 'It's not fair,' I gasped. 'I'm terribly upset, you don't understand. . . .'

And then I burst out about Poll and my mother, and our father running away and how awful it would have been if Ellen had decided to get rid of Poll before she was born. In the beginning part of me was standing by and watching the effect this was having on Gus, but about halfway through that part disappeared and I was crying properly, with real wretchedness, until I felt weak and empty and comfortable, the way you feel when you are still in bed ill, but your temperature has gone down.

Gus was hovering round me. 'Poor little Katey, poor little Katey,' he kept saying. As I quietened, he held his handkerchief to my nose. 'Blow,' he said. I blew, and smiled at him shakily.

A small fat woman with a bulging, mock-leather shopping bag, came into the shelter and looked at me curiously as she sat down, her little feet in stumpy shoes riding clear of the ground. Gus steered me out of the shelter. We walked without speaking for a little. I felt quiet and almost happy now, but Gus looked worried: his face was screwed up and

154

there were crow's feet round his eyes. At last he said, abruptly, 'Kate, don't talk to anyone outside your family about this. It doesn't matter, your telling me, but now you've got it off your chest you must keep quiet about it.'

He went on, it seemed uncomfortably, to say that although he was quite sure my father had done nothing wrong, he might be displeased if it got about. I wouldn't want to upset him, would I? Then for the rest of the way he spoke earnestly about the dangers of rumour and bearing false witness which we had discussed at our last Fellowship meeting.

Chapter Thirteen

'Of course the trouble with Poll is that she's like me, basically insecure,' Joanna said.

She had been reading books on child psychology and found from them that we had all been brought up quite wrongly. She did not keep this discovery to herself, but lectured Ellen constantly on her failings as a parent, following her from room to room and speaking in a low, furious voice. Joanna was doing badly at school and chose to blame Ellen for having expected too much of her and pushed her too hard when she was younger. Ellen was over-anxious. She was distrustful of life. Her own narrow upbringing had disinclined her to allow us to experiment and develop our qualities to the full. Of course, Joanna was only telling Ellen these home truths in order to prevent her ruining my life, and Poll's, as far as she, Joanna, was concerned, it was certainly too late. 'It's probably too late for Kate, too,' she said, speaking with the savage calm she seemed to find in the contemplation of despair, 'but it might help Poll. Though

155

only up to a point, of course, too much damage has been done already.' She looked at Ellen meaningfully. 'After all, *you* should know why she gets into her states. . . .'

Poll was an April child, all lowering storm one minute and cheerful sunshine the next. She had lately discovered an irritating amusement which consisted of belching loudly and then saying, 'Come in, Vicar'; it was a joke which palled on everyone, but it drove Joanna wild. 'You never stop her, you just smile and she goes on and on thinking it funny. It's the same all the time, belching and awful table manners and lavatory jokes. If you don't put your foot down, how's she ever to learn they're disgusting?'

This, though intolerant, was not actually unreasonable, but it seemed to me that what really offended Joanna was Poll's general cheerfulness: whenever she laughed or sang *Abide With Me*, her favourite hymn, Joanna would put on a martyred expression and complain of a headache, or shout at her in a frenzy, 'Shut *up*, what do you think this is? A parrot house?'

In contrast, when Poll wept, or had a nightmare, Joanna was all loving attention, sweeping her into her arms and casting baleful, I-told-you-so glances at Ellen. At this time, Poll was deeply concerned about the number of hedgehogs that died on the roads: she sobbed over each little, crushed body, and determined to cut down the slaughter by removing all the live hedgehogs from the tarmac and depositing them in the safety of our garden. Though she never found a hedgehog, she rescued a number of woolly caterpillars and placed them tenderly on the pavements. This minor obsession was normal, at her age I had felt a similar anxiety about spiders, but it was Poll's nature to carry everything to extremes. At four o'clock one morning she was discovered in the hall, weeping, and trying to draw the stiff bolt on the front door so that she could go into the street on her errand of mercy.

'I ask you, what normal, secure child would do that?' Joanna asked in bitter, satirical tones.

'I think it was because she'd wet her bed,' Ellen said,

having on this occasion decided to please Joanna by sitting down and carrying on the argument. 'She was upset and trying to create a diversion.'

Joanna gave an incredulous laugh. In all these exchanges she spoke and acted rather like the sinister villain in a Victorian melodrama. 'Ah – but *why* does she wet her bed?'

Patiently, Ellen tried to explain what Boyd believed, that it was a straightforward physical disability and she would grow out of it, but Joanna merely rolled her eyes to heaven in answer, and embarked on an incredibly overdone routine of shrugs and sighs. 'Oh, it's no use talking to you. You don't want to find out the truth about Poll, or me, or anyone. You only want to go on pretending everything in the garden is lovely.'

I was astonished by Ellen's tolerant reception of Joanna's behaviour: *I* would not have got away with such rudeness so easily. In fact, I think Ellen was sorry for Joanna who was as miserable as anyone could be. Will Saxon's defection had been a bad blow to her pride and her self-conscious retreat into the studious life had not helped to mend it but had made her more bitterly aware of failure: Greek, which had once opened windows for her, had become nothing but a stiflingly dull exercise, a sterile boredom. Our parents, and her teachers, said what they had been saying for some time, that she should change from classics to medicine: this is what she really wanted to do and, ultimately, did do, but now she repudiated the suggestion with an almost hysterical violence, as if all she wanted was to be completely empty of purpose. It must have seemed to her that all her work had been useless, all her instruction false, all her enthusiasm wasted; her plan of life had gone wrong and she needed time to gather courage for the difficult task of making a new one. Meantime, she goaded Ellen, the way a bored child will pull the wings off flies.

Joanna was not stupid, not even emotionally stupid, the way some clever people are. She did not really believe Poll was insecure because she had never known our father, nor,

I think, did she feel so insecure herself: it was simply that at this frustrating period in her life she found release in the luxury of a fictionalised emotion. She had to blame someone. She was using our absent father as an excuse – how could she be expected to work hard and do well when she had *this* to disturb her? – and also as a weapon against Ellen whom she hated with the violence unhappy people often hate those who love them most: you turn on the ones who love you, because no one else would care.

Of course she did not actually come out with it. She did not once mention our father to Ellen or to Boyd and her innuendoes were so theatrical, were surrounded with such a cloud of murky, hinted menace, that it is possible they did not understand what she was at. Indeed, more than possible. Since we had always been encouraged to be straightforward and honest, to state a problem and accept help in finding a solution, it is almost certain that Joanna's spiteful deviousness missed the mark altogether, as maybe, in her heart, she intended it to do: if our parents had once understood her argument, it would have faded like the shadow it was in the sensible, clear light they would have brought to bear upon it. Even left alone, it is doubtful if it would have survived long. Joanna's basic lack of dramatic imagination, or, more positively, her natural vitality and good sense, would have starved it out of existence if she had not turned to Aunt Hat for fuel to feed it on.

It is because she turned to Aunt Hat that I think Joanna was more to blame for what happened than anyone held her to be. Joanna knew – she had seen it for herself, earlier on – that Aunt Hat wat unaware of the difference between a false emotion and a true one. Or perhaps it would be fairer to say that Aunt Hat was unaware that there was any difference, was unaware that falsity, that worm in the bud, existed even: there was no feeling too tinny, too worked over or second-hand, that Aunt Hat could not accept, and treat, as purest gold. It would never occur to her that emotion could be used as a device for getting attention, or merely for one's private pleasure.

I don't mean I understood clearly, at the time, the extent of Joanna's miserable folly, nor the way it was changing her, turning her from a bright, confident girl into an unhappy, useless kind of person, dangerous to herself and to everyone else. But I did see that she was working herself up into a fine, theatrical state, as I had done over Walter's mother's abortion, and for much the same reason: she was trying on a role which had just enough truth in it to be viable, and playing it to an audience she knew would be taken in.

And of course Aunt Hat was taken in, though, as always, Joanna played her part badly. She took to drooping and sighing and smiling in a bitter, mysterious way at the most commonplace remarks as if she alone could read their double meaning.

One afternoon we played Monopoly after tea with Aunt Hat and Poll. Both were irritating players, Aunt Hat because she pretended not to notice when we landed on her 'sites', and Poll because she was a plain, ordinary cheat, a failing which Joanna and I did our best to correct. This afternoon, the game ended when we caught her filching money from the bank. She upset the board and left the room, roaring like a bull. Aunt Hat pursued her, but she locked herself in the lavatory.

'Don't fuss over her,' Joanna said, when Aunt Hat came back. 'She's got to learn or it'll be a great handicap in after life.' She gave one of her sighs. 'I wish I knew why she cheated.'

'She wants to win,' I said.

'That's not the real reason.'

'What is, then?'

Unable to answer me, Joanna took refuge in obscurity. 'Nothing is ever what it seems. You'd know that if you read a decent book sometimes instead of those old comics. I can't think why Ellen allows it.'

'M.Y.O.B.' I said.

'It is my business. How do you think I feel, seeing my sister acting like a silly baby and growing up ignorant.'

'I don't care.'

The bitter, knowing smile twisted her mouth. 'I believe you don't. You have no family feeling. None at all.'

'Now, now,' Aunt Hat said. 'Birds in their little nests agree.'

Temporarily drawn together by this dreadful remark, Joanna and I smiled naturally at each other.

I began to collect the spilled Monopoly money. 'Give us a hand, then,' I said, but Joanna seemed to have fallen into a trance staring into the sleepy fire. Aunt Hat got down on her knees at once and put all the money and the cards into the box but in the wrong place, so that later on I had to sort them out again.

The room was quiet. A spurt of gas flared in the fire and Joanna got up to look at herself in the glass over the fireplace. Turning the lovely oval of her face this way and that, she said wistfully, 'Sometimes I look in the mirror and it seems as if there's nothing there. . . .'

'You must be going blind.'

She ignored me. 'It's a funny feeling, not knowing who you are. Sometimes I lie awake all night. . . .'

'You shouldn't lie awake,' Aunt Hat said. 'Growing girls need their sleep.'

'I've stopped growing. One's physical health isn't important, anyway. Not beside other things.' She sighed and smiled, twisting her bright, slippery hair into a high knot on the top of her head; whatever she said, she was clearly seeing herself now, and the sight gave her pleasure. She went on in a soft, dreaming voice. 'I lie awake and think of all of us here, in this house, and how we're just faces and voices to each other. That's all I am, a face and a voice. And then I think about walking out in the street and seeing all the other people passing by, and they don't know me and I don't know them and there's no way of telling who they are and they can't tell who I am, either. We just pass by and I go one way and they go another. It frightens me. I mean, suppose I was out somewhere and I saw' – she darted a pregnant glance at Aunt Hat – 'a *certain person*, would we know each other? You'd think there ought to be some difference, some way of telling, but I think about the people in this house and then the people in the street, and there's none I can see.'

Aunt Hat gave a nervous little cough, and looked at me.

Joanna let her hair fall and shook her head so that it swung silkily and straight. Then she sat down, very gracefully, one foot pointed in front of the other, and gazed intently into the fire. 'I've been thinking a lot lately. One of the things I've been thinking about is Will. He was quite wrong for me, I see that now, but the other thing I'm beginning to see that it wasn't *him* broke it up, it was me.' She glanced at me and added quickly, '*Basically*, I mean. It was never a satisfactory relationship and though he saw that before I did, it was my fault it wasn't satisfactory. It was as if part of me was holding back all the time – almost as if part of me was missing!'

'You just didn't love him, dear,' Aunt Hat said. 'All girls like to have a boy friend, that's natural, but you can't expect to find Mr Right first time round, so to speak. He'll come along, one of these days, and then you'll feel quite differently.'

'I doubt that,' Joanna said in a gentle voice, 'I'm afraid I really do doubt that! I shall never love anyone, Aunt Hat.' She smiled bravely. 'One thing I've begun to realize is that I shall never be able to have a proper relationship with anyone, because I'm not a whole person!' Suddenly she dropped the suffering smile and the droopy voice and said briskly, as if she had decided to cut the cackle and come to the hosses, 'It's been proved that children who have lost a parent are permanently crippled – just as much as if they'd lost a leg or an arm.'

I couldn't bear this frightful, ham performance another minute. 'You look as if you'd got all your legs and arms to me.'

'You . . .' She turned on me. 'You haven't any feelings, you never think, only about your own stupid, rotten *self*.'

'Shut your trap.' I stuck my fingers in my ears but not very hard, and I could hear her long, tired sigh.

'I think all the time.' The colour came up into her face.

'When they give out those things on the radio – you know, when they say someone's dying in a hospital and they ask for their family to get into touch – well, I think one day it might be *him*, dying there all alone with no one to care, and thinking about his children, and longing to see them just once and put out his hands and touch them, and about me, not knowing, and not being there to hold his hand . . . and him thinking I don't care and it being too late. . . .' She caught her breath. 'You don't know how terrible I feel.'

'I know you make *me* feel terrible. You make me feel sick,' I said.

Her face crumpled suddenly into the ugliness of genuine grief. 'I hate you,' she cried. She got up, all her gracefulness gone, and lurched out of the room.

'Silly fool,' I shouted after her. The house shook as her bedroom door slammed. 'It makes me sick, listening to her silly talk,' I muttered, 'lot of made-up nonsense.'

'I don't think it's made up, dear,' Aunt Hāt said. 'After all, it could be the way she says. Dying alone . . .' Her cheeks were pink, her cow-brown eyes dampened, and I could tell from her soft, dreaming quietness that she was carried back in her mind to the man who had fallen dead on her doorstep, long ago. I felt a sudden, queer uneasiness I could not place or name. 'She's unhappy,' Aunt Hat said. 'She's got all this on her mind just now and there's no way she can work it off. She can't talk to Ellen, you see, it would hurt her, and of course she doesn't want to hurt her mother.'

'Joanna doesn't mind about not hurting people. She just knows Ellen would stop her making a fool of herself and she's enjoying herself too much to want that.'

'Aren't you being a teeny bit unkind, dear? You're only a little girl, you don't really understand. Poor Joanna has this feeling about things being too late, you're too young to understand that, it's a dreadful feeling. Aunt Hat's felt it more times than she cares to name. . . .' The dreaming look misted her face. 'When Dick's poor father passed away – when I got the news, I mean – that was the worst time of all. The day he left to go to France we had a terrible quarrel, he'd

162

been drinking and he came in the kitchen, needling me, and I threw the mixing bowl at him, it caught him on the side of his head . . . it didn't hurt him but the cake mixture spilled out and down his uniform. He didn't go for me – he wasn't violent like poor Jack, it was only words with him – he only swore and went off to the bathroom to clean up and I waited in the kitchen, cooling myself down and meaning to make it up in a while, but he just came straight down from upstairs and went out through the front door without a word. I ran out in the street in my apron, but he'd gone. It was the end. He stepped on a mine at Dunkirk and there'd not been a word written or spoken between us since that day. I tell you, Kate, it was a cold, bitter feeling. When I got this telegram I forgot all the hard things we'd said to each other – it was drink and woman trouble mostly – and just remembered all the good times we'd had once and all the things I wished I'd said and done. . . .'

'Joanna doesn't feel like that,' I said. 'She just wants to be unhappy.'

Aunt Hat went up to Joanna and I crept up after them and tried to hear what they were saying, but the bedroom door was closed and they were speaking softly: all I could hear was a gentle sea-like murmur.

I went into Poll who had dressed up in an old blue dress of Ellen's and a pair of pink satin high-heeled shoes. She had rouged her cheeks and put lipstick on and a piece of veiling over her face fastened with hair slides. On top of her head, she wore the cardboard crown. She was the Queen and we played at Coronations for a while. Poll had a great deal of information about the ceremony from Miss Carter who, unlike Aunt Hat and Mr Fantom, was devoted to the Monarchy: I was, in turn, the Archbishop, the Gold Stick in Waiting and Prince Philip, kneeling before Poll and vowing to be her liege lord of life and limb. These secondary roles became boring eventually and I suggested we play Personalities. I began with Miss Carter, acting in dumb show all her grotesque, nervous habits, winking and grimacing and working my jaw. Poll guessed her and then did Mr Saxon, stretching her neck like a stiff giraffe, sucking in her cheeks and drooping her eyelids. That was all she seemed to do, and yet – Poll's art was spare and baffling as a good cartoonist's – I could *see* Mr Saxon's boney, sagging face above the pink plastic collar.

'You guessed too quickly,' she complained.

'Only because you're so good.' I felt no envy: Poll's gifts were so superior to mine that envy was somehow inappropriate.

She pouted. 'S'not fair. I want another turn.'

'It *was* fair. But you can if you like.'

She took off the veil and crown, climbed on to the bed, pulled the eiderdown over her and lay flat and still for a minute. Then her head began to move slowly from side to side. Her plump face became hollow and grooved, her eyes gleamed through half-closed lids, her mouth wrinkled up into a little, drawn purse that opened, bubbling out a little spit, and closed again. 'I don't know, Poll,' I said, and then, suddenly, 'Don't do it any more – it's *horrible*.'

Her face smoothed out and she opened one eye. 'Give up?'

'No . . . *yes*,' I cried, as the dreadful impersonation began again.

She spoke up, beaming. 'Miss Fantom,' she said.

'That's not fair,' I said, outraged. 'She's not like that.'

'She is. When she gets sick, she's like that.'

'How d'you know?'

'I saw the other day.' She looked at me and went scarlet. 'I did, so there! I was in talking to Mr Fantom and I went to get his silly old newspaper and her door was open so I went in. She was in bed, just like that.'

'Where was the nurse, then?' I asked, speaking sceptically, not because I disbelieved Poll, but for the sake of discipline.

'In the bathroom.'

'Did she see you?'

'Course not. I ran soon as she pulled the chain.'

'You'll catch it if anyone knows you went in there.'

'I won't. I told Mr Fantom and I asked what was wrong

164

with her and he said she was just sick, the old bitch, and it was time for her medicine.'

'You shouldn't call her an old bitch.'

'I didn't. He did. I was just saying what he said.'

'You shouldn't talk to him. He shouldn't use swear words in front of a little girl. It just shows how beastly he is.'

'He is not beastly.' She glared at me and then said, unwillingly, 'He's a bit beastly, though. It isn't fair, he cheats at draughts. He always wins when we play draughts because he always cheats.'

'You cheat too.'

'I don't cheat. Not at draughts. I don't have to, I always win when I play with you, don't I?'

'Only because I let you.'

Her face began to puff up with rage and I said quickly, because I didn't want to quarrel over nothing, 'Let's play something else. We'll play hospitals, if you like.'

'Only if I can be surgeon,' Poll said. Since she was quite ready to quarrel, she was able to drive a hard bargain. I lay submissively on the bed while she performed bloodthirsty rituals on my bare stomach with a plastic knife that disappeared into the hilt when you pressed it. 'Forceps, Sister,' she said grimly, and she looked so silly, bending over me in the blue dress, her face smudged with lipstick, that I began to giggle. 'It's no good,' I gasped. 'You're not dressed properly.'

Though there was an old surgeon's gown and mask in our dressing up chest, Poll refused to abandon her glamorous attire. She decided she would be a lady instead, visiting her little boy in hospital. 'You can be my husband,' she said. 'Your name's Arthur and mine's Louise, and our little boy is George.'

We laid George, the bear, in the cot and tucked the cover under his chin. 'Poor George, he's had his appendix out,' I said, but this was not dramatic enough for Poll.

'He's much iller than that,' she insisted.

After a long discussion, we decided that George had double pneumonia. 'He's dying,' Poll said.

165

'You don't die of pneumonia nowadays.' Poll stuck out her lower lip. 'All right,' I said hastily. I put my arm round her and lowered my voice. 'I'm afraid there's no hope. The doctors have asked me to break it to you, Louise, dear.'

'Dying!' Poll cried. 'Oh, no Arthur, no!'

'Don't distress yourself, Louise. Everything that could be done has been done. Medical science can do no more.'

Poll sank to her knees beside the cot. 'Speak to me, my baby, my little George! Speak to me once more.'

'He can't speak. That was his death rattle. Louise, our first-born has passed away.'

'But he is too young to die!'

'The good die young, the Lord giveth and the Lord taketh away.'

Poll's tears fell thick and fast. Her face showed such pure and beautiful grief that a lump rose in my own throat. From the cot George regarded us with his unwinking, button eyes, one more loosely tethered than the other, giving him a lopsided appearance.

'Don't cry, Louise.' I put my arm round her. 'He is not suffering any more. He has passed from this vale of tears to a happier land.'

'My George has gone to be with God and Jesus.' Poll cast herself into my arms. My stomach heaved and we wept together.

'What is going on?' Ellen asked, from the door. She stood there, in her outdoor clothes, blinking at this tragic scene. Feeling foolish, I released Poll who ran to Ellen and buried her face in her stomach. 'Oh,' she wailed, 'we're having such a lovely game.'

Chapter Fourteen

'It was only a sort of game,' I mumbled.

My sins had come home to roost. As I came into the house I met Gus Lightwater coming out, ushered by Boyd. Smiling in an oddly nervous fashion, Gus asked me if I had been swimming again. 'Well, keep up the good work,' he said, and jerked his pipe stem upwards in farewell.

Boyd closed the front door and beckoned me into the dining room. One look at his face disabused me of the temporary hope that Gus had come to pledge his love and ask my hand.

While Boyd spoke, I stared at the Turkey carpet that had come from his uncle's house, like so much of our furniture. It was a hideous carpet, worn in places. I was conscious of myself, standing on a particularly threadbare patch, as a dark triangle with a pinpoint head. In front of me Boyd was another triangle, looking against the pale rectangle of the window. Outside, the spring twilight was green and lasting and still.

'I can see you might have been acting it up a little,' Boyd said. 'But that's a poor excuse, isn't it, for breach of confidence? You know that a doctor's family must never gossip about the patients. If it was just a game, as you say, then you have behaved very badly. But I can't believe that. You must have been really upset. You were upset, weren't you, Kate, not just pretending to be?'

I looked at him. His face was hurt and troubled and that surprised me because his voice had been so calm. I thought back but I could not remember. 'I don't know, it was a bit of both, I expect.'

'Umm. I'm sorry, Kate. I blame myself. There's nothing

wrong in what I did, I can only ask you to believe that, but I should never have told you about it. You couldn't be expected to understand.'

Mortified, I averted my gaze and took refuge in mumbling childishness. 'It was all right your telling me. I mean I asked, didn't I? And you've always said you ought to tell children things when they ask.'

'Perhaps I was wrong.'

'No.' I could see what he was making me do and suddenly I was glad of it. 'The only thing wrong was me going off and gabbing to Gus. That was just . . . I mean . . . I only did it to . . .'

'To get it off your chest?' Boyd said quickly – to spare me, to test me? – 'I can see that perhaps you needed to do that, though I wish you'd come to me instead.'

'I didn't *need* anything,' I said crossly. 'I just wanted Gus to take notice of me. The enormity of this admission brought the blood pounding in my ears. 'Oh, that was *horrible*.'

Boyd smiled slightly. 'Not particularly. Nobody's motives are ever pure. What was wrong, as you rightly said, was gabbing to Gus. Not why you did it.'

My face burned. 'What can I do?'

'Nothing.'

'*You*, then . . .' He raised his eyebrows. '*Hit* me, or something. . . '

Boyd looked thoughtful. 'That wouldn't change anything, would it?'

'Oh . . . I *hate* myself,' I cried.

'Don't do that.'

'Why not? I *do* . . .'

'Because it doesn't help,' Boyd said. 'When you've done something, it's done. All you can do is to live with it. Hating yourself doesn't help you do that. In fact, it's an easy way out.'

I was discovering this for myself, though I hardly realized it then: self-disgust had soothed my conscience and made way for healing indignation. 'I think it was real mean of Gus to come and tell you. *That* was a breach of confidence, too, wasn't it? I mean, he's a sort of priest, in a way, and a priest is like a doctor.'

'You mustn't blame Gus. He felt it his duty to come. His duty as your . . . er . . . spiritual adviser.'

'He's a fool. A big, fat, stupid fool.' I screwed up my face and made a spitting noise.

Boyd said, rather coldly, 'I don't really think so. He was concerned for you. And, incidentally, for my professional reputation. It may be a minor point beside the moral issue, but he said you seemed to believe Mrs Tanner's abortion was . . . well . . . not strictly lawful, and he was worried in case you spread this around. *Did* you believe that, Kate?'

'Well . . . doing *that* . . . I mean, it is against the law, isn't it?' I muttered, hoping that I looked and sounded convincingly innocent.

'It can be. It wasn't, in this case. Not in my opinion, nor in the opinion of the other doctors who examined Mrs Tanner. But you haven't answered my question, have you?'

I couldn't. I couldn't meet his eyes.

'I see . . . You just thought it made for a more dramatic story? Gus thought that might be the case, but he couldn't be sure. He said you seemed really upset, but then the poor chap was at something of a disadvantage. He's not been acquainted with your theatrical imagination as long as I have.'

He sounded flat and weary. I felt desperately ashamed and anxious to redeem myself in his eyes. 'I really was awfully upset . . . it wasn't Mrs Tanner, not really . . . I was upset about *Poll.*' I stumbled, and, for a brief second, saw clearly that I had fallen into the same old trap I had fallen into with Gus, of producing, for the effect it would have on Boyd's opinion of me, what I knew he would accept and welcome as pitiable truth. But I saw this only for that second: the next, his swift nod of satisfaction – for though Boyd had more insight than Gus he was human, too, and anxious to seize upon something straightforward that he could deal with – released in me a sweet uprush of sadness and heavenly relief. He comforted me while I sobbed in his arms, blowing my nose on his clean handkerchief and saying that it was a good thing, if one had a tendency to dress up one's feelings, to check them occasionally against the facts: there was no point in generating heat over things that had never happened. 'Poll is nearly eight now. You can take it from me that her survival was never in question.' He tilted my blubbered face and kissed my eyes. 'Like a game of chess? I think we've time before tea.'

We set out the good ivory set and sat before the sitting-room fire. Ellen was rattling china in the kitchen; Poll bellowing hymns upstairs.

I told Boyd that Poll had been in to see Miss Fantom. 'She looked awful, Poll showed me. Is she very sick?'

He was silent for a moment. Then, 'That was a bit care-less, wasn't it?' He leaned over to take my queen. 'She died this morning,' he said.

The clock ticked. A piece of coal fell on to the hearth. I looked at Boyd and was surprised to see his face was just as it had always been.

'Look at the board. No,' – as my hand moved – 'think again.'

I thought. 'Check.'

'Good girl. Not Mate, though. . . .'

'What did she die of?'

'Terminal pneumonia.'

'I thought pneumonia didn't kill people nowadays.'

'It does sometimes. When they're old and very ill.'

'Were you there when she . . .?'

'Yes.'

'Was Aunt Hat?'

He nodded.

'Did she die after we'd gone to school?'

I thought of us going to school. We had been late this morning and had to run: I thought of all the people in the world running and walking or sitting in buses and trains, moving, scurrying round the earth, and then of the dead, lying still. I had not thought about death for a long time; now, for a concentrated minute, I thought of it. I wasn't afraid but coldly aware, as you are aware of a large, empty space in the dark. I wanted to ask Boyd something but as soon as I had said, 'Did she . . . does dying hurt much?' I knew that this wasn't, really, what I wanted to know.

'Not much, not nowadays.' Boyd looked at me intently. 'Does it worry you?'

'I think so.'

He stared into the fire for a little before he said softly, 'The worst that can befall thee, measured right, is a sound slumber and a long good-night.'

I was astonished to hear Boyd quote poetry, for he was a most unpoetic man.

Boyd and Ellen went out to supper and a film and took Joanna with them. They often took her out at this time and I was sometimes jealous, but not this evening: I was anxious for the details of Miss Fantom's death-bed and knew I would get them, once I had Aunt Hat alone.

But we were not alone long. Poll was in bed and we were settling by the fire with a tray of tea and Marie biscuits, when the doorbell rang.

'Why, you're quite a stranger, Ethel,' I heard Aunt Hat say. Miss Carter answered something low and Aunt Hat said, 'Nonsense, of course you must come in, dear. There's only Kate and me.'

Miss Carter stood in the doorway. 'I'm sure I don't want to intrude.' She spoke to Aunt Hat but the spite in her voice was intended for me.

I got out of my chair at once and said, '*Do* sit here, Miss Carter,' hoping to imply by my innocent welcome that I had forgotten the last time we sat together in this room.

Her long nose, red at the tip, seemed to quiver suspiciously like a rat's whiskers, but she came into the room and perched on the edge of the chair, keeping on her outdoor clothes to make it clear that her departure was imminent. In response to Aunt Hat's coaxing she relented so far as to un-button her coat but refused tea. She had just heard about Miss Fantom, she explained, and had felt she must pop in. I saw the greed in her eyes and knew we were sisters under the skin.

Aunt Hat's eyes filled. 'It was a merciful release. She went off very peacefully – just slipped away. After all that pain and trouble no one could wish anything else. I sat up with her all night, Ethel, and I couldn't help thinking how different things are from what they used to be. There she lay, sleeping like a baby, and I thought of my poor old grandmother moaning and crying the week *she* died. On and on, night and day. My mother put cotton wool plugs in my ears to help me sleep but of course they didn't work and I heard everything. Oh – things are so different now! They've got all these wonderful drugs and it's better for those left behind, too. It's not easy to see someone you love to go off like that . . .'

Miss Carter nodded sympathetically. She glanced at me and I stuck my nose in my book.

'My old Dad went the best way,' Aunt Hat said. 'He'd never had a day's illness in his life, I never knew him take to his bed except at the end. It was after he'd gone blind. It was cataract. I took him up to the hospital and the doctor said they could operate, but he didn't hold out much hope. We went home on the bus and I tried to cheer him up but he didn't seem to listen. Then, when we got back, he asked me to take him a walk round the garden. He had this little orchard he'd planted and I led him round and he touched every tree. Then he went back in and said, 'I think I'll go to bed now, Hattie.' Well, I was surprised, you know, because it wasn't like him and I said, 'Come on, Dad, you're not ill, just sit by the fire first and have your bit of supper,' but he said no, he'd had a good innings and there was no point in hanging around any longer. I didn't get his meaning at first, though I wondered at him being so quiet, but the next day when he wouldn't get up breakfast time, I fetched the doctor. He talked to Dad and examined him and then he sent me away and talked a bit longer, and when he came downstairs he said he was afraid there was nothing he could do. I asked him what was wrong and he said there was nothing at all but that Dad was dying. 'He wants to go and that's that,' he said. 'He's a strong-willed old man; used to getting his own way and he'll get it over this, or I'm a Dutchman.' I couldn't believe my ears, you know, but he was right. Dad was dead in two days and conscious and cheerful right up to the last. I tried to have it out with him but he said, 'I'll die in my own time, my girl, if it's the last thing I do.' Then he laughed and said, 'Which of course it's likely to be. So don't try and hinder me.' When he went, in the end, it was just as if he'd switched off the light and gone out of the room at the end of the day.'

'Mind over matter,' Miss Carter said. 'That's the remarkable thing. I believe in some primitive tribes . . .' She went on to tell Aunt Hat how in some backward parts of the world, people could will themselves to die. Aunt Hat listened with the strained look she always wore when anyone tried to give her interesting general information. Her eyes were fixed wide open and staring at Miss Carter's mouth as if she were a deaf person lip-reading. She didn't relax until Miss Carter stopped talking about primitive people and spoke of her mother.

'She had . . . well, the same trouble as Miss Fantom,' Miss Carter said with a quick look at me, and I knew she didn't mean pneumonia.

Apparently Mrs Carter had been a very house-proud woman and when she got ill she lay in bed and worried about the dust. 'We had a daily woman look after her while I was at school,' Miss Carter said, 'and every afternoon when I came in, the first thing she said was, 'Has she done the drawing room?' One day the woman broke a vase my mother had been particularly fond of and I remember I was terrified she'd get out of bed one day and go downstairs and find it was gone. Of course she never did, but I used to wake up in the middle of the night and worry about it. She suffered cruelly at the end. She used to say, *Oh, why can't I die?* The doctor gave her stuff to take but it wasn't enough. I begged him for more but he said no, he was afraid it might shorten her life. Afraid for his own skin is more like it! Doctors! Oh, I've got no patience with them, they're all alike!' She snorted vigorously and with more malevolence, I thought uncomfortably, than could be accounted for by her memories.

There was a little silence. Then Aunt Hat said, 'Oh, it's pain and grief coming into the world and pain and grief going out of it.' Her voice held a rich, enjoyable sadness.

In contrast, Miss Carter's was harsh and rasping. 'Sometimes I think it's a pity we're not allowed to do for human beings what we would do for a dog!' She gave one of her loud laughs, snatched off her glasses, polished them energetically on her skirt and put them back, twitching her nose rabbit-fashion to settle them into place. Her nose was flushed; above it, her high forehead looked more than usually white and polished.

'Well, of course most doctors do what they can,' Aunt Hat said. She looked very pretty, her plump hands resting comfortably in her lap. 'I don't know you'd find many nowadays who'd be like your poor mother's man, and he sounds plain callous, if you don't mind my saying so. I must say Doctor Boyd's not like that. None of that awful measuring and clock watching. He gave me extra doses for the night – give it her any time she needs it, he said, there's no need to let her suffer now. 'Oh, he was good to her, Ethel, she said to me more than once, 'He's like a son to me, like my own flesh and blood. And he was, nothing was too much trouble.' She loosed a deep, happy sigh. 'Oh, if they were all like Doctor Boyd, things would be a sight different.'

'Of course, if he had been her own son, he wouldn't have attended her, that's medical ethics,' Miss Carter said. 'Even as it is, if I understand you correctly, he was taking a risk, wasn't he?' Her eyes rested on Aunt Hat, suddenly slyly thoughtful as if assessing how far she dared go. 'After all, I'm sure he was . . . well . . . *especially attentive* to Miss Fantom, but we know he had a particular interest in *her* case, don't we?'

'Well, he'd known her most of his life, Ethel, he was very fond of her, but it's unfair to suggest . . .' Aunt Hat's voice trailed away and her colour mantled: though she seemed unsure what Miss Carter's suggestion had been, she met it as a challenge. 'Doctor Boyd doesn't make any difference between his patients. What he does for one, he does for all. I can't tell you the trouble he goes to for the most ordinary people.'

'I'm sure he has a charming bedside manner,' Miss Carter said, coldly playful.

'Oh, it's more than that, believe me . . . .' Flushed with partisanship, Aunt Hat sat bolt upright in her chair. 'He's not *that* kind of doctor, soft words and pink medicine and no real help in trouble. . . . I can tell you, Ethel, I know least one poor soul who's been glad she had him to turn to. . . .'

I sneezed. Aunt Hat gave a start. '*Kate*. Good heavens, just look at the time, Aunt Hat had quite forgotten you were there, you naughty girl, sitting so quiet, your nose stuck in that old book. . . .'

I pleaded that it wasn't very late and anyway it was Saturday tomorrow, but I didn't plead very hard: I had heard Aunt Hat's enthusiastic eulogies of Boyd before. 'Befordshire for you, chick-a-biddy,' Aunt Hat cried, 'up the little wooden stair.' Her face was suddenly anxious and when she came up ten minutes later to kiss me good-night, I thought I understood why. 'Katey, love,' she said, 'I do hope you weren't upset by all that old morbid talk. . . .'

I shook my head. I hadn't been. In fact, hearing about all those people dying had made me less afraid of death than I had been before. Since it was something everyone had to go through, it couldn't be so bad.

Boyd went to Miss Fantom's funeral. He went alone, although Joanna and I had begged to be allowed to accompany him. We had never been to a funeral, standing beside the open grave while the earth crumbled on the coffin and the preacher spoke those beautiful words. Joanna said it was an experience we ought to have, but Boyd said it was one we could do without for the time being and that, anyway, Miss Fantom's coffin was not being lowered into a grave but placed in the family vault where her mother lay, and her father, and all her brothers and sisters who had died in infancy and who swarmed round the base of the stone monument, disguised as cherubs.

The funeral took place on Monday while we were at school. Monday was a busy day for Boyd and when he came home after tea, he was still wearing his dark suit and black tie. He had had no time to change, no time for lunch: though Ellen protested, he said all he could manage now was a glass of milk and a sandwich. Drinking the milk standing up, he said, 'Where's Poll? Be a good girl, Kate, and see if she's in the camp, will you? I don't want her to play over there just at the moment.'

'Why not?' I asked – since Mr Fantom had not liked his sister, Boyd could hardly be afraid Poll would disturb him in his sorrow – but Boyd only said, 'Never mind, do as I say for once,' and hurried off to his evening surgery.

Poll wasn't in the camp, so I crept up to the house. Even if Poll was there, I had no intention of going in to fetch her, but I peeped in the window to see.

There was no sign of Poll but Miss Carter was sitting there with Mr Fantom. There was a fire lit and tea spread on a low table in front of it. The pads on Mr Fantom's cheeks looked very hot and he was sucking his pipe and staring at Miss Carter who was talking away in her most grotesquely jaw-wrenching fashion. She was wearing a crepe dress, beige with purple flowers on it, and a wide-brimmed black hat that she must have rushed home from school to put on before going out to tea. Had Mr Fantom asked her, I wondered, but dismissed the absurd idea at once: Miss Carter had simply dropped in to condole with him, that was why she was wearing the black hat. But why was he giving her tea? Like his sister, Mr Fantom did not entertain. Mystified, I chewed at the side of my thumb. I had a feeling of faint uneasiness, light as the spring wind on my cheek.

I wandered through the garden, calling Poll. I found her, busy digging a hole by the fence. The earth was peaty and wet and had spattered her face, lumps of it clung to her hair.

176

'What are you doing?' I hissed. 'You shouldn't be here. You know poor Miss Fantom's dead.'

'So's her cat,' she said impatiently. Out of breath, she leaned for a minute on the heavy spade she had purloined from somewhere, and I saw she was a grave-digger. The Abyssinian cat lay beside her, partially wrapped in a piece of sheeting. Insects crawled over its dusty, open eyes.

'What happened to it?' I asked, and she shrugged her shoulder.

'How'd I know? I found it by the dustbins.'

'What were you doing there.'

'Just looking. I thought something might have been thrown out I could use for the camp. But there wasn't anything, only the cat, so I thought I'd better bury it.' She paused. 'I expect it ate something,' she said.

Chapter Fifteen

'Well, your father won't have to do the pools any more, will he?' Jane Owen said.

She was no longer my best friend, but since neither of us had found another, a barbed truce had been declared between us. We were walking through the town, this wet afternoon, looking in the confectioner's windows and debating what Easter eggs we should buy for our families. Having made this curious remark, Jane looked at me expectantly, her head on one side: the rain had wisped her feathery blonde hair round her small, rather beaky face, and she looked like a wet canary.

'Boyd's never done the football pools,' I said, surprised, but cautious: catching each other out was one of our main activities.

She giggled and went red. 'Well, he won't have to start then.'

'I'm sure I don't know what you mean.'

'Don't you?'

'I said so, didn't I?'

She giggled again. 'Most people would.'

'Only if they were pretty odd.'

'*I* think you'd have to be pretty odd *not* to know.'

I tossed my head and concentrated on working out whether I could afford to buy the scarlet-wrapped egg displayed in the centre of Jock's window for Ellen. It had gold ribbon round it and was more expensive than I had planned for, but it was the only one I had seen so far that was made of plain chocolate and Ellen did not like milk. I had time to review my finances before Jane spoke again. She had used the interlude to work out a new form of attack. 'I thought your parents told you everything.'

This was an unkind reminder of an occasion last year when I had told Jane what the word homosexual meant. She had repeated my explanation to her mother who had telephoned Ellen and said perhaps she would kindly ask me to keep that sort of information to myself in future: there were some parents who liked to keep their children's minds pure.

'They do,' I said shortly.

'You can't be sure they do, because you wouldn't know what they didn't tell you, would you?'

Defeated by the cleverness of this argument, I affected boredom.

'Well, what *is* it all about then?'

'You mean you really don't know?'

'No – I mean, yes.'

'What *do* you mean, yes or no?'

'Yes. Yes, I really don't know.'

She looked at me, eyebrows raised and smiling. For some curious reason she kept her lips clamped together and turned the corners of her mouth down: it made her look like an imbecile. 'I don't know that I ought to tell you. . . .'

'Why not?'

'If your parents don't want you to know . . .'

I capitulated. '*Please*, Jane.'

'Oh, all right then. Your father's come into a fortune. That was why I said he wouldn't have to. . . .'

'*What?*'

She sighed, clicking her tongue against her teeth in an exasperated way. 'Old Miss Fantom left him all her money. Do you really mean you didn't *know*?'

I shook my head. I couldn't speak.

'Well, I must say . . .' Jane lifted her pointed profile and addressed the darkening air. 'I mean, I must say your parents are funny people. They tell you all sorts of funny things but they don't tell you the sort of things most parents tell their children. I mean it *is* funny.'

'Ha, ha,' I said witlessly.

'I meant funny *peculiar*. After all, I should've thought they'd have been pleased to tell you they'd come into a lot of money. I'd have thought it would have been the sort of thing most *ordinary* parents would have been pleased to tell their children.'

'My parents aren't ordinary,' was the best retort I could manage.

Jane Owen was wrong on two counts. Miss Fantom had not left Boyd all her money. She had left him fifteen thousand pounds; the rest of her estate went to charity. And neither Boyd nor Ellen were pleased about it. Boyd said that he was sorry I had been made to look foolish but that he had been somewhat embarrassed by the bequest and had not wanted to talk about it.

'Why were you embarrassed?' I asked. 'Jane Owen says she'd have thought you'd be pleased to be left all that money.'

'Miss Fantom was my patient, that's one reason. Another is that she left her brother nothing. After all, he's entitled to . . .'

'He's entitled to nothing!' Ellen cried. 'Look how he treated her!'

'He's entitled to feel aggrieved,' Boyd said mildly. 'And he can contest the will, I suppose, though Starling says . . .'

'You've spoken to Starling?' A frightened look came into Ellen's eyes; it vanished when she saw I was watching her.

'Well . . . it's an awkward position.' He turned away from me and said something low, ending with the words, 'Undue influence.'

'What's that?' I asked, indignantly remembering times he had told me it was bad manners to mumble.

Ellen turned on me with a flash of temper. 'Oh – do be quiet, Kate. This doesn't concern you.'

'It does, though,' Boyd said. 'Sorry, but if there's going to be talk, she'd better know what it's about. Kate, when some-one's had a long illness, their doctor's likely to be an important person in their lives. Particularly if they're old and lonely. So if they leave the doctor money when they die, people are likely to say that he . . . well, that he influenced . . .'

'You mean they'll say you were nice to Miss Fantom because you were after her money?'

Boyd laughed but Ellen gave a shocked exclamation. She was looking nervous, screwing up her eyes. 'Kate! No one could possibly say such a monstrous thing! Why, your father's the last person . . . let me tell you, he's the most honourable, least self-seeking man you're ever likely to meet. Most people know that, there's no one round here more respected, more looked up to . . .' Her voice faltered; there were tears in her eyes.

Boyd's mouth gaped open. Mine, too. It must have been the first time either of us had ever heard Ellen speak so approvingly of anyone.

I said, 'I only meant it was what people might say. But it wouldn't be true, anyway, would it?' I tugged at Boyd's sleeve and he turned to me. He had reddened and his eyes looked bright and shy. 'I mean, she didn't leave you money because you were her doctor, but because she'd known you all that time, ever since you were a boy.' Boyd was frowning and I thought he didn't understand my point so I went on, 'I mean you were such good friends and so close to each other, even though you were different ages and people thought it funny. She thought of you like a son, didn't she? She treasured you . . .'

'Shut up, Kate,' Boyd said abruptly.

'Well, she *said* that. *I treasured Arthur*, that's what she said.'

Ellen gasped. She went to the fireplace and stood stiffly, her back to us. Boyd went up to her and put his hand on her shoulder but she wriggled and he let it fall.

She said, without turning round, 'I won't touch a penny of her bloody money.'

I was flabbergasted. I had never heard Ellen swear before. She raised her fists and brought them down hard on the mantelpiece so that the clock jangled.

'The old bitch,' she said. 'Turning you into a sort of . . . oh, I don't know. Her son! Oh . . . it's disgusting. It disgusts me.'

'Ellen,' Boyd said. 'Ellen . . . we didn't quarrel over her when she was alive, don't let's start now she's dead.'

Ellen turned. Her face was lined like an old woman's. 'It's no good. I can't keep it in any longer. How do you think I felt, day after day . . .? If it had just been for pity, I could have borne it . . .'

Boyd said nothing.

Ellen gave a little moan. 'Oh . . . that's not fair. You were right to be fond of her, there's nothing wrong in that . . . but it was more than affection and pity, wasn't it? *Wasn't* it? You felt *guilty*. . . .'

'She did so much for me,' Boyd said.

'*That* wasn't why you felt guilty, was it?'

There was a pause. 'No,' Boyd said, very low.

Ellen's voice was triumphant. 'She loved you . . . and not like a son. You knew that . . . even as a boy you must have guessed it. Oh . . . I could bear that, if she hadn't made such a fool of you . . . how could you let her? She made a fool of you and you let her . . . you *liked* it. You *liked* having a place where you could escape from us. . . .'

'Not from you. From myself, perhaps. From this species, Suburban Man.' He smiled. She didn't respond and his smile faded. 'Ellen,' he said gently, 'Who doesn't want to get away sometimes? Don't you ever think of the person you might have been, dream that you might go back, start at the beginning again?'

'I didn't realize you found your life so unsatisfactory.'

'That isn't it, don't you see? Oh, Lord, Ellen, if I had the years over again I'd not make one different choice. But that doesn't mean it mightn't be pleasant, sometimes, to feel like a young man again with the choices not made yet. . . .' He laughed, suddenly and good-humouredly, but Ellen only stared.

She said, 'So that's how it was, of course I should have known.' She held the back of her hand against her cheek, which had flamed red. 'She made you feel ill-used. A brave bull, gelded. *She* knew you better. . . .'

'It wasn't like that.'

'No? She didn't take you in? You just let her think she had . . . you felt you owed it to her? All right . . . you don't have to tell me which it was. But you let her dish it out and you lapped it up. So close to each other . . . her treasure. The *doting* old fool. My God, didn't it disgust you?'

'No. I told you, *it wasn't like that.*' He stopped, his face went tight, like a mask. 'Even if it had been, what could I have done? Left her alone, turned away? Should I have said, how dare you love me, you diseased, you *old* woman. . . .'

I fled up to Joanna who was standing at the top of the stairs, white as paper. 'Thank God Poll's out,' she said.

We had never heard them quarrel before and were not hardened. I clutched at Joanna who shook me off, went into her room and lay down on the bed.

I stood at the door. After a minute I said, 'It's all right, they've stopped.'

She rolled over, groaned loudly, and stared at the ceiling. 'I want to get away.'

'Boyd says everyone does.' It was as if a pit had suddenly opened before my feet.

Joanna scowled. 'What's stopping him? We're not his family, are we?'

They were very gentle with each other all evening. They laughed attentively at each other's jokes and touched hands when they passed but we were not comforted: this was too much like the determined demonstrations of good will children go in for, when they fear they have lost someone's regard.

Washing up in the kitchen after supper, Joanna told Aunt Hat about their quarrel. She said how upset she had been but for once Aunt Hat was not sympathetic. 'What's a little quarrel? You don't know you're born, my duck. You've had suffering angels, not parents . . . good heavens, Aunt Hat could tell you some tales!'

'Please don't.' Quivering with resentment, Joanna said in her most prissy voice, 'Parents should never fight in front of their children, it makes them insecure.'

'A bit of insecurity won't hurt you,' Aunt Hat said bracingly. 'Think of them. It's just as well they've had it out, it's been tearing them in pieces these last months and no one's fault, it seems to me. Ellen couldn't help feeling the way she did and he couldn't do anything but what *he* did.'

Joanna polished a plate with excessive care. 'Ellen says she won't touch her money. *I* won't, either.'

'I should cross that bridge when you come to it. Maybe you won't be offered any.'

'*He* shouldn't touch it. It's made a lot of talk.'

'Oh, it'll be a nine days' wonder,' Aunt Hat said.

She was wrong. Miss Fantom had been rich enough to be newsworthy. One evening paper carried a photograph of Boyd leaving the evening surgery. He had put up his hand to his face, he said to stop a sudden sneeze, but he looked like a criminal evading identification. The local *Gazette* had a long obituary on the 'Daughter of Monks Ford's Most Eminent Benefactor'. 'Local Doctor is Not Forgotten,' it said, and, under a sub-heading 'The Quality of Mercy is not Strain'd.' published a smudged photograph of Joanna as Portia in last year's school play and spoke of Boyd's well-known devotion to his patients.

We had a heavy post. 'Begging letters,' Boyd said, and refused to let us see them. But he could not prevent us answering the telephone. It rang five times one evening when Boyd and Ellen were out and a man's voice asked how many rich old ladies the doctor had on his list. 'Filthy-minded pig,' Joanna shouted, when it was her turn to receive this charming enquiry. She put down the telephone and burst into tears. 'You shouldn't have said anything, it's not dignified,' Aunt Hat said, but dignified or not, it seemed to have worked: the telephone rang no more that night.

When Ellen went out, women stopped her in the stores or on the streets and either congratulated her on Boyd's inheritance, or condoled with her on the death of 'such an old family friend.' Several times she returned from shopping trips pale and nerve-wracked: Aunt Hat made her take aspirin and lie down in a darkened room. She seemed, suddenly, always to be tired or not well. 'I can't think what she's got to be ill about,' I grumbled. 'It's just that she hasn't got the temperament for the limelight,' Joanna explained. She said that from now on we must do the shopping for her: we had plenty of time to be helpful, now the Easter holidays had begun.

Since she had overheard our parents' quarrel, Joanna had stopped tormenting Ellen and begun to treat her with a grave, exalted tenderness that seemed to me almost as perverse as her previous behaviour: she cooked and washed dishes unobtrusively enough but went about all the time with a rapt, faraway expression as if she were pursuing half-formed fancies that had no relation to anything she was doing in this life. Irritably seeing this as yet another of her tedious affectations, I was surprised to find that I could not goad her out of it: she answered my sneers with a puzzled gentleness as if she had no idea why I should want to hurt her or make her angry, and after a while I grew bored and left her alone. Even this classic remedy failed to work. She continued to keep her distance, and not only from me: when Boyd or Ellen spoke to her she smiled and answered in a soft, even voice, but always after an interval, as if she were a

184

foreigner who needed time to translate what they had said before she properly understood it. She talked, voluntarily, only to Aunt Hat who was sleeping in the house again: shut up in my bedroom that smelt of her powder and icing-sugary scent, they had long, murmuring conversations from which Joanna emerged with the fixed, drifting look of a sleep walker.

She took to solitary drinking and smoking. One day I found her lying on her bed, holding a tooth mug half full of whisky in one hand and a cigarette in the other. 'They'll smell your breath,' I said, quickly closing the door.

She sighed deeply. 'I can't get through the day without alcohol,' she said, heaving lazily on to her elbow and stubbing out the cigarette which, I realized from subsequent observation, she had probably smoked very little of: she held Passing Clouds at an angle between her fingers in order to acquire a nicotine stain. Similarly, some of the whisky went down the plug as I discovered one night when I bent over the wash basin to clean my teeth and was met by the smell, powerful as a drunkard's breath. All the same, she drank enough to look unnaturally bright-eyed sometimes, enough to make me alarmed about my own responsibilities. How could I stand by and watch her become an alcoholic? She would never listen to me. If only Gus had not betrayed me, I could have talked to him. I day-dreamed several highly satisfactory conversations with him in which I proudly disclosed that my sister had become a secret drinker, before I realized, reluctantly, that on past evidence he would merely feel it his duty to inform our parents. And to tell *them*, of course, was unthinkable.

They appeared to suspect nothing, which surprised me because I imagined Joanna must have made noticeable in-roads on the household liquor supply. It was at this time that Boyd suddenly began to offer Joanna a glass of sherry before the evening meal. When she refused, he seemed disappointed. He said she was quite old enough, now, to drink a little occasionally, but she still shook her head, smiling demurely, and saying she did not think she would like the taste. 'One can't mix the grain and the grape,' she explained afterwards, when I looked in on her, before going to bed. She spoke in her new, gentle voice, and took out the old blackcurrant juice bottle that she kept hidden behind the shoe rack in the wardrobe.

I prayed for her that night. Clutching the blankets suffocatingly over my head. I prayed as loudly as I dared, superstitiously believing that spoken prayers had more chance of being listened to than silent ones, and so effectively that I made myself cry. And having cried, I slept peacefully until morning.

I woke early. Joanna's dissolute behaviour temporarily forgotten, I turned my attention on to the problem of Easter eggs. I had nine shillings and fivepence and five eggs to buy. Traditionally in our family, we each spent most money on Ellen's egg and then divided the remainder between the others: unfortunately, the chocolate egg in Jock's window that I had marked down for her this year was five and sixpence, which left a niggardly amount. I lay in bed for a while and then got up to check the contents of my money box in case I had underestimated my resources. I had not. Sighing, I went to the bathroom. When I came back Poll was awake and similarly occupied with her financial position: I found her squatting beside her bed with coins heaped in five neat piles on the linoleum in front of her. She looked up as I came in but barely saw me: her eyes were glazed, her lips moved in calculation.

After breakfast I decided that the time had come to burn my boats and make my purchases. Going out, I met Will Saxon on the doorstep. He was spottier than ever and red as a boiled beet. 'Do you want Joanna?' I asked, as he opened and closed his mouth silently. He shook his head, turning an even richer colour as he did so, and whipped a bunch of wilting tulips from behind his back. His hand, holding it, looked enormous: a huge, overgrown fruit sprouting from the shrunken stalk of his tweed jacket. 'For your mother,' he said in a hoarse growl and walked backwards, as if leaving a royal presence. He stumbled over a stone, recovered himself
186

and shot out of the gateway where he stopped to wave awkwardly at me and shoot a hunted glance at the upper windows of our house before vanishing down the street at a gallop.

'How kind,' Ellen said when I gave her his offering, 'but why?'

'Perhaps he really meant them for Joanna but didn't like to say,' I suggested. This seemed likely to be true, both because I knew it was how I would have behaved in Will's position, and because I suddenly wanted it to be: if Will were to make up their quarrel, Joanna might be diverted from the bottle. Perhaps, I thought excitedly, Will's appearance was a direct answer to my last night's prayers. 'Give them to her *now*,' I urged.

Ellen looked surprised. 'But suppose you're wrong? It might be embarrassing for her, don't you think?'

She was smiling, but the skin under her eyes was dark and she looked tired and older than she usually did. It seemed to me that she looked wistfully at the tulips and my anxiety for Joanna's reformation disappeared in a wave of remorse: poor Ellen, I thought, no one brings her flowers any more.

I said awkwardly, 'I expect it would. I expect I was wrong, anyway. I expect he did mean them for you, really.'

I hesitated, wondering why, and was visited by inspiration. 'I expect he remembers how nice you were to him when his father was in that trouble.'

'That was a long time ago,' Ellen said.

'I expect he remembers, though. I mean, it's not a thing you'd forget. And now . . .' I stopped, wondering if Will could have heard about the horrible telephone calls and the begging letters. 'I expect he wanted to cheer you up,' I said.

Ellen gave a queer little laugh. 'Why should he think I needed it?' She looked sad, suddenly, and I saw my tactless mistake: it wasn't flattering to think someone had brought you flowers just because they were sorry for you.

I thought of a better thing to say. 'Perhaps he's secretly in love with you.'

Ellen laughed, properly this time, and said, 'Get along, you silly baggage.'

I went to Jock's and bought Ellen's egg. It looked more beautiful close to than it had done in the window and the thread in the tinsel ribbon shone like real gold. It was the best egg I had ever seen. The girl who sold it to me found a cardboard box to put it in and some tissue paper and said, 'I guessed you'd be coming in. I've seen you looking in the window. Is the egg for your Mummy?' Though I knew she meant to be nice, I was embarrassed because she had said 'Mummy' as if I were a child and other people waiting to be served had heard her, so I shook my head and said no, I would be eating it myself, and counted my change frowningly, as if I suspected her of cheating me.

The cardboard box was clumsy and kept slipping. I had one bad moment when I crossed the street and stumbled on the kerb. I spent threepence on a carrier bag from the greengrocer's: this cut down the risk of breaking the egg, but it also left my finances seriously diminished.

I went into Woolworth's. Jane Owen was standing by the jewellery counter, trying the effect of brass hoop earrings against her narrow face. I told her they looked stupid on her and went to buy a chocolate nest with five candied eggs in it, for Poll. I got Aunt Hat a nest too, because they were cheap and pretty, a cream-filled egg with a real shell round it for Boyd, and a chocolate rabbit for Joanna. Left with a penny, I bought two halfpenny chews and gave one to Jane who had followed me over to the sweet counter, because I had been unkind about the earrings.

She thanked me, rather absently, and we left the store. I thought she was still angry with me, so I showed her Ellen's egg, to be friendly. She was polite but not very interested: while I re-packed the egg and arranged the rest of my purchases carefully in the carrier bag, she stood silent, watching me with a funny little smile on her face.

I thought she had decided not to speak until she had had a formal apology, so I said I was sorry about the earrings,

188

they really hadn't looked bad at all. 'I just thought they were a bit big for your face.'

She looked vague. 'Oh, I wasn't thinking about that, I wasn't going to buy them anyway. I was thinking about something else.' The mysterious smile hovered on her lips while she waited for me to ask her what it was.

I determined not to give her that pleasure, since I could see from her smile and sly, darting looks that it was something she was burning to tell me. As we walked down the street, I stared straight ahead of me and hummed under my breath with elaborate unconcern.

She held out until we reached the intersection where our ways parted. Then she coloured brightly and said she didn't suppose I knew, but there had been a dreadful scene here yesterday afternoon: on this very spot, Mr Claud Fantom had stood in front of Boyd's car while he waited at the traffic lights, banged with his walking stick on the bonnet and shouted that he would have the law on him for doing away with his sister.

Chapter Sixteen

Boyd complained that Mr Fantom had dented his bonnet. 'You should have stopped him,' I said, shocked. Jane Owen, who claimed to have been there and seen it all, had said that the traffic lights had changed twice before a policeman appeared to persuade Mr Fantom to move out of Boyd's way, and, all the time he had been cursing and thumping the bonnet and a crowd gathered, Boyd had just sat there behind the wheel, waiting, saying nothing.

'Why on earth didn't you tell me?' Ellen cried. She got up from her chair and went to the door to listen.

'It's all right, Poll's in the kitchen with Aunt Hat. They're making fudge,' Joanna said.

Ellen closed the door and came slowly back to sit on the edge of her chair. She smoothed her skirt nervously over her knees as she looked at Boyd.

'Why didn't I tell you?' Boyd smiled. 'It hardly seemed worth mentioning.'

'Not worth . . . ' Ellen expelled a long breath. 'The man must be raving mad!'

Joanna emerged from her cloistered silence in a burst of indignation. 'You ought to have the law on *him*. He can't go round saying things like that, it's libel.'

'Slander,' Boyd said.

'He ought to be sent to prison!'

'That's silly, you can't send a person to prison just because he says Boyd went to his sister's funeral,' I said reasonably.

They all stared at me. I stared at the carpet, unfocusing my eyes, so that the colours swam together. Boyd cleared his throat. 'Joanna, look at his side for a moment. They didn't get on, of course, but he thought he had been doing his best for his sister. I even think he had honestly come to believe they were poor. People have had stranger delusions and he had some grounds for this one. He'd kept the house going for years – she didn't contribute a penny. When I came along poking my nose in, it made him look either a fraud or a fool. Neither is pleasant.'

Ellen spoke with impatient anger. 'Oh, I can see he might have had it in for you. But to suggest . . .'

'It's *horrible*. He *must* be mad . . .' Joanna's voice made me tremble. Boyd went to her and put his arm round her shoulders.

'No,' he said. 'Just a man with a grievance.' He looked down at her thoughtfully. 'Though I agree, he wasn't exactly in a state of reason . . .'

Joanna said breathlessly, 'But there was a crowd there, everyone heard him. What will people think?'

Boyd laughed out loud. 'Whatever they were thinking

190

before, I daresay. Don't worry about it. It was a foolish incident, I hardly think he'll repeat it.'

'Let's hope he's got it out of his system,' Ellen said.

Joanna looked from one to the other. 'But don't you *see*? I mean, suppose he goes to the police?'

'Don't be silly, Joanna,' Boyd said. He spoke lightly, almost gaily, and I felt a warm surge of inexplicable relief – inexplicable because if I had known the second Jane told me that there was a darker interpretation to Mr Fantom's words than the one I had immediately and confidently produced, I had obliterated the knowledge in that same fragment of time, shut it off so completely that I could hardly be said to know it now. All that remained from that monstrously embarrassing moment was this sudden feeling of comfort and safety that enfolded me when Boyd spoke in that cheerful, unworried way. It was as if I had woken in the night frightened of some vague shape in the corner of the room and he had come in and switched on the light to show me there was no shadow there.

Ellen said, 'Katey, dear, why don't you take Poll down to the park? It's such a lovely day.'

'You only call me Katey dear when you want to get rid of me,' I observed coldly, but I went just the same. When we came back, they were all still sitting there. Ellen and Boyd seemed very cheerful and Joanna was drinking a glass of sherry.

I asked her what they had talked about while I was at the park with Poll, but, 'You're a silly oaf to listen to that stupid Jane Owen,' was all she would say. 'Making bloody mountains out of molehills. I tell you one sure thing, Kate Boyd, when I grow up I'm not going to live in a ghastly bloody suburb like Monks Ford full of ghastly awful people who are so sick and bored with their own mean, messy little lives that all they can find to do is muck up other people's. Mutter, mutter, mutter, do you know what the so-and-so did, *did* he *really*, well, who'd have thought it? God Almighty. People are so shoddy I can't bear it.'

'Where would you like to live then, London?'

London's too provincial nowadays. I'd want to live in Europe – Rome or Paris. Not New York. Americans have refrigerators but no souls. I couldn't bear to live in a materialistic society. Maybe I shall withdraw from the world altogether and go into a convent.'

I thought she sounded more normal than she had done for a long time.

Later that night I got up to get a glass of water and heard my parents talking in their bedroom.

'. . . but needs not strive, officiously to keep alive,' I heard Boyd say, and then, 'It's not what I did, but what I didn't do.'

I thought it strange that he should have taken to quoting poetry in his old age and was about to pad on, to the bathroom, when he said something that riveted my attention. 'Oh, I agree . . . better if she'd left the lot to a cat's home.'

Ellen murmured something; the bedsprings creaked. 'No, that's very unlikely,' Boyd said. 'On the other hand, he can bring a case himself, you know, he has the right, though I can't think it could come to anything. Withholding antibiotics in a case like this can hardly be called criminal neglect. but it might make things awkward if he maintains I knew of my financial expectations!

'That's ridiculous,' Ellen said. 'He can't say that.'

'Can't prove it, no. But I can't prove I didn't, can I?' He sighed, there was a click as he turned off the light.

'But you've done nothing,' Ellen said, her voice light and strained, 'nothing that any decent doctor wouldn't . . .'

Boyd said, very dryly, 'Oh, my conscience is clear.'

I had cramp in my left foot. I shifted my position and a board creaked, not loud enough to alert them but loud enough to scare me. I crept back to bed and lay uncomfortably awake. It seemed to me that Boyd was in trouble and that it was all my fault. Mr Fantom was going to have the law on him because Miss Fantom had left him that money; Mr Fantom had shouted at Boyd and thumped the car because

192

he believed Boyd had known she was going to leave it to him and this was against the law. Mr Fantom couldn't prove it, Boyd said, but I knew that he could: he could prove it because I had lied. Behind the red screen of my closed eyelids Mr Fantom danced, black, faceless, a jerky figure in a shadow show, he waved his arms and shouted, *undue influence*, *I know you were only after her money because Miss Carter told me so*, I moaned and opened my eyes. In the bed beside me, Poll was making a loud, sucking sound in her sleep. I moaned a little louder. Nothing happened. I broke into affected sobs.

The landing light switched on and Boyd came in to me, his bare feet squeaking on the linoleum. He crouched and asked me what I was crying for.

My tears were real now. Murmuring, he slid one arm under my neck, lifting my head from the pillow. 'What's the matter?' he asked – and I didn't tell him. Not from fear, forgiveness was as close as his warm shoulder, but because, in that split second my head left the pillow and came to rest against him, I suddenly thought, *this won't change it*. I say, in that split second, but it wasn't really a revelation, it was something I already knew, a lesson I could have learned before if I had been ready to. I had lied to Miss Carter and nothing could change that, nothing *had* changed it: none of the other lies and deceptions with which I had tried to cover it up had changed, or ever would change, that original lie. To confess and be forgiven was no earthly use, could undo nothing, comfort no one except myself. And at this point the memory came up as if it had been waiting to meet me here: Boyd saying, *you have to learn to live with what you do*. I hadn't understood it then: I understood it now.

I told the first lie of my adult life. 'I've got the most horrible tummy ache,' I said.

Aunt Hat had made pounds of lemon curd. No one except Poll liked lemon curd and a great many jars stood reproachfully in the cupboard. When Aunt Hat was out shopping, Ellen said, 'I wonder if Miss Carter would like a jar. Take one in to her, will you, Kate?'

My heart thumped. 'Must I?'

'Why not?'

'Perhaps she doesn't like lemon curd.'

'She'll be pleased, anyway. I feel a bit guilty; we've not seen much of her lately,' Ellen said.

I walked up our neighbour's front path as if going to the gallows. My hand shook so much that it was an effort to pull at the Austrian cow bell, dangling at the side of her porch. She opened the door. It was ten o'clock in the morning and she was doing her housework in a flowered wrapper. There was a smudge of stove black on her forehead.

'Ellen wondered if you'd like some lemon curd.' She frowned at me. 'Aunt Hat made it, it's very good,' I said, and she wiped her hands down the front of her wrapper and took the jar.

'Thank your mother,' she said coldly, and waited for me to go.

I didn't move. They say hatred is akin to love and, remembering how I felt about Miss Carter, I know it to be true: hatred draws you to your enemy, compels you to observe every detail of their appearance with fascinated attention. Everything about Miss Carter was repulsive to me – the bleached moustache on her upper lip, her stiff, frayed hair, every knob and ridge of bone beneath her pallid skin that had a slight, surface dampness like the sweat on cheese – and yet I couldn't take my eyes off her.

My fixed stare made her uneasy. She said, avoiding my eyes, 'I suppose you want a glass of lemonade?'

I nodded, ignoring her grudging tone. 'Oh, well . . .' she said, shrugging her shoulders a little so that the cotton wrapper fell away from her neck, disclosing a pink, knitted vest.

I followed her into her front living room which was the same size as ours but appeared smaller, owing to the set of heavy Jacobean dining chairs that lined the walls and the dominating presence of a grand piano on which photographs were arranged: her mother as a bride, in lace; as a young matron with her plain daughter on her lap; as an old lady

194

with her hair in stiff, white waves and a large Cairngorm brooch pinning the neck of her dress. Miss Carter's mother had been good looking in a severe way; her father, after whom Miss Carter took, was not. There was only one photograph of him, angular in plus-fours, and beside it, another photograph I had not seen before, of a stern, rather mournful-looking man in uniform.

I examined this photograph while she left me to fetch a glass of lemon squash and a Marie biscuit. Sipping my squash, which was watery, I felt nervously impelled to make conversation. 'He's awfully handsome, isn't he?'

'A very distinguished face.' Miss Carter moved the picture a little, to put it in alignment with the others.

I gulped at the lemonade while she watched me. Almost before I had finished she held out her hand for the glass. Her lack of enthusiasm for my company made me desperate to ingratiate myself. 'Is he a friend?' I asked, jerking my head at the photograph and smiling idiotically.

'Yes. A very dear friend.'

'He looks awfully nice.'

'Yes.'

'Is he . . .' Something about the set of the eyes inspired me. 'Is he a foreigner?'

'Yes.' Miss Carter looked at me: her working mouth betrayed an inward struggle. Intellect warned her to remain on guard, but her need to talk was stronger. 'A Polish Count from a very fine old family. We met during the war when he was serving in the R.A.F.' She put her head on one side and pushed back a straying wisp of hair with a preening movement. 'That doesn't really do him justice, though. He's not smiling, and he had a beautiful smile.'

'Have you got any other pictures? I'd love to see them.'

'Well, I have one, I think.'

Her smile, shy and eager, had lost all trace of suspicion. She rummaged in the bookcase for a red leather album and we sat side by side on two of the Jacobean chairs, while she turned the pages. The album was devoted to Miss Carter's career in the W.A.A.F. All teeth and boney knees, she was photographed with other women in uniform, standing in front of huts, aeroplane hangars, and once, daringly, at an indoor bar with a tankard of beer in her hand. 'Taken by flash, of course,' Miss Carter said.

The snapshot of the Count came near the end. He stood between Miss Carter and another, prettier, woman. 'The girl with us was my friend Clara,' Miss Carter said. With *us*? I wondered. The Count was definitely hugging Clara: round Miss Carter's shoulders, his other arm seemed only casually draped.

Miss Carter closed the album on a reminiscent sigh. 'Oh – those were happy days.'

'Was he your boy friend?' I asked, slyly.

She looked at me, lips parted. 'We loved each other,' she said.

A pleasurable excitement rose up in me. 'Why didn't you marry him, then?'

'He had a wife in Poland.' She got up from her chair and stood, the album clasped to her chest, her profile dreamily raised. 'It was hard for us both when the war ended, and he had to go home.'

She seemed to have fallen into a kind of trance. I was embarrassed for her. I coughed and said, 'He's terribly handsome, like a film star. But he looks rather sad in that picture – the one on the piano.'

Miss Carter lifted her shoulders and pouted her mouth in a foreign way. 'Oh – that exile's look! You often see it in men who are forced to live away from the country they love.' She bent to put the album away. When she straightened up, she was a little flushed and not entirely, I fancied, from stooping. 'Claud – Mr Fantom – has it,' she said in a hushed, excited voice.

I could only stare.

'Yes,' she mused, 'he has it! It was one of the things I first noticed. India is *his* country. And of course *he* has no chance of going back.'

'But he's not an Indian.'

Miss Carter smiled. 'It is the country where his heart lies.

I know that now. We've had one or two really good old talks. He needs someone to talk to, alone in that great old house, I flatter myself that I've been able to cheer him up.'

My pulse had begun to beat painfully. I mumbled, 'It was awfully sad about his sister, wasn't it?'

'Sad? Yes, I suppose so.'

She tossed her head with a loud laugh and, plumping on her knees before the bookcase, began to pull out books and bang them together to get rid of the dust. I saw that she felt she had been making a fool of herself and was trying, as I would have done in her place, to erase the memory from her mind by a show of energetic behaviour. Coughing with the dust, she went on, 'Of course Mr Fantom is deeply hurt. He doesn't say so, he's very proud, but I can see how he feels. And understand it too – to my mind, she treated him abominably. After all those years of devotion, one can hardly credit it! Her will was a terrible shock to him, though not to other people, apparently.' As she completed this sentence she paused, books all about her, on the floor, in her lap, and gave me an unfriendly but conspiratorial smile. 'You were right about that, Miss, weren't you?'

I clasped my hands together. They felt wet and horribly slippery. My voice came out thick and hoarse. 'My father didn't know anything about the money,' I said.

She raised her eyebrows and pulled down the corners of her mouth in an expression of satirical disbelief. She looked at me steadily, her muscles fixed for about fifty seconds in this unattractive grimace, before she said, 'Well, that's hardly something I can discuss with a little girl, is it?' She craned her neck backwards to look at the mahogany clock that stood on the mantelshelf, flanked by two green plaster cats. 'Goodness, is that the *time*?'

Her joints cracked as she got up to shepherd me into the hall. One hand on the front door latch, she cleared her throat and said, 'Kate – did your father tell you to come?'

Here was my chance. I could have told her the truth, then. She would have believed me: I knew, in spite of everything, that she was not really a fool. But her hand was on my shoulder, her face was close to mine, and I was overtaken by such complete physical aversion that I felt dizzy and sick: I was afraid that if I stayed a second longer, I might *be* sick. 'No, Ellen did,' was all I could gasp.

The afternoon was wet. After tea, Aunt Hat said she thought she might make one of her apple pies for supper; would Poll and I like to make a pastry man?

We were in the kitchen when Miss Carter came. We heard Ellen answer the door and call upstairs to Boyd. There was a murmur of voices: the dining room door closed and Ellen came into the kitchen, looking puzzled. She admired Poll's man which had been worked on so hard that it was grey and sweaty, and began to peel potatoes.

Aunt Hat peeled apples, taking off the skins in one long coil and giving them to Poll and me to throw over our shoulders; when they fell, they were supposed to form the initials of the man you were going to marry.

'Your's is a "G" I think,' Aunt Hat said to me, her brown eyes shining with the secret she thought we shared. Sorry I had ever mentioned Gus to her, I stared back blankly and said it didn't look like that to me.

'Mine's a "W",' Poll said. 'That means I'm going to marry Walter. He said he wouldn't, last week, but I'll ask him again next time he comes to tea.'

'You'll have to live in a caravan if you marry Walter.'

'I'd like to live in a caravan.'

'With a horse and dog, like the Pedlar man,' Aunt Hat suddenly sang.

'I'd hate it, personally,' I said coldly, looking out of the kitchen window at the sad, rainy garden. '*Personally*, I'm going to marry a business tycoon and live in the South of France. I'm fed up with this damned country.'

'Don't talk in that silly voice,' Ellen said, from the sink.

Glowering, I thumped my pastry man viciously.

'Oh, look now, you've spoiled him, duckie,' Aunt Hat said.

'He's my damn pastry man.'

'Now, now, naughty words,' Aunt Hat said.

198

'*I* don't swear.' Poll knelt on the chair to reach the raisins. 'It's not nice manners. I've got nice manners. I don't swear and I always say thank you for having me. Can Walter come to tea tomorrow?'

'If you like.'

'You always say yes when *Poll* asks,' I complained. 'It's always no dear, another time, when *I* do. It's not fair.'

'I've got more friends than you have,' Poll said. 'I've got six friends. You've only got silly old Jane Owen.'

'That's not true,' I screamed, and advanced on her.

'Oh, do *stop it*,' Ellen said, waving the potato knife, half angry, half pretending to be.

Poll said, 'I've got six friends. Walter and Gilly and Hermione and Richard and Angela Harris and David Crosbie. They've got to be my friends because they're in my gang and I'm the head of the gang and Walter's the second head. They all have to do what I say when I'm there and when I'm not they have to do what Walter says. Jessie wanted to be in our gang because ours is the top gang in the whole school but we wouldn't let her because she's a cry baby bunting. She cries when you do the Chinese burn . . .'

The dining-room door opened and we heard voices. Miss Carter's, the words inaudible, and then Boyd's. He said, speaking loudly and precisely, 'You must do whatever your conscience tells you, Miss Carter.'

Poll said, '*I* don't cry when people do tortures on me.'

The front door shut with a slam.

'I can light matches and put my fingers in the flame, I can't keep them there long yet, but I expect I shall if I practise.'

Boyd stood in the kitchen doorway. His face was white and sharp-looking as if he had suddenly gone thinner.

'Did you know Fantom was a chum of Miss Carter's?' he asked Ellen. He seemed hardly conscious that anyone else was in the room.

Ellen turned from the sink. She said slowly, 'I didn't know he had any friends.'

There was a muscle twitching below Boyd's eye. He must

have been conscious of it because he put up his hand and dragged at his cheek, exposing the red under-lid. 'It seems she's his confidante and . . . well . . . his informer, I rather gathered, though it was very delicately put. So delicately, that it was some time before I realized I was being accused . . .' His eye swept the room and lighted on Poll who was kneeling on the chair again. Head bent and breathing hard, she was placing a row of raisin buttons down the centre of her pastry man. Boyd smiled, coldly. 'Not directly, of course. She came to warn me. She felt it her duty.'

'I know that kind of duty.' Ellen was standing in the middle of the room, hugging her arms across her chest as if she were cold.

'Yes. She said that certain things about my treatment of my patient had come to her attention, and she thought it right to approach me.'

Ellen made a small, choked sound. She went up to Boyd and seemed to lean against him.

'Oh dear,' Aunt Hat said in a worried voice. 'I do hope it was nothing' I said.

Boyd looked at her thoughtfully. Then he put his hand on Ellen's shoulder and led her out of the kitchen.

Aunt Hat stared after them. She looked shabby; her pink cheeks fell in little pouches. She wiped her hands down her apron and said, 'That's a lovely man, Poll.'

'He's Mr Fantom,' Poll said. 'You can tell because I've put two fat currants to make his nose.'

I slipped out of the kitchen, closed the door, and hovered in the hall. The sitting room door was open.

'. . . told her that when pneumonia sets in at this juncture, you just thank God for his mercy,' Boyd was saying. 'That no one in their senses would have wanted her dragged back. Trouble is, I suppose, that he's not in his senses. And it wasn't, anyway, all she had to say. . . .' There was the click of the drinks cupboard and the pop and hiss as Boyd opened a bottle of beer. 'She took some time to get round to her other suggestion. Which is that I was . . . well . . . over-generous with drugs. . . .'

Ellen said something I couldn't catch. Her voice had a furry sound as if she had a mouthful of cotton wool.

Boyd said, 'She had some long story about her mother. It was hardly relevant . . . though perhaps it was, to *her*.' He paused, and went on in a thoughtful, considering tone. 'Of course there *is* an argument . . . as a patient acquires tolerance to a drug you have to give progressively larger doses and morphine, for example, will depress the respiratory centre. It's a nice point . . . whether in that sort of case, death is caused by the pneumonia, or by the drug. . . .'

'You didn't tell *her* that?' Ellen cried.

'No. I merely said that I gave my patient what I thought necessary to relieve her pain. That, at this stage in her illness, it was my only consideration as it would have been for any decent, humane physician. She was kind enough to say that she, personally, didn't doubt my probity as a doctor, but that it might be difficult to convince Claud . . . they're on Christian name terms, apparently. She said she had only come because she was worried about his attitude and wanted to know how best to advise him. Really, of course, she just wanted the pleasure of telling me. . . .'

'*Could* she be so malicious?'

'That did surprise me. She seemed so . . . personally hostile.'

'Oh, God,' Ellen said. 'But no one would listen to her, surely? Or to *him*. A malicious woman and that . . . that crackpot?'

'Malice, indiscretion . . . that's the way these things happen.'

'Gossip, yes. But *legally* . . .?'

'Oh . . . the law is a sprung trap,' Boyd said. He sounded very tired. 'Of course he can get someone to listen. In a way, it would be wrong if he couldn't. The most likely thing, I suppose, is an action for professional neglect. He could argue . . . it's not impossible . . . that if she'd lived a few days longer, she might have changed her will.' He laughed suddenly, without amusement.

Ellen's voice shook. 'No one could believe that!'

'I hope not. But if you throw mud, some will stick. . . .'

There was a silence. The sofa squeaked; one of them must be leaning forward to get their drink.

'What can we do?' Ellen said.

'Nothing.'

'*Nothing?* But we can't just wait. . . .'

'We have to. There really is nothing we can do.'

'You could talk to him, get him to see reason. . . .'

'No. I've done nothing I'm ashamed to have done. I'd rather it came out than stayed festering.'

'*You'd* rather? I was thinking of the children.'

'D'you think I'm not?' There was a *thump* as Boyd's feet hit the floor. D'you think I wouldn't want to spare them? But not *this* way. Oh, I daresay I could crawl, beg him to keep his mouth shut. What good would that do? D'you think they wouldn't find out, in the end? And what do you think they'd learn then . . . that I was afraid to let the truth come out! That I'd done something wrong and tried to hide it!'

Ellen said bitterly, 'You're thinking of their opinion of you?'

'No. *Yes* . . . but not in the way you mean. We've tried to bring them up honestly, haven't we? You can't tell children one thing and do another.'

Ellen was crying. 'It's the publicity . . . it would be in all the papers, wouldn't it? Oh . . . you know what I'm afraid of . . .'

Boyd's voice was suddenly gentle. 'You've been frightened of that too long. You've made a kind of prison for yourself.'

'Only for the children's sake.'

'Maybe that was wrong. Not in the beginning, perhaps, but maybe it's wrong now. They're growing, they're curious, you can't shut them up safe for ever, or you'll make a prison for them, too.'

'Poll's only seven.' Her voice broke with sudden anger. 'Oh . . . I could *kill* Hat. . . .'

My legs had begun to shake. I went back into the kitchen and slipped out the back door. The rain had stopped and the sky arched over me, green and clear. It was like being inside a crystal ball.

Poll came out after me. 'My man's cooking,' she said. 'Let's play hopscotch.'

We played hopscotch until Aunt Hat called us in, standing on the back doorstep and saying, Someone had just telephoned her, we couldn't guess who, could we?

Ellen was in the kitchen. My chest felt tight at the sight of her, but she was looking quite ordinary and smiling at Aunt Hat as if she wasn't angry with her at all, only pleased that her stepson's ship had just docked at Tilbury, and that he would soon be coming to see us all.

Chapter Seventeen

Aunt Hat cried when Dick came: he patted her shoulder affectionately and said, 'Turn off the waterworks, Mum, home is the sailor and all that. . . .'

He was a sturdy, sandy young man with clean square hands, and well-kept nails with beautiful half-moons. He was not the figure of tragedy I had expected nor the dashing lover that Aunt Hat had inevitably suggested to Joanna that he might be. 'Oh, you'll like my Dick, take my word for it, you two will get on like a house on fire,' she promised her at frequent intervals during the two days that had to pass before his visit. To me she was more explicit. 'He's not bookish, dear, but that's not everything, is it? In other ways he's just Joanna's type. It would be nice if they really took to each other, wouldn't it?'

The result of this romantic speculation was that when Dick arrived Joanna was so stupefied with shyness that she could barely speak to him and when she did, it was so abruptly that Ellen raised her eyebrows. Dick did not seem to mind this, if indeed he noticed it: all his attention was focused on Aunt Hat whom he teased all the time in a gentle, loving way that made her preen herself like a girl. With the rest of us, he was rather silent. He played Halma and Monopoly with Poll and me but, though he listened attentively when Ellen or Boyd spoke to him and answered all their questions with painstaking politeness, he appeared most of the time distant and abstracted as if he had something much more important on his mind. Once or twice I found him sitting alone, his mouth moving silently and his eyes fixed on a point directly in front of him as if he were having an imaginary conversation with a ghost in the opposite chair. 'Potty,' was Joanna's verdict when I told her of this curious behaviour. 'I expect that biff on the head damaged his brain.'

It was not so desperate. What was troubling him, it turned out, was how to suggest to Ellen and Boyd that he might be allowed to pay for Aunt Hat's board, while she had been staying with us. Of course he knew it could only be a token, he said, bursting out with it about an hour before the end of his three-day visit and speaking rapidly and shyly; he could never repay them for all they had done, he knew that, please don't think he didn't, but he had saved money on this voyage for just this purpose. He had been worrying for weeks how best to put it to them and he knew he wasn't doing it very well. . . .

Once over the first fence he became so voluble that it was difficult for Boyd to get a word in. It was also difficult for him to refuse Dick's offer without appearing grand: in the end he said that Dick was very kind but that the indebtedness was really on our side since Aunt Hat had been a great help to us and had more than paid for her keep. When the boy's face fell – and he wasn't much more than a boy I realize now, though I didn't then – Boyd went on to say that if he had really saved a little and wanted to help his stepmother, he was sure there would be plenty of opportunity in the future. Dick said, shyly, that he had thought of that.

Perhaps now 'Mum' was stronger, though he knew she would be sorry to leave us, she might like to have somewhere of her own, a flat, or a cottage: he had saved enough, he said, for the first few months' rent.

The tears came into Aunt Hat's eyes. She said he was a dear, good boy, but of course once she was on her feet and really settled, she wouldn't take a penny from him: she was a young woman, not an old crock, she could earn her living. Dick said, quite crossly, that this was nonsense, he was responsible for her and he intended to see she was looked after. He hesitated a minute before he went on to say that he hoped she had no idea of going back to Jack when he came out of prison, if she had, she was to put it out of her mind at once. Aunt Hat looked vague at this and merely repeated that he was a dear, good boy, but his gentle bullying seemed to make her happy. I was hurt because her happiness seemed to be occasioned by the prospect of leaving us and only slightly mollified when she gathered Poll and me into her arms and said she couldn't bear the thought of leaving us, she really couldn't, but when she did find a little place of her own, somewhere in the country, perhaps, we would be her very first visitors, wouldn't we? 'But I don't want you to go,' Poll cried, winding her arms tight round Aunt Hat's neck and hiding her face in her scented shoulder.

Dick's departure took place in an atmosphere thick with goodwill. After he had gone, Boyd and Ellen said a great many complimentary things about him to Aunt Hat, which made her eyes shine. I was in that weepy state that sad but joyful emotion usually produces, and, when Ellen shouted angrily at me before supper because I stumbled carrying a vegetable dish into the dining room and dropped it on the floor, I actually burst into tears and rushed upstairs. Since Poll was already asleep, I took refuge in Joanna's room, slamming the door.

I sat on her bed and waited. Ellen was often sharp with us but she was just: I had broken the dish by accident and as soon as she realized she had been unfair, she would come up and say so. I blew my nose and got up to fetch Joanna's hand mirror which I propped up on its shank against the Greek dictionary on her desk. I sat down, pulled open the desk drawer, and twisted the Anglepoise lamp forward. These strategic preparations completed, I crouched so that I could get a good view of my face and was disappointed to see that it was not as ravaged as I had hoped. Forcing myself to yawn, I managed to squeeze out a few more tears and then froze: someone was at the door. In one swift, practised movement, I pushed the mirror into the drawer, closed it, and leaned my forehead wearily on my hand.

But it was only Joanna who opened the door on this despairing scene and she was unimpressed. 'Supper,' she said coldly. I followed her downstairs and slipped into my place at the table, stiff with indignation. 'Can you eat two potatoes?' Ellen asked, spoon poised.

' I don't want any supper.'

Silently, she filled my plate and passed it to me. I sat and looked at it. Everyone else began to eat. I sniffed audibly once or twice, but no one took any notice.

I said, 'I didn't mean to break that old dish.'

Ellen looked at me as if she hardly saw me. Her eyes were vacant. 'You might have said you were sorry.'

I stared. I *had* said I was sorry – before she shouted at me. 'Eat your supper,' she said.

I pushed my plate away. The gravy slopped on to the cloth.

'Eat your supper.' She was not eating her's, but sitting motionless, the serving spoon still clasped tightly in her hand. 'Eat your supper, eat your supper' – she repeated the words in a strange, sing-song chant and then, very slowly, put the spoon down on the table before her. It looked as if her fingers were stuck round the handle and she had to try very hard to unloose them.

Childish rage burned up inside me, rage that was not caused altogether by her unfairness, but had some roots in jealousy: she had said so many pleasant things about Dick this afternoon, when had she ever said them about *me*?

'You should have said *you* were sorry,' I shouted.

Her eyes focused on me briefly, then she made a little sound midway between a moan and a cough and bowed her head forward so that her hair was almost in her untouched plate of stew.

'You didn't even come *up*,' I wailed. Joanna kicked me under the table and Boyd said, loudly, 'Leave the room this minute, Kate.'

I went without a word. He followed me into the dark kitchen where I stood with my face buried in the roller towel on the back door. He switched on the light. 'What's all this about?'

'I *told* you . . .'

He said yes, yes, he knew all that, but I was making rather a fuss about very little, wasn't I? He was not unkind, but his kindness was perfunctory and his eyes fell on me with a restless, flickering look as if, like Ellen, he wasn't really seeing me.

'She's unfair,' I complained hotly, twisting my hand in the roller towel and yanking it viciously backwards and forwards. 'She hates me, she wishes I were *dead*. . . .'

'Stop being stupid,' he commanded, and then, making an effort to control his irritability, said that he thought I was old enough to be a bit more sensible. Ellen was tired, surely I could see that? He seemed to hesitate. Then, 'She's got a great deal to worry her at the moment, try not to ride her too hard.'

His return to gentleness made my eyes smart. 'I don't see what she's got . . .' I began mutinously and then stopped, terrified by a sensation that I had only had before in dreams: that I was being forced to open a door that I knew gave on to darkness. 'She doesn't have to be so beastly,' I cried, pouting like Poll – and knowing I was pouting like Poll.

'That's enough,' Boyd said. 'Since you don't want any supper, Kate, you had better go to bed. Perhaps you will be in a more amiable frame of mind in the morning.'

In fact, the morning found me in a mood of revenge. My parents had behaved unfairly to me – well, let them take the consequences! Since they cared so little about me, I would show them how little *I* cared. From henceforward, I would take no more part in family life.

Pursuing this resolve, I faced them at breakfast with cold politeness. When they spoke to me, I answered in bleak monosyllables and, since I had decided that only a full-blown apology could earn my forgiveness, responded to smiles with a poker face.

If they noticed my withdrawal, they did not comment upon it. This roused me to fresh excesses of righteous anger. That morning, I left my bed unmade and determined that for the rest of the time I was forced by law to remain under my parent's roof, I would come home only for meals and at night, to sleep.

Though my resolution wavered after the first day, I did, for a while, draw a veil between me and them. And not altogether out of spite, I see now: it was, in a way, a measure of self-protection.

Easter was over, the holidays ended, the days lengthened. I gave up going to Fellowship: my love for Gus was dead and with it, my desire for religion. Instead, I took to sex, hanging round the rustic-oak park shelters with other girls, giggling and talking in loud voices for the benefit of the boys who leaned against their gleaming bicycles a few yards away. Occasionally one of us would be offered a boiled sweet or a piece of gum, or a girl would leave the group and walk home with a boy, the girl on the pavement, the boy straddling his bicycle in the gutter. Sometimes, following this courtship ritual to its logical conclusion, I imagined myself becoming pregnant, though, for all our parents' instruction, the actual process by which this would be achieved was foggy in my mind. It would serve Ellen and Boyd right, I thought. But no one even offered to take me home though one boy, whose name I have forgotten, took to walking by our house those spring evenings, looking up at the windows and loudly whistling a popular tune. I remember that I hid behind the bedroom curtains to watch him pass.

It seemed an age went by, but it can only have been about two weeks.

One Saturday morning in May, Mr Fantom appeared at our back door with Poll in his arms. She was bleeding from a cut below her left eye. In short, barking sentences Mr Fantom informed Ellen that she had gone up to the tower and climbing up to fetch an old newspaper from the top of the tank, had slipped and fallen, cutting her face on the corner of a tin trunk. Red in the face, Poll began to sob. 'More fear than anything,' Ellen said, and handed her to Joanna who bore her off to the bathroom.

Mr Fantom remained on the back doorstep. 'I really don't understand what Poll was doing,' Ellen said. 'She'd been told . . .' She stopped: I suppose it hardly seemed polite to tell Mr Fantom that Poll had been warned to keep out of his way.

Mr Fantom did not reply. He stood woodenly in the doorway. The top of his forehead was white, as if he always wore a hat when out in the sun.

Ellen rubbed her hands up and down her skirt and screwed up her eyes. Then she asked him, stiffly, if he would like a cup of tea. He looked at her in a puzzled way as if she had spoken in a foreign language. Then he came into the kitchen.

'Won't you sit down?' I asked politely, and he sat down at the kitchen table, his hands on his spread knees, and stared straight in front of him.

Ellen put the kettle on. Blinking nervously, she jerked her head at me to go away, but I pretended not to see.

Nothing happened. A fly buzzed on the sticky paper over the sink. The kettle began to steam.

Ellen said, 'I was very s-sorry about your sister.'

Mr Fantom appeared not to have heard her. Then, after a long silence, he said, 'I wish I'd been better to the old bitch when she was alive.' He lifted his arms, spread them flat on the table and bowed his head between them. He stayed there like that, not moving.

Ellen made the tea. She took a blue and white cup from

209

the dresser and filled it. She put the cup, the jug of milk, the bowl of sugar, down by Mr Fantom's elbow. Then she looked at me.

This time I left, shutting the kitchen door. I went upstairs and looked out of the landing window. It was a grey day, and beyond Lock View the gulls, whirling near the river, looked very white.

I stood there a long time, until Mr Fantom came out of the house and went across the lawn to the hole in the fence which he had broken open further, so that he could climb through with Poll. He stepped through, replaced the swinging board, and vanished.

Ellen came singing up the stairs. Her face looked fuller and softer. She went into the bathroom where Joanna was still bathing Poll's cut and fussed over Poll, calling her, 'poor little twiddle-puss.' Then she came out, opened the landing window and leaned out to breathe in great gulps of air. 'What was she doing, the silly child?' she said, but there was an abstracted, smiling look on her face and I knew she did not really want an answer.

Mr Fantom never came to our house again, but he had lifted a shadow from it. I don't think I knew until that morning what a bad time it had been – or perhaps I had simply not dared to admit that I knew, until the time had passed.

But now it had, things were not the same. I discovered this slowly, with surprise. Although I had not clearly understood what was wrong – and had, in fact, deliberately closed my eyes to what I did understand, deliberately and childishly using ignorance as a shield – I could not help seeing that whatever had threatened us, Boyd and Ellen were powerless to prevent it. I had seen them as set apart, strong, invulnerable: now I knew they were no different from the rest of us, creatures that some blind mischance could destroy. This discovery every child makes sooner or later, if it came harder on me than is usual, it is because Boyd himself held to, and had passed on to us, his own belief in the strength of personal virtue: it was not only right to be good, but also

210

safer. Now, though I could still admire him for this and perhaps, even, loved him more, I saw it as an old-fashioned and innocent delusion that people wiser in the ways of the world had discarded. Rectitude, honour, goodness, were no protection against malicious chance: what you needed for real security I didn't know, but I suspected luck and cunning.

Cunning I could not supply, but luck I could do something about. I began to jump cracked paving stones, count green lorries, touch every third gatepost. I had not done such things for years: when Boyd caught me one morning, walking along the main street with my eyes closed – I had to count to five hundred before I opened them – he was puzzled. I might have wandered into the road and got run over, he said, and then questioned me. Were things all right at school, was I worried or upset about something? I said I just did these things for luck. He smiled and said he'd rather thought I had grown out of that sort of thing, and gave me a little lecture on superstition to which I attended with sophisticated tolerance.

Chapter Eighteen

The rhododendrons were out in the Fantom's garden; our camp – Poll's and Walter's camp now – was carpeted with their petals. One afternoon Mr Fantom cut armfuls of the mauve, waxy flowers and carried them into the house. Arrayed in a butcher's apron, his shirt sleeves rolled up, he hung Persian carpets over the line by the kitchen door and pounded them with what looked like an old tennis racket with most of the strings gone. I stood on the edge of the lawn that was white with fowl droppings, but he did not notice me. He worked in the determined way of a man of action, his expression absorbed, his colour fresh and high.

'He's spring-cleaning,' Poll told me when I asked her about this unaccustomed activity. 'He's going to tidy up the house and then he's going to advertise for a lodger. He says it will help to pay the rates.'

'It's a good thing he's got something to take his mind off things,' Aunt Hat said. 'There's nothing like an interest to take your mind off grief.'

Ellen said that grief was not quite the word she would have chosen, though she was sure Mr Fantom missed his sister: she had kept his adrenalin flowing.

Aunt Hat pulled a reproachful face as if Ellen had spoken ill of the dead and Ellen grew belligerent as honest people are often forced to do when truth runs counter to conventional sentiment. 'There's absolutely no point in pretending he loved her, Hat. But he was tied to her just the same, hating her kept him going. When she died there was nothing to stiffen him, nothing to pit himself against. Perhaps that was why he . . . what was really behind . . .'

She glanced at me and stopped. She and Aunt Hat were turning out the kitchen. Ellen climbed on to the steps and looked with some despair at the top shelf of the kitchen cupboard. 'Why all those tins of beetroot?' she muttered.

'That *other business*?' Aunt Hat finished for her, speaking in a meaning tone.

Ellen looked down at her, a clutch of tins in her arms.

Aunt Hat's coppery curls bounced as she shook her head. 'Oh, we don't have to look far for a reason for *that*, do we? Give me those tins, dear, and I'll pass up the dish cloth. That woman! Well, she's had her come-uppance all right, she's had her marching orders!'

Ellen dropped a tin. She got down off the steps and picked it up. 'How do you know, Hat?'

'Well, it seems Poll was in there, helping him dust and get things a bit tidy and My Lady came to the door. She'd brought some jam but he didn't want it, nor her. He told her to clear off quick-sharp. The old bitch, he said. Mind you, I don't think he should have spoken like that in front of the child, though I must say as far as she's concerned it's water off a duck's back, but I can hardly be sorry he's seen her for what she is. I daresay it was what made him turn around – looking at *her*, he could see how low and spiteful *he* was behaving!'

Ellen was rubbing the rust off a tin of beetroot, polishing it slowly and lovingly as if it were a piece of old silver.

'Poor woman,' she said.

'Poor woman!' Aunt Hat echoed. 'Really, Ellen.'

'She needs friends,' Ellen said, and blew some specks of rust off the top of the tin.

Aunt Hat snorted. 'Funny way to set about it, then. I told her a thing or two, I can tell you.'

Ellen looked at her with a faint air of wonder. She said, 'I wouldn't want you to lose a friend out of loyalty to us.'

'Oh, you can't run with the hare and hunt with the hounds.'

Ellen murmured, with a smile, that this was rather an unfortunate simile, wasn't it? Aunt Hat tossed her curls and said, 'Oh, she knows what *I* think, all right.'

Ellen sighed. 'She's got no one. It must be terrible, to be so alone.'

'Who's alone?' Joanna asked, coming in. She had been bicycling to get her hips down and looked pink and pretty.

'Don't pick up fag ends,' I said.

'Shut up. Who's alone?'

'Miss Carter.' Ellen climbed on the steps again and began to wipe the top shelf with a cloth. Her voice was muffled inside the cupboard. 'I was saying it must be sad to live on one's own.'

'Oh.' Joanna reflected, pushing her pale hair behind one red ear. Her face was blank at first but took on a queer, conniving expression as she looked at Aunt Hat and said, 'She's not the *only* person alone in this world.'

Miss Carter passed us in the street with lowered eyes and a mantling colour. But whatever shame and misery she privately felt, it had not diminished her loyal fervour. She was organizing a Coronation Pageant at the school, representing the Monarchy through the ages. Poll was to be Queen Elizabeth the First and Walter, Henry the Eighth. Ellen had volunteered to make both costumes and the dining table was covered with shiny satin and braid. 'It's not fair, *I'd* like to be Henry the Eighth. Off with her head,' Poll cried, making passes in the air with the kitchen knife.

'Queen Elizabeth executed plenty of people too,' Ellen said.

Aunt Hat clicked her tongue. 'You couldn't be Henry the Eighth. You're a little girl, it would look wrong.'

'It would *not*. I look like a boy. I'm flat in the chest.'

I giggled. 'Just being flat there doesn't make a boy.'

'I could stick something inside my trousers. I just hate being a horrible old girl.'

'Don't be silly, lambie-pie,' Aunt Hat said. 'Why it's nice being a little girl. Sugar and spice and all things nice, that's what little girls are made of.'

'Who cares? I'd rather be a bloody boy.'

'Penis-envy,' Joanna said in a light, remote voice.

Ellen took off the glasses she wore for sewing and said, 'Kate, why don't you and Poll go down to the field? They're setting up the marquee and the fair. It should be interesting.'

In Poll's floody field, the heavy lorries had already churned up the coarse, rank grass and the flowering hedges were filling up with empty tins, old tyres, newspapers, half-eaten sandwiches, broken bottles. Dogs barked round the heels of tethered horses, dark men in caps and coloured scarves moved purposefully between their caravans and converted buses and the still-shrouded amusements: the steam roundabout, the flying chairs, the rifle ranges, the lucky dips, the ping-pong balls that danced on a jet of water and the fishing ducks where you got a prize every time. One part of the field, marked out with pegs and string, was to be devoted to local effort: bring and buy stalls, guessing the Vicar's weight, a bucket of water into which you dropped pennies to try to cover the silver florin at the bottom. None of these entertainments would be set up until the day itself but the men from the council were busy on the red, white and blue marquee and the barbecue for the ox-roasting and had already erected the Public Conveniences, Elsan buckets behind canvas screens, next to the large notice which said: This Field is the Property of the Water Company. Please Leave no Litter.

Poll and I had a good time. I had two halfpenny chews and two blackjacks in my pocket: we divided them, one of each kind for each, and wandered round the field, idle and free, like visitors to a strange country. It was a warm day and the air was soft and syrupy, though the grey sky promised rain. Everything was slow-moving and relaxed beneath that high, soft arc of sky: men with soggy, loose-packed cigarettes sticking to their lips, laughed and shouted to each other, women stood on the steps of their caravans and dreamed or gossiped while their babies tumbled in the mud. A group of fairground boys whistled at me in a good-humoured way that was not embarrassing but produced a warm, opening-out feeling inside me as if the whole world had suddenly flowered open and friendly, with everyone knowing and liking each other. Poll seemed happy, too. She swung my hand and sang hymns in her loud, rather hoarse voice.

The worst things always happen when you are at your most vulnerable. Or maybe that is a kind of self-pity: you look back at something terrible that has happened and cry, oh, but I was so happy before. But it is true, too. Things happen like that. We came back to the house, giggling at nothing, our mouths dark with blackjack, jumping cracked paving stones for amusement only, not for luck and ran up the front path between the budding roses quite unpre-pared, unguarded, wide open with happiness.

And in the hall we stopped at once, still as stone.

We knew there was something wrong before we heard Aunt Hat crying upstairs: I could swear that before we registered that fact, Poll's hard little fist had doubled up tight inside my bigger hand. Perhaps children smell fear like animals, perhaps it is only that looking back, memory is falsified by later knowledge, but there is one thing I am sure of, would hold to until my dying day: when the door closed, muffling that dreary sobbing, and Boyd came hurrying down the stairs towards us, smiling at us, smiling *for* us because there was no other reason to smile except for our reassurance and comfort, and said, 'Someone's coming to see you – good heavens, what a pair of tramps, I'd better clean you up, hadn't I?' I knew that the someone was my father.

And it wasn't a matter of timing, either, no momentary confusion of place and time like the confusion that comes when you dive off the side into the bath and find yourself for a split second in two places at once, poised on the side and cleaving the water, because he didn't tell us then, didn't tell us for a good five minutes. What he did, immediately, was to stand between us. We loosed our hands and he stood between us hugging us close – the mark of his jacket button was still on my cheek when I looked in the glass to comb my hair a little later – and then he put his hands on our shoulders and pushed us forward. 'Upstairs with you,' he said. He drove us up the stairs and into the bathroom, closing the door. There were now two closed doors between us and Aunt Hat's weeping which we could still hear until he began to run the hot-water tap. The bathroom was small for the three of us and Boyd had to sit on the lavatory seat before he could comfortably wring out a flannel in the running water. He tilted my chin to clean my face, an indignity I had not had to suffer for years and only endured now because of the frozen helplessness that my foreknowledge had induced in me, and then said in a bright, unreal voice, the kind of voice he had never used to us before, 'Your father's coming to see you. Isn't that a surprise? Ellen's gone to meet him at the station, they'll be here in a minute. We must get you looking presentable, mustn't we?' That nanny's remark touches me more in retrospect than anything else he ever said or did, perhaps because it is the only time in my memory of him

216

that this self-effacing man ever betrayed a selfishly trivial impulse: he did not want *his* children to appear dirty-faced before their father. He went on, scrubbing away at the black line on my lips like Ellen at a dirty saucepan and said, 'He was just passing through, he rang up from the station and said he'd like to come and see you.' Monks Ford was at the end of a branch line; no one passed through it to anywhere, but I suppose it was the best lie he could think of at that moment. He gave my face a final wipe then held me away, between his knees, and looked at me critically. 'There, that's better, though I think you'd better comb your hair.' He looked at me and I looked at him. Or, rather, I looked at certain small things on his face: the red scratch where he had shaved badly, the flesh-coloured mole on his upper lip – remembering the faces he pulled when he cut the stiff hairs that grew out of it – and the lines that crinkled the pouches under his eyes. 'Well,' he said. 'Now, Poll,' and he pushed me away and stood up awkwardly in front of the basin to run more hot water in. He didn't look at her: I realized, suddenly, that since we came into the bathroom, he had not once looked at Poll.

He would have been forced to it now, of course, if the telephone hadn't rung. He was out of the bathroom before it had rung twice. We stood there, poised, not saying a word, but all we heard him say was, 'Yes, yes, yes, of course, yes, I think it's a good idea.' And then almost, if gently, irritated, 'Yes, of course I can manage lunch.'

He came to the bathroom door and said, 'Kate, wash Poll, will you? Ellen's gone out to lunch. They'll be along after.'

He went downstairs. I handed Poll the flannel and told her to wash her own silly face. Then I went into the bedroom and stood in front of the glass, looking at myself. I don't remember what I thought, just that I stood there and looked at myself and noticed the mark Boyd's button had made on my cheek. I brushed my hair. Then I took off my shorts and T shirt and took my party dress out of the wardrobe and put it on. I brushed my hair again and sat down on my bed, wondering if I should change my muddy shoes and for some reason not having the energy or the desire to do so. I felt nothing that I can now recall except when Boyd called from the kitchen and I went downstairs I had the strangest feeling that this was not *me*, this body walking down the stairs in a party frock and muddy shoes: it was just a kind of shell that I was temporarily using in the way that some sea creatures will slip into any old housing, as shelter, or disguise.

Poll had not washed her face. Boyd, dishing up straight from the oven on to the kitchen table, made no comment on this, nor on my festive attire. Only Joanna, coming in last, said, 'Oh, for God's sake,' and sat down at the deal table, first staring glumly at the scratched surface and then pulling a sick face when Boyd put down a plateful of mutton stew in front of her. She had a flushed, miserable air and looked, both younger than usual and also more like Ellen than I had ever seen her look before. Her face seemed thinner and her nose more prominent.

'I *hate* carrots,' Poll said. 'Aunt Hat's crying.'

'Well, you cry sometimes, don't you?' Boyd said. 'Carrots are good for you.'

Joanna picked up her knife and fork and put them down again. 'It wasn't Aunt Hat's fault,' she said. 'Ellen shouldn't have bullied her.'

Boyd frowned at her but she went on, 'Aunt Hat didn't know I was going to do it. I found an old address book among her things. I wrote and told her after. And she was awfully upset, she said I shouldn't have done it and it was all her fault for talking to me – you know the way she always thinks everything's her fault?'

'Yes,' Boyd said.

'Well . . . she said it probably wouldn't get to him anyway, so we'd best say nothing about it. It was an old address in Leamington Spa.'

'Don't let's discuss it now,' Boyd said.

Joanna set her jaw. 'I don't see it was wrong. He's got a right, hasn't he? I mean I just told him about all of us because I thought it would be a comfort to him to know, I didn't ask for anything. It's all Ellen's fault, making such a silly mystery.'

'Don't blame your mother. You don't understand,' Boyd said.

'Well, *she* never thought of him, did she? She didn't think he might be lonely, living in some terrible digs somewhere and eating his heart out.'

'Like that man in the film,' I suggested.

'What film?'

'Oh, any film,' I said, and Boyd looked at me in a surprised way as if there was something about me he hadn't noticed before. I thought it was my party frock and bent over my plate, muttering, 'Well, you told me to smarten myself up, didn't you?'

'What? Oh – a very good idea,' Boyd said heartily. 'You look fine, just fine.'

'I never thought he'd come, though,' Joanna said. She was pushing her food round her plate and making a castle of potato with a moat of gravy round it, the way Poll did sometimes.

'What did you expect?' Boyd asked.

Joanna patted the top of the castle with the flat of her knife. I waited for her to produce something fancy, like she had thought our father might come along and take her off to travel the world with him, but she didn't. Instead she said, sounding much younger – years younger – 'I thought he might send me a postcard. Or something.'

Boyd's face showed such pity that sadness wrenched at my heart and I had to pull the corners of my mouth down to stop myself crying.

Joanna said, 'Ellen says he's not coming to see us. She says he's probably seen about you and Miss Fantom's will in the newspapers and thinks he's on to a good thing.'

Boyd said firmly, 'Ellen was upset, she didn't mean that. Of course he's coming to see you.'

Suddenly Poll said, 'Who's my father?' She looked at Boyd, her dark-dilated eyes unfathomable. 'You're my father,' she said.

The scrape of Boyd's chair as he pushed back from the table set my teeth on edge. He turned to the stove. 'Joanna, hadn't you better take a tray up to Aunt Hat? She'll be hungry. I think Poll and I will take a turn round the garden.'

'I've got to go to the lavatory in a hurry,' Poll said.

When they had both gone, Boyd and I cleared the table. I said, 'I wish he wasn't coming.'

Boyd bent over the sink and jabbed awkwardly at the potato saucepan with a wire brush. 'You'd like to see him, wouldn't you?'

'I feel sick inside. What did she have to go and write to him for?'

'She felt she wanted to. It's natural to feel . . .'

'Joanna doesn't really feel anything. She makes things up. She thinks she feels things but she doesn't really.'

Boyd abandoned the saucepan, putting it in the sink and turning both taps on full blast so that the water splashed over his waistcoat. 'How can you tell the difference between what you feel and what you think you feel?'

It took me a minute to sort that out. 'There just is a difference,' I said, obstinate suddenly, because although I did not know what the difference was, there had to be one, otherwise there was nothing, no certainty, no reality, no truth. I said, 'If you're acting something, that's not real. You can make yourself sad till you cry, but it isn't real.'

'Isn't it?' Boyd mopped at his waistcoat. 'Reality is made up of illusions,' he said.

'I don't know what you mean.'

'No? Put it this way. If you have a feeling it only stays . . . well, pure, if you like, for a fraction of a second because the moment you recognize what you feel you put it into words and then it's changed already, mixed up with things you've read, heard other people say, films you've seen . . .' He looked at me. 'Or if you talk to someone . . .'

I said indignantly, 'Joanna told Aunt Hat she was unhappy about our father and talking about it made her think she really was. I mean it would, wouldn't it? You know what Aunt Hat is!'

'Mmm. I daresay what Joanna felt became exaggerated a little. That doesn't mean she didn't feel it. When you cry at a play, that's real, isn't it?'

'But you know afterwards it was just a play. Like when I . . .' I wriggled with shame, but I had to say it. 'Like when I talked to Gus. I knew *afterwards* . . .'

Boyd was smiling. I cried, 'But you can't just sit and do nothing or say nothing *ever*, like . . . like that man in the barrel!'

'Only if the search for truth was the only thing you wanted. Most of us want more so we have to get along with less.' He laughed and touched my cheek. 'Action and half-truths are our portion. So don't blame Joanna and maybe you'd better change those shoes if you want to create a good impression. I must have a word with Poll. Poll . . .'

He went out of the kitchen, calling her. I stood at the sink to finish the saucepan he had left and, through the window, watched them walk down the garden together. Poll was hanging her head and dragging her feet. Her back view looked mulish. Boyd was holding her hand and bending over her.

Aunt Hat came into the kitchen, carrying the tray Joanna had taken her. The plate of food was untouched. Her hair was disordered, her curls limp, copper corkscrews. She stood at the sink beside me, such a picture of misery that all the misery went out of me and I wanted to laugh. 'Cheer up, droopy-drawers,' I said, repeating the silly phrase she used to us when we were down in the mouth. She looked at me, her cow eyes hurt and sad. I put my arms round her and hugged her tight. She hugged me back and her tears fell on to my shoulder, warm rain through the thin stuff of my party dress. 'Cheer up,' I said, awkwardly patting. After about a minute, she stopped heaving and drew away, fumbling in the neck of her blouse for a handkerchief. She drew out a small, sopping ball and dabbed at her eyes. 'Oh, Katey-ducky, you know I didn't mean any harm, don't you?'

She seemed no older than Poll. 'Don't be upset,' I said. 'If Ellen's been cross, don't worry. Her bark's worse than her bite.'

'I wish I'd never opened my mouth. I'd have cut off my right hand . . .'

I was very grown-up. 'Don't be silly. Nothing really awful's happened. Just that my `. . . that *he's* coming. There's no harm in that,' I said grandly, though my mouth had gone dry.'

'Ellen says it's my fault. Oh, Kate . . . the way she looked at me! *If he makes trouble for Boyd or takes the children away, it'll be your fault,* she said. And looked at me as if she wished I was dead. *I* wish I was dead . . .'

'No one can take us anywhere,' I said, frightened. 'We live here.'

'Oh, but he's your legal guardian, dear. And of course Boyd's in a delicate position, being a doctor. They have to be so careful.' She began to cry again. 'I swear I didn't know, I swear it, Kate! I'd no idea they hadn't fixed things up properly . . . no one would guess it, knowing your mother and her prim and proper ways. Though of course if I'd *thought* . . . I knew she'd not been in touch with him from that day to this. But why didn't she tell me? She could have trusted me, couldn't she . . . I'd not have breathed one word . . .'

'They're coming,' Joanna said, from the door, and my heart was like a stone turning inside me. 'You go,' she said, 'I can't . . .' Her forehead was pearly with sweat. She turned and ran heavily up the stairs.

'Get Boyd,' I said, to Aunt Hat, and walked on rubbery legs to open the front door.

Ellen's coat was undone and she was all legs and arms. She stumbled over the brick step at the gate and had to clutch at the gatepost to stop herself falling and I was ashamed because the man getting out of the car had seen how clumsy she was. I was so ashamed for her that I couldn't look but stood back, holding the front door wide while she came running up the path. She collided with Boyd in the hall.

He caught her elbows steadying her, and she said, 'Oh, it's no good, he means to . . .'

I looked up then and saw her face, white and staring, and heard Boyd say sharply, 'Hold on . . .' and then, still grasping her elbow, he moved forward, bulking between me and the light, and said, loudly, 'I hope they gave you a good lunch at the Crown.'

'The lunch was nothing special,' my father said. 'But the occasion was. It's a long time since I had the pleasure of taking my wife out to lunch.'

Even had I wanted to, I couldn't look at him. Ellen and Boyd stood in front of me. I ran into the living room and flung myself down on the floor behind the sofa. The front door banged. I heard voices in the hall and they moved closer, following me into the room. Frantically, I stuffed my fingers in my ears so hard that I could hear nothing except the drumming in my own head. I stayed, screwed up and sick, until all my muscles began to ache. I took my fingers out of my ears, keeping my eyes shut.

'. . . that's the situation, then?' I heard Boyd say.

'I suppose it's a fair assessment,' my father said. 'Though I'm not at all sure that I care for the accusing tone. Most people would consider I was the injured party.'

'There are other things to consider too,' Boyd said.

'Ellen has put them to me. She didn't waste time making me feel welcome.'

'Did you expect it?'

'No.' My father laughed. He had a pleasant, young laugh.

Boyd was walking the floor. His steps jarred a board under my head. 'Why did you come?'

'Why would you have come in my place?' My father spoke in a light, teasing tone. In contrast, Boyd's voice sounded thick and tired as if he had a heavy cold.

'I find it difficult to put myself in your place,' he said. 'Curiosity, perhaps?'

'Ellen was less kind.'

My nose had begun to itch from the dust in the carpet. I held my breath and put my finger on my upper lip to stop myself sneezing. My head swelled with holding my breath, then, slowly, the urge to sneeze died away.

'. . . any truth in it?' Boyd was saying.

My father laughed again. He seemed a man easily amused. 'Well . . . the idea of compensation had crossed my mind. After all, it might be said I had been deprived of a great deal. My wife's affection . . .'

'You left her,' Boyd said.

'True. I'm not pretending it was a successful marriage. But she might have done me the courtesy of letting me know . . .'

'When we met, she'd not heard from you for over a year. She didn't know where to find you.'

'Did she try?'

Boyd said nothing for a moment. Then, 'She was afraid you wouldn't let her go.'

'Oh, my dear chap! Did she need my co-operation to divorce me for desertion?'

'That takes three years.'

'I daresay I could have supplied other grounds.' He went on, in a tone of pure surprise. 'Why the hell didn't she ask me?'

'I said she was afraid. That was an understatement. She was terrified you'd make trouble.'

'And you believed this story of the bogey man?'

'To some extent it may have been a rationalization. It hardly matters. The fear was real.' Boyd cleared his throat but his voice remained hoarse. 'In a way, she'd closed her mind. Denied your existence. It was the only way she could bear the situation.'

'She felt guilty! That's my Ellen!'

Boyd said stiffly, 'If she did, you will admit, I hope, that she had no reason to. The fact is, she was at breaking point. The thought of trying to trace you drove her to such a pitch . . .'

'And afterwards?' my father said.

'What do you mean?'

'Once she was no longer at breaking point, as you put it. Once she was cosily settled? It could have been arranged discreetly. Didn't she want security?'

'She had it.'

'Yes. I can see that's one answer. But there's another one,

too. Once she'd moved in with you, her position wasn't so unassailable, was it? Oh, not in *my* view. . . . I'm not a moral man, as she's told me often enough, . . . but in *her*s. She wouldn't, you know, have cared to be on the wrong foot with me. . . .'

'Go on,' Boyd said.

'You don't agree with me? Well, why should you? It's only a worm's eye view.' He paused. 'A little while back, you asked me why I came. Well, I'll admit I was interested to discover my errant wife had shacked up with a richer man, but it was a titillating thought, no more. You suggested curiosity. Naturally, I *was* curious. But I suppose I chiefly came to settle a grudge.'

'After eight years?'

'Oh . . . I'd not hugged a grievance all that time, but I'd not forgotten. Ellen's puritan conscience and I are old acquaintances. . . . I was the whipping boy, she flayed me raw! She made me feel like an animal, some ravening beast. I daresay you're not much interested in my side, so I won't bore you. Just let me say I'd been on the receiving end so long, that when I found she'd settled down in a glass house, I was tempted to cast the first stone.' He chuckled suddenly: it was a disconcerting sound. 'My dear chap . . . what *would* the neighbours say?'

There was a silence.

'What do you want?' Boyd said.

My father didn't answer.

'I suppose you can ruin me professionally,' Boyd said. Then he spoke in a way I had never heard before. His voice shook with passion. 'If you do one thing, say one word, I will break you. You will pay me back every penny these girls have cost me since you abandoned them . . . every penny, if I have to fight you through every court in the land. . . .'

My hands were clenched on the carpet and my hot tears ran over them.

'Ellen said you were so fond of them,' my father said uncertainly.

'Fond?' Boyd repeated, and his voice was like ice breaking. 'We weren't talking of affection. Only of what other people would consider the situation to be. On those terms, your wife, your children, are not my responsibility. Take them, provide for them, I'll not stand in your way. I have no right to, after all.'

'My God, you dirty bastard,' my father said. There was a creak as he got out of his chair.

'I'll give you twenty-four hours to get them out of my house,' Boyd said.

A long, hiccoughing sob burst out of me. Boyd's long arm came behind the sofa and scooped me up. I began to wail, keeping my eyes tight shut and he shook me to make me open them. 'Kate,' he said, 'Kate,' and then, when he saw I was looking at him, 'Listeners hear no good of themselves.' He smiled, though he was deathly white. Then he took out his handkerchief and spread it open for me to blow my nose, keeping one hand on the back of my neck and pressing it gently, as if he were trying to tell me something through his fingers.

'Well, so this is Kate,' my father said. He was standing, one elbow resting on the mantelshelf and smiling at me. I looked at him, at first self-conscious about my rumpled party dress and muddy shoes and then, forgetting my appearance, I just looked at him.

He looked, as of course I had known he would, like Poll. The beauty of his complexion, the almost waxy thickness of his skin was like hers, as were his eyes, those dark, blue eyes, and his dark, limp hair.

He smiled at me pleasantly. His smile made him look young, too young to be anyone's father. 'So you're Kate,' he said. 'How do you do?'

'I'm very well, thank you.'

He looked at me, still smiling, and I felt I should say something polite. 'Did you have a good lunch?' I asked, and then, as soon as I had spoken, remembered the answer he had given to that question before, and shuddered.

But he only said yes, thank you, and then told me what he

had had to eat: shrimp cocktail, roast beef and ice-cream. 'I believe you're very fond of ice-cream,' he said, and I went cold, wondering what else he had been told about me.

'I used to be when I was younger,' I said, 'but it always makes me sick.'

'Poor girl,' he said, smiling again, but not really interested I suddenly saw – or no more interested than any stranger who had no connection with me and no responsibility for what I ate and drank. This comforted me so that I felt able to treat him like an ordinary visitor. I tried to think of something polite to say.

'Are you acting at the moment?'

'Resting,' he said, 'temporarily resting.'

'Oh.' I knew what that meant. 'I expect you'll get a good part soon, though,' I said kindly.

'Why should you think that?'

'Well, because good actors are never out of a job for long, are they?'

'How do you know I'm good?' he asked.

'I don't know, I suppose. But Boyd said you were.' He had stopped smiling, but he appeared to be still interested and listening. I racked my brains to remember what else Boyd had said. 'He said he'd never seen you act, but he'd heard you were awfully good and promising. He said we ought to be proud of you.'

My father sat down in a chair. He looked winded. Behind me, Boyd cleared his throat with a rasping sound. Neither of them spoke, and it seemed I had to go on, carrying the social burden. 'Poll and I are quite good at acting. Poll's better than me. She's Elizabeth the First in the Coronation Pageant. Her friend Walter's Henry the Eighth. Boyd said we're lucky to take after you.'

I stopped. I could think of nothing more to say. It seemed that no one else could, either. The silence in the room was long and uncomfortable.

Then my father jerked his wrist forward and looked at his watch.

'How do the trains go?' he asked.

Boyd did not answer and I kicked surreptitiously back-wards at his shin to remind him of his duty as host. He did not respond so I said, 'Wouldn't you like a cup of tea, or something?'

'Well . . . something, perhaps,' my father said.

Boyd stood up. 'Whisky?'

'Please.' My father looked at him. 'If I may, I'd like to meet the rest of your family before I go.'

Chapter Nineteen

Joanna and Poll were sitting on the floor of Poll's room, doing a jigsaw puzzle.

'You've got to go down,' I said.

Joanna's face was blank. 'No,' she said, bending over the puzzle and trying to force two unmatched pieces of sky together.

'You have to. Boyd said.'

'I can't.' She bowed her head so that her hair hid her face. 'What can I *say*?'

I felt her misery like a ball in my stomach. I wanted to tell her that it was all right; to explain how he had looked at me and acknowledged me but without any feeling of connec-tion. But all I could find to say was, 'Just hallo – he only wants to say hallo.'

Poll got to her feet. 'Come on, then we can come back and finish the jigsaw after.'

Joanna stared at her and then looked away. Her face flamed scarlet. 'Do you know who it is downstairs?'

' 'Course I know. He's my biological father,' Poll said with scornful calm. 'And if you're not coming, I'm going by myself.'

'Go then,' Joanna said.

Poll lifted her shoulders and rolled her eyes. 'Lazybones,' she said, and went out, closing the door. I held my breath and walked with her in my mind, down the stairs, into the sitting-room. . . .

'It's not fair to make her go alone,' I said.

'Poll's all right, she doesn't . . .' Then she asked urgently, piteously, *'What's he like?'*

'Like Poll. I mean Poll's like him.' The sick heavy feeling returned to my stomach as I thought of him watching Poll come into the room, seeing his eyes look out at him from her child's face and feeling . . . feeling what? Thinking about it frightened me.

'I didn't mean what does he look like. I mean – oh, *you* know. Ellen said . . . well, you'd think he was a sort of monster.'

'No. He's quite nice, really.'

'*I can't go.*' Joanna thumped her fists on the floor and the jigsaw pieces danced.

'You've got to.' I swallowed hard to conquer the sick feeling. Then I began to be angry. 'You started it, you've got to go through with it, it's not fair if you don't.'

'I can't, it's terrible,' she moaned, but she was getting up from her knees to look in Poll's mirror, hung too low on the wall for her so she had to bend to see her face in it, and I knew she would go in the end. 'It's a terrible situation, you don't understand,' she said, widening her eyes at her reflection and lovingly patting her hair straight. Then she stood upright and looked at me. 'You might as well know,' she began, and I knew what she was going to say and started to snigger, stupidly, unable to stop myself as I was unable to stop her saying what I knew already and did not want to hear made explicit. 'They're living in sin,' she hissed, and the dramatic tone of her voice as well as the words she used, made me gasp hysterically. I collapsed on the floor and stuffed my fist into my mouth.

'Don't laugh, it's not funny,' Joanna said and kicked me on the thigh.

'I'm not laughing,' I choked, which was true: I was, as I said, sniggering in that dry-eyed, put-on way children do at some ludicrous, embarrassing, grown-up mystery that is thrust at them before they have any proper place in their minds to put it. Ellen and Boyd not being married was one of those things like birth and death and all the in-between adult processes which, though I knew about theoretically, I was still young enough to think of as the private habits of a different species, strange, faintly absurd, nothing to do with me. And, as like all children I was unwilling to think of my own parents taking part in those processes, doing the things other people did, I sniggered in self-defence and Joanna kicked me again, hard.

'Shut up, filthy beast,' she cried. Tears stood in her eyes, her voice shook. *'Living together*. It's the sort of thing common people do!'

I didn't laugh at this because I saw that this ridiculous, irrelevant idea really did distress her. Instead I said, trying to comfort her in the way she seemed to need comfort, 'Perhaps now he's come, Ellen will get a divorce and then they can get married. We could all be bridesmaids.'

Joanna's face stiffened, coloured, became a puffed-up mask. 'That would be awful,' she burst out, 'worse than anything, can't you see why? Everyone would have to know.' She exhaled slowly, like a dying balloon, and looked thoughtful. 'They'll have to leave things as they are, there's nothing else they can do that I can see, and we . . . well, we'll just have to be sensible about it.' She sighed again, with dramatic gentleness, and looked at me. 'We must never tell Poll and you must never tell Ellen that you know. It'll be bad enough for her knowing I know, but I've made up my mind, Kate, I shall never say anything to her about it.' Comforted by this pious resolve, she walked to the door with a little smile on her mouth, but stopped on the threshold: she had thought of a better way of putting it. 'I shall never reproach her,' she said, and went downstairs to see our father.

I sat on the floor and finished the jigsaw puzzle which was

of five female rabbits dressed in frocks and bonnets sitting under a tree and having a picnic.

He left about twenty minutes later. Boyd offered to drive him to the station: he said he had his afternoon visits to make and he wouldn't be back for tea.

We stood on the front doorstep with Ellen and waved him off like any other visitor. He waved back, very cheerfully. A light rain had begun to fall and Miss Carter passed by our gate in a green mackintosh. She looked at the car curiously as it drew away.

Joanna began to laugh, in great, painful whoops. '*Hoo, hooo*, if *she* . . . *hoo*, *hoo*.'

Ellen took her arm and drew her indoors and closed the door. Joanna leaned against the wall, doubled up as if she had a pain in her stomach and Ellen looked at her in a way that might have been afraid or ashamed, but I don't think it could have been either, because she said, 'For heaven's sake, pull yourself together, Joanna,' in a perfectly ordinary, sharp voice.

Aunt Hat, hovering in the back of the hall, said timidly, 'Shall I make tea, Ellen? A cup of tea would be nice, don't you think?'

And a little later we had tea, with bread and butter and raspberry jam and chocolate cake on the trolley, sitting in the living room and making conversation about the weather.

Aunt Hat said what a pity it was so wet and cold, she did hope it would clear up for the Coronation, how dreadfully sad it would be if it didn't. Ellen said she hoped it would clear up too, though she doubted it, knowing this country, and Aunt Hat cried breathlessly that she *did* hope Ellen wasn't right! All those beautiful clothes, and the poor people waiting on the pavements all night!

Then Poll got a raspberry pip stuck between her back teeth and when she had finished fussing and was sent off to the bathroom to get rid of it with a piece of cotton, Aunt Hat went suddenly very pink, and, looking suspiciously round the room as if she feared there might be interlopers lurking behind the furniture, said in a low, earnest voice, 'Well, it didn't go off too badly, all things considered, did it?'

I couldn't understand why Ellen and Joanna should smile at this remark. Ellen did not answer it, but she said, quickly, as if to make amends for the smile, 'Why, Hattie, you haven't eaten a thing,' and offered her a piece of chocolate cake. 'Just a little piece won't hurt you, Hattie,' she said, coaxing her gently, just as she had coaxed her the day she came, as if nothing had happened between that first day and this, as if nothing had changed at all. . . .

At seven o'clock Ellen called Poll for her bath, but she wasn't in the house.

'She'll be in the camp,' I said.

It was raining harder now, in cold, sharp needles. I went into the garden and found Boyd there, standing in the rain and looking speculatively at a rose bush. Seeing him, I stopped still. He looked up and saw me. I stayed where I was, feeling ashamed and afraid, not because there was any difference in him, but because he stood there, unchanged, and it suddenly seemed wrong to me. He should have changed, what we had done should have changed him.

'You're awfully wet,' I said, across the distance between us.

He didn't answer and I wondered for a horrible moment if he had decided to go away and leave us and thought of asking him not to, but then I thought, *I can't ask him anything, anymore.* How could I? He had given us everything, without asking, and we had given him nothing; he had looked after us, and we had grown, taking his youth with us; he taught us things, played with us, held bowls for us to be sick in, and we had done nothing back. We had not even thought of him, we had lied, deceived, and between us brought him to the edge of ruin and disgrace, but we had not even thought of him now: we had been sitting drinking tea and eating chocolate cake.

He was looking at me. 'You're wet too. What are you doing?'

232

'Looking for Poll. I thought she might be in the camp.'

'Shall we go and see?' He lifted his hand in a tentative, awkward movement, and I ran across the squeaky, wet grass and took it. His coat sleeve felt sodden as if he had been out in the rain for hours. We walked down to the bottom of the garden.

When we got to the fence, we could hear her crying. She was lying on her face on the ground, surrounded by disintegrating cardboard boxes. Boyd bent to pick her up but she resisted him, kicking out with all her strength and going purple in the face. He hung on to her, soothing her in a droning voice until her sobs quietened and she said, hiccoughing, 'Walter says he won't marry me. I asked him again yesterday and he said he wouldn't because I told him I wet my bed sometimes.'

That was a lie, of course, and Boyd must have known it was a lie. I mean, it might have been true, but it wasn't why she was crying because Poll never cried about things that had happened yesterday. But Boyd held her close and said, 'Don't worry about that, it'll stop, I told you, don't you believe me?' and then, when she began to cry again, burrowing her face into his neck, he stroked her soaking hair and said, 'Don't cry any more, my darling, there's quite enough water about as it is!'

He shifted her weight so he had a free hand for me, and said, 'We'd better go in. If we don't, Aunt Hat will begin to imagine all kinds of calamity.'

VIRAGO MODERN CLASSICS

The first Virago Modern Classic, *Frost in May* by Antonia White, was published in 1978. It launched a list dedicated to the celebration of women writers and to the rediscovery and reprinting of their works. Its aim was, and is, to demonstrate the existence of a female tradition in fiction which is both enriching and enjoyable, and to broaden the sometimes narrow academic definition of a 'classic' which has often led to the neglect of a large number of interesting secondary works of fiction. In calling the series 'Modern Classics' we do not necessarily mean 'great' — although this is often the case. Published with new critical and biographical introductions, books are chosen for many reasons: sometimes for their importance in literary history; sometimes because they illuminate particular aspects of women's lives, both personal and public. They may be classics of comedy or storytelling; their interest can be historical, feminist, political or literary.

Initially the Virago Modern Classics concentrated on English novels and short stories published in the early decades of this century. As the series has grown it has broadened to include works of fiction from different centuries, different countries, cultures and literary traditions, many of which have been suggested by our readers.

Also by Nina Bawden

TORTOISE BY CANDLELIGHT

'An exceptional picture of disorganised family life . . .
Imaginative, tender, with a welcome undercurrent of
toughness' — *Observer*

With the ferocity of a mother tiger defending her cubs,
fourteen-year-old Emmie Bean watches over her
household, her amiable drunken father, her gaunt,
evangelical grandmother, her beautiful, wayward sister
Alice and, most precious of all, eight-year-old Oliver,
who has the countenance of an angel and the ethical
sense of a cobra. But with the arrival of new neighbours,
the outside world intrudes into the isolated privacy of
family life and Emmie's Kingdom is no longer secure.
Combining the guile of a young child with the
desperation of adolescence, Emmie fights to stave off
the changes — and the revelations — that growing up
necessarily brings. Powerful, heart rending, but never
sentimental, *Tortoise by Candlelight* is a captivating
excursion into the landscape of youth.

THE BIRDS ON THE TREES

'Few women novelists are writing better' — *Punch*

The expulsion from school of their eldest son shatters
the middle-class security of Maggie, a writer, and Charlie,
a journalist. Since childhood, Toby has been diffident
and self-absorbed, but the threat of drug-taking and his
refusal (or inability) to discuss his evident unhappiness,
disturbs them sufficiently to seek professional help.
Veering between private agony and desperate public
cheerfulness, Maggie and Charlie struggle to support
their son and to cope with the reactions — and advice
— of friends and relatives. Noted for the acuity with
which she reaches into the heart of relationships, Nina
Bawden here excels in revealing the painful, intimate
truths of a family in crisis. Toby's situation is explored
with great tenderness, while Maggie's grief and self-
recrimination are rigorously, if compassionately, observed.
It is a novel that raises fundamental questions about
parents and their children, and offers tentative hope
but no tidy solutions.